THE LIMITS OF MY WORLD

THE LIMITS OF MY WORLD

a novel

Gregory Coles

WALKING CARNIVAL
W|C
"Make Readers Happy."

The Limits of My World
Softcover ISBN 978-1-939953-20-9
e-Book ISBN 978-1-939953-36-0
Large Print ISBN 978-1-939953-37-7

Published by Walking Carnival Books
a book packaging imprint of Nappaland Communications Inc.
1437 Denver Ave. #193, Loveland, CO 80538

Editorial: Mike Nappa
Cover Design: Anna Filbert
Interior Design: WC Creative

Walking Carnival™ and the Walking Carnival colophon are trademarks of Nappaland Communications Inc.

www.WalkingCarnival.com
www.Nappaland.com

First Edition

1 2 3 4 5 6 7 • • • 2026 2025 2024 2023

"Make Readers Happy"

For Curry Kennedy,
kindred interpreter of Babel's inheritance—
"Stagger onward rejoicing."

The Lord came down to see the city and the tower, which the children of man had built. And the Lord said, "Behold, they are one people, and they have all one language, and this is only the beginning of what they will do. And nothing that they propose to do will now be impossible for them. Come, let us go down and there confuse their language, so that they may not understand one another's speech."

~ Genesis 11:5-7 (ESV)

The limits of my language are the limits of my world.

~ Ludwig Wittgenstein
Tractatus Logico-Philosophicus (5.6)

TRANSLATOR'S NOTE

In the pages that follow, only those chapters rendered in italics were originally written in English. The rest of the narrative has been translated into English from the two languages spoken by its protagonists, known to linguists as Lugha and Taal. The authentic sense of these original languages has been preserved whenever possible, even in cases where such preservation may contradict the typical English meanings of words used.

Nowhere is this tension more evident than in the use of pronouns. Lugha contains the pronouns "he" and "she" but makes no distinction in meaning between the two. Although a few Lugha speakers use both pronouns as interchangeable synonyms, most pick one pronoun or the other and use it exclusively. As such, readers will see the same individuals variously referred to as both "he" and "she." This is not to say that these persons should be read as genderfluid—certainly not in the way such a term might be employed by English speakers. Imposing that concept onto this text would be anachronistic at best and colonizing at worst. The concerns that occupy these pages are dictated by the words and experiences available to the individuals represented within them.

As for Taal, this language follows syntax rules which, if copied into English unaltered, would inhibit clear reading. Some passages from Taal have been translated as literally and woodenly as possible in order to heighten distinctions in meaning. In other cases, Taal syntax has been reproduced in easily readable English in order to mimic the ease with which the words were understood by their original hearers.

Where passages within the manuscript represent a blurring between Lugha and Taal, or a moment of polysemy at the overlap of the two languages, pains have been taken within the body of the text to attune readers to such textual complexities. Cumbersome footnotes, deserved though they may be, must wait for a future edition of the work.

ACT ONE

The forceps of our minds are clumsy forceps, and crush
the truth a little in taking hold of it.

~ H. G. Wells
A Modern Utopia

1

KANAN

WHEN SHE GOT HER NEW SKIN, Kanan would be able to run the perimeter of the universe in seventeen minutes. Her current skin could make the circuit in twenty-two minutes, as long as all the access gates were left open and she didn't trip on any seams between compartments. But her new skin—her Final skin—would never trip on seams. Its stride would be longer, its muscles stronger, its joints more perfectly aligned.

"If you're this fast in fledgling skin," Kanan's mentor had gushed, "you'll be faster as a newborn Final than most of us ever become. Seventeen minutes, easy. With a little training in Final skin, probably under fifteen."

"Fifteen!" Kanan's eyes widened. "You think so? If I get a Final skin—"

"Don't say *if*," Mentor interrupted sternly. "Say *when*. *When* you are born into your new skin. *When* you become a Final."

"But not everyone becomes—"

"No, not everyone. But you will."

That was a mentor's job. To make each fledgling believe she was destined for Finalization. To persuade her she was the finest egg ever hatched into the universe, and then to make her act like it. Kanan's thirty-nine agemates had no doubt been told the very same thing by their own mentors: "You're better than the others. Smarter. More reliable. More agile. A harder worker. You're sure to be chosen as one of the Finals. You have to be."

Not that there was any shame in being archived. Of the one hundred eggs hatched in each cohort, thirty were archived before being born into junior fledgling skins. Thirty of the remaining seventy were archived when their agemates were reborn as senior fledglings. Only ten senior fledglings from each cohort were Finalized, and even those ten would be archived in the end, once their service to humanity was finished.

"The Final skin is a high honor," said Captain Buru at each aging ceremony, standing at a gleaming silver podium atop a pyramid of steps in the center of the assembly room. "But the archive is also an honor. As long as you remain a member of the human race you were hatched into, our honor is your honor. The only dishonor is in ceasing to be human. The only dishonor is in deletion."

"Our honor is your honor," the assembly chanted in reply, a thousand voices in practiced solemn unison. "Your honor is our honor."

Still, no matter how honorable archiving was supposed to be, everyone worked and wished and begged to stay in skin as long as possible. Junior fledglings who weren't selected for rebirth into the next skin would cry silently as they clutched their mentors' arms, stumbling toward the ominous grey curtain that hung below the captain's podium and veiled the entrance into the heart of the pyramid. Sometimes they let out an audible wail from behind the privacy of the curtain as they shed their skin for the first and last time.

The senior fledglings not chosen as Finals had more self-control. They held their heads high and stretched their lips into blade-thin smiles when their names were called. They had already shed their skins and seen their hideous underflesh once before. They knew what was expected of them, what honor demanded. But no amount of self-control could keep their eyes from twitching, keep their breath from turning shallow and ragged.

No amount of self-control could keep them from losing their skin.

And without skin—even with the whole digiscape at their disposal—they would never again know what it felt like to breathe unarchived air, to run the perimeter of the universe until their lungs strained against their chests.

Kanan spent most of her leisure evenings running laps around the universe. And maybe, she thought, this was why she ran so often—because running proved she was still in skin. It proved she hadn't been archived yet.

Sometimes her agemate Tei would join, and the two of them would jog slowly side by side, talking in sentences as long as Tei's wheezing allowed. But more often than not, Tei logged into the digiscape with the rest of their cohort, where she could run at pace with Kanan's fastest sprint for hours without a hint of wheezing.

"You should join us," Tei would say, as Kanan peeled away from their cohort after the evening meal. "You and I could go on a digiscape mission together. It could be fun."

"Fun won't make us Finals," Kanan would reply grimly.

Tei would smile and wink, as she always did, no matter how grim the subject matter. "There's more to humanity than

Finalization," she would say. "And even if there isn't, there's more to Finalization than agility."

That last part was undeniably true. Being human—the kind of human worth keeping in skin—required all kinds of skills, some of which could only be learned in the digiscape. Mathematics. Chemistry. History. Skincare. Marksmanship. Coding. Aviation. Engineering. The tutors for these subjects had all been archived generations ago, because the digiscape made an ideal classroom. Of all the hundreds of humans who played a role in each fledgling's training, only mentors needed a skin.

Like every dutiful senior fledgling, Kanan spent the time she was required to spend in the digiscape. She learned the history of humankind by talking to members of archived generations, all the way back to the very first generation, the first humans born in skin after the creation of the universe. She learned the properties of chemicals: how to safely mix them together and extract them from one another, which ones could be used to make a meal in the galley, which could melt the silica earth under their feet. She practiced loading and firing the small handheld strykers carried by orderkeepers, weapons powerful enough to blow a hole through Final skin. She practiced skincare by binding up the wounds of archived humans she had just attacked.

"No hard feelings," she would say, bent over their bleeding forms, as she cleaned their wounds and poured ointment and wrapped them in bandages.

"Of course not," they would answer kindly. "It's all part of the learning process. It's what we're here for."

Sometimes their wounds would be too great for Kanan to mend, and their skins would fail in her arms. But each time she logged out of the digiscape and logged in again, they would be returned to their former selves, none the worse for wear.

Everything was safe in the digiscape. No error was fatal, no mistake irreparable. Fledglings could be trained without risking skin damage, without wasting resources. Finals could hone specialized job skills, consult with the archived humans who had held their jobs in generations past. And everyone, fledgling and Final alike, could log into the digiscape to spend their leisure time however they pleased, limited only by their imaginations and their skills in coding.

Kanan was no stranger to leisure in the digiscape. Sometimes it was Tei who coaxed her, weaving a long creative tale about the adventure they might go on together. Sometimes Mentor insisted: "It's not natural to keep skin out of water all the time. Especially not at your age." But with each new aging ceremony, as Kanan's cohort of senior fledglings drew closer to their Finalization or archiving, she found it harder to be at ease in the digiscape.

"Isn't this what it feels like to be archived?" she asked Mentor once. The two of them were fording an icy digiscape river, bundles of supplies held above their heads by trembling arms.

Mentor kept her eyes fixed on the snowy shore ahead of them. "Archiving is just another name for moving permanently into the digiscape."

"And we don't *want* to be archived, do we?" Water rushed around Kanan's armpits, lapping at her throat. Her words felt stiff and brittle.

"We're all archived in the end," said Mentor. "But no one wants to be archived when there's skin available for them."

"Then why do we spend our leisure here? Isn't that like archiving ourselves ahead of schedule?"

Before Mentor could answer, Kanan's foot caught on a bit of jagged, slippery rock. The current pulled her off-balance, sending her and her supplies toppling into the water. She thrashed and tried to regain her footing as the river dragged her away.

"Swim," said Mentor, watching her intensely without moving, both hands still clasping her own bundle. "You've learned how to swim."

"Too cold," Kanan gasped. Her head sank underwater. She took a mouthful of water and reemerged sputtering, two skin-lengths further from Mentor than she had been before. "I can't breathe."

Mentor turned away, resumed walking. "I disabled your gills, remember? No one said training exercises should come easy. If you want to stay in skin, start acting like a Final."

Kanan fought the current until her limbs were too numb to continue. Her head bobbed above and below the water line, the skyline toggling between sharp snowcapped mountains and swirling blue-grey bubbles. She choked over a second mouthful of water, a third, a fourth. A scream no one could hear escaped her lips in a trail of bubbles.

Four excruciating minutes later, she woke up in skin again.

She never forgot the feeling of drowning. The gills that refused to open, the water in her lungs where air should have been. The terror even though there was nothing to be afraid of.

Other fledglings had drowned too. They'd been burned to ashes, bled out beyond recovery, felt their necks snap and their eyes roll back into their skulls. Skin failure was all part of the training. Mentors allowed fledglings to suffer disaster so they would understand the weight of their responsibility as humans in skin. And yet none of the fledglings seemed to fear the digiscape as much as Kanan did.

Almost none of them.

Nine aging ceremonies ago, so far back Kanan could barely remember it, a junior fledgling named Jerik had been assigned to the archive. In the middle of the archiving ritual, after she was already stripped of her skin behind the privacy of the grey curtain, Jerik burst back into the assembly and began racing toward the nearest access gate. The pitch of her frightened screams and the grotesque sight of her bare underflesh burned themselves into Kanan's memory.

Two orderkeepers and Jerik's mentor had chased after her, easily outrunning Jerik's small skinless legs. One of the orderkeepers tackled her and pinned her to the ground as she screamed and kicked. A thousand pairs of eyes watched in stunned silence.

"There's nothing to be afraid of," Jerik's mentor had said, gentle and soothing but somehow loud enough for the whole assembly to hear. "The digiscape won't hurt you. You'll see us there the same way you always have. And you'll be honored there. Our honor is your honor."

The second orderkeeper—the one whose hands weren't full of Jerik's wriggling limbs—tucked a sheet of russet fabric over the skinless fledgling. With the sheet in place, Kanan could see Jerik only from the neck up. A nest of matted black threads sat on top of her head where skin should have been, just above her terrified eyes. And beneath the sheet, the contours of Jerik's skinless form were still faintly visible, like the rough beginnings of a sketch Kanan's eyes would never forget how to complete.

Jerik's underflesh was the first underflesh Kanan saw. The second was her own, two aging ceremonies later. Her junior mentor had walked proudly with her, hand in hand, through the applauding assembly and past the grey curtain when her name was called for rebirth. Behind the curtain, lit by two suns in the hollow pyramid's belly, a hydropod full of sticky green water lay open like a salivating mouth. Fresh skins, bulbous and limp without occupants, hung from the surrounding walls.

"It's best if you close your eyes," Kanan's junior mentor had said, as her newly assigned senior mentor and an orderkeeper set their hands on her shoulders. "And hold still. It won't hurt. But you've never felt anything like it."

Kanan nodded and closed her eyes. When the first flap of skin tore away from her scalp, her eyes sprang open again in shock, and no one told her to close them a second time.

Humanity didn't have words—didn't need words—for what Kanan saw as her junior fledgling skin was peeled away. Her underflesh was as grotesque as Jerik's had been, only darker in color—closer to the carbon sheen of the universe's edges than to the glowing yellow of the suns. If she had touched the thing she saw beneath her skin, she felt sure it would be soft and malleable against her fingers. Like pudding, perhaps, or gelatin. Whereas skin was consistent in style and texture across the whole body, underflesh seemed to be stitched together from a dozen different materials, all protruding and sinking inward at random.

"It's not you you're seeing and feeling right now," her new mentor whispered into her ear, as four pairs of hands tugged at her. "Skin is you. Digiscape is you. This is just the almost-you, the thing between births."

"I still have a heartbeat," Kanan whispered back, feeling the rhythm pounding in her ears. "Is that part of me?"

"It was," said Mentor. "It will be."

No sooner had the last bit of skin been pulled away from her feet than the pairs of hands began binding a new skin around her. The old skin had been torn off piece by piece, but this new skin was already fitted together, a complex mesh of gleaming blue muscle dangling from a rubbery central backnerve. Each flap that fused against her brought with it a fresh surge of strength—more strength than the muscles of her junior fledgling skin could have achieved no matter how hard she trained. These new muscles slowly swallowed up her underflesh in their warm grip.

"Now," said Mentor, no longer whispering, "you are a senior fledgling."

Kanan was so transfixed by her new skin at first, so obsessed with its strength and speed, that underflesh completely disappeared from her mind. But as the seasons and aging ceremonies passed, the memories of her own underflesh and Jerik's slowly resurfaced.

Underflesh was somehow the opposite of the digiscape. Underflesh didn't exist in the archive, because it couldn't be digitized. It was like skin that way—perhaps more like skin than skin itself.

Running made Kanan feel near to her underflesh again. It may have hidden invisibly beneath her skin, but Kanan was convinced that it was still there. Still part of her, no matter what Mentor had said. When she ran as far and fast as her skin could carry her, she felt her heartbeat in her ears, the way she had felt it behind the grey curtain in that split second when her junior fledgling skin was entirely stripped away and her senior fledgling skin still dangled in pieces from Mentor's hands.

The leisure evening before her Final aging ceremony—the one that mattered, the one where she would be either archived or reborn into Final skin—Kanan ran her last laps around the universe as a fledgling. Twenty-two minutes and four seconds. Twenty-two minutes and one second. Twenty-two minutes and twelve seconds.

After each circuit, she slowed to a walk, placing a hand over the skin of her chest to feel its rapid swelling outward and its heavy falling inward. Her other hand trailed along the pitch-black boundary of the universe, fingers tracing the cool carbon walls that stood between humanity and Nothing.

"Tomorrow," she said aloud. "Seventeen minutes." Seventeen minutes, or never again.

Don't say if. Say when. When you become a Final.

Kanan programmed her dormitory hydropod for a dreamless sleep that night. But because of a malfunction—it must have been a malfunction—she dreamed anyway. Not one of the default dreams imported from the digiscape. Certainly not a dream she would have customized for herself.

She dreamed of aging ceremonies past and future, of the grey curtain and the gaping green mouth that smelled of chlorine and fear. Chanting voices. Trembling lips. Blade-thin smiles. Unfamiliar hands holding her against the silica earth as Mentor peeled the skin away from her, piece by piece.

2

TEI

EYES WERE BEST. As for the rest of skin, Tei couldn't understand what the fuss was about. Most days he preferred the
digiscape: an adventure without boundary, the only massive
thing in an otherwise claustrophobic universe. Skin had rules
and limits. In the digiscape you could do anything, go anywhere, be anyone.

But there was something about eyes. Human eyes in skin
were a magic spell, a flicker of starlight on a clear night, a
tunnel mouth welcoming you into the echoing underground.
Eyes in skin always seemed to be going somewhere, taking you
on an adventure, even if the skin around them sat motionless.

In the digiscape, eyes never looked quite right. Their colors
were correct, and their shapes, and everything that should
have made them identical to the world in skin. Their coding
was flawless. But still they seemed flat, shallow. Instead of a
tunnel mouth, digiscape eyes were just a hole in the dirt, leading nowhere.

When Tei was archived, it was eyes he would miss most. His own eyes, staring back at him in murky reflection from the carbon walls. His agemates' eyes. Mentor's eyes.

Kanan's eyes.

If eyes were a magic spell, then Kanan was a sorcerer, casting a raging inferno that put the others' flint-and-tinder sparks to shame. Kanan's eyes made proximity delicious and distance unbearable. Sometimes—though Tei would admit it only in the privacy of his own hydropod, as he coded his dreams—even their two skins felt like a barrier to the kind of closeness he wanted. To draw nearer and nearer until there was no gap, no air between them, until they fit inside the same skin and answered to the same name.

But the Kanan of the digiscape—the Kanan of Tei's carefully programmed dreams—didn't have the same eyes as Kanan in skin. Digiscape-Kanan's eyes were shallow, holes in the dirt, identical to everyone else's. It was only in skin, sitting across from Tei in the mess hall or glancing over at him as they jogged the perimeter of the universe, that Kanan became a sorcerer.

When Tei was archived, it was eyes he would miss most.

"Don't say *if*," Mentor had lectured him, the same way every mentor lectured every fledgling. "Say *when*." Tei had taken the lecture to heart, following the letter of the law if not the spirit. He said *when* to anticipate the future he knew was coming. And he knew, as sure as he knew the distance around the universe, that no Final skin would be waiting for him at today's aging ceremony.

Skin selection always had an element of chance, of course. No one was guaranteed a new skin. It depended which current Finals were being archived, opening up their careers to newborns. If you weren't suited to the open careers, there was nowhere to go except the archive, no matter how remarkable you were.

Still, no matter which careers opened up, Tei wouldn't be the best candidate for any of them. Finalization wasn't like the upgrade to senior fledgling skin, where you only needed to stay slightly above average to ensure you weren't archived. Being one of a cohort's ten Finals meant being exceptional, being so remarkable that the rest of the world in skin felt they needed you.

Tei was the sort of person everybody liked, but nobody needed.

He was no Kanan, setting records in agility and mastering the use of skin. He was no Yerima, carrying himself with such confidence and perfection that their whole cohort whispered he was sure to become captain someday. Tei didn't have a mechanic's mind or a caregiver's instincts or a galley chemist's patience. He felt most at home in the digiscape, making up stories for his agemates and customizing happy dreams for himself. He enjoyed learning the history of the universe from the lips of the archived people who had experienced it, coding scenes from their memories into the fabric of the digiscape so future fledgling cohorts could experience them again and again.

Tei belonged in the archive. No sense fighting it. There was honor in the archive—not as much as in Finalization, but enough for Tei's appetite—and plenty of adventure as well.

All he would miss was eyes.

§ § §

Air smelled different on the morning of an aging ceremony. Hints of a feast wafted out of the galley, filling the universe's vents with the promise of fat and spice and sweetness. There was, said Captain Buru, no better way to inaugurate a new mouth than by filling it with bricklecream.

Everyone smelled the feast, but not everyone would taste it. Thirty junior fledglings, thirty senior fledglings, and ten Finals would no longer have a mouth in skin by the time the mess hall tables were set and the feast was served. Freshly archived, they'd feast in the digiscape instead, where food was unnecessary but always available for those willing to program it.

Tei lay in the water of his hydropod far longer than necessary, planning the feast he would code for himself and twenty-nine of his agemates after they were archived. First the roast, a thick slab of darkmeat turned slowly over glowing coals, thinly sliced and draped across steaming biscuits. Crisp greens with nutmeal and slivers of redfruit, drizzled with citrus and vinegar. Finally, a thick fig pudding, sticky and almost black, soaked in dragonsbreath and set on fire so it glowed blue. It would be extravagant as only a digiscape feast could be, with none of the regulations or supply limitations that vexed the galley chemists.

The dormitory was nearly empty when Tei finally sat up and blinked away water. Only three of his cohort's hydropods were still closed. The rest hung open and empty, gleaming green against the black walls. Mornings before aging ceremonies were leisure mornings for fledglings, but most chose to volunteer their time in the galley or the rowing room. The threat of the archive was enough to turn them into temporary philanthropists.

"Checkers?"

The voice behind him came so abruptly that Tei nearly fell off the bunk ladder, slithering unceremoniously past three hydropods on his way down to earth.

Kanan sat against the wall, smirking. Between his akimbo legs, a square of gingham fabric laid flat. "Checkers?" he said again.

"No volunteering for you either?" Tei sat cross-legged in front of his agemate. Their skins were nearly touching, Tei's knees against Kanan's splayed feet.

"My mentor says the decisions are already made. No sense wasting our last morning on a few hundred watts when we could be playing checkers." Kanan emptied a pouch of aluminum scraps onto the ground and began sorting them into two piles. "Lines or circles?"

"Lines," said Tei, reaching for the slenderer pile. "I still don't know why you like this game. A whole digiscape of entertainment, and you'd rather slide scrap metal around a piece of cloth."

"You know why." Kanan glanced toward the access gate, his eyes narrowing. "Today, of all days, you know why."

"And you, of all people, have nothing to worry about. If anyone was ever guaranteed to be a Final—"

"No one ever was," shot back Kanan.

They finished setting up the game in silence and began to play.

"Besides," said Kanan, "it's not just me I'm worried about." His eyes met Tei's, their magic as strong as ever.

"Promise me," Tei began, and then found his throat was empty. He looked down at the checkerboard, breaking the spell. "When you're in Final skin, promise you'll come visit me. I know you hate the digiscape. But promise me you'll come, when it's the only place we see each other."

Kanan shook his head fiercely. "Don't. Don't say that."

"I don't mind it. Really I don't. I'm good at coding. But I don't want to have to code you the way I do in dreams. I want you really there. As much of you as I can get." *Everything but the eyes.*

Kanan's head still shook. "No. You're more than good at coding. You're the best. Maybe the committee will see that, and they'll—"

"Just promise me."

More silence. They slid aluminum across gingham, leaping each other's pieces, slowly emptying the board.

"Wherever you are," said Kanan at last, "wherever I am, we'll find each other. I promise."

"Good enough," said Tei. For a moment, he almost believed it was.

§ § §

For cohorts not under evaluation, aging ceremonies had the impatient thrill of a carnival. Music filled the air, regal horns and soaring strings and pounding drums blaring out of the digiscape. Fledglings jostled each other as they took their seats in the assembly room. They whispered and smirked, avoiding their mentors' disapproving glares. Some of the older ones had no doubt placed wagers on who would be archived and reborn, gambling with keepsakes or contraband backrubs or extra bites of the coming feast.

Tei sat with his cohort at the head of the senior fledglings' aisle. On one side sat Kanan; on the other, an agemate named Obel. Obel's odds for Finalization would be good. He was quiet but well-spoken, clever with his fingers, the sort usually selected for careers in maintenance or engineering or craftsmanship. Tei imagined he was seeing Obel's head from behind, evaluating his agemate at a distance, as if he were seated among the ones placing wagers instead of the ones being wagered on.

Of the fledglings with skin in jeopardy, some shook visibly; some carried themselves stiff as steel plates; some simply looked weary or resigned. Every Final Tei could see—even the ones recently born, with decades in skin likely still ahead of them—sat in the bleachers with solemn faces. Mentors looked doubly stern, worrying for their mentees' skin as well as their own.

When the whole assembly was seated, Captain Buru climbed to the podium. His checkered skin gleamed brighter as he drew closer to the suns. "Another season come and gone," he began. His amplified voice rumbled through the room like a drumroll as the digiscape music faded. "And the fate of humanity looks brighter than ever."

Tei turned to Kanan, to Obel. Both had firm chins and eyes fixed ahead. They appeared to be listening intently. *Appeared*—that was what mattered. It made no difference whether they heard a single word the captain spoke. All they needed to do was stare in the right direction and remember to join the corporate refrain: "Our honor is your honor. Your honor is our honor."

After the captain's opening remarks came the naming of newborn junior fledglings. One by one they emerged from behind the grey curtain, tentative and unsteady, taking their inaugural steps in skin. The first sound they heard outside the digiscape was the sound of their own name, read in the captain's booming voice and greeted by a sea of cheers.

When the last newborn had emerged, the captain held up his hand for silence. "Newborn junior fledglings," he said, "we welcome you. You've already learned inside the digiscape how to walk and speak and think like a human. Today, you start putting this knowledge into practice. You are human now, and your honor is our honor. Welcome to your first skin. Welcome to the human race."

In this first part of the ceremony—only this part—there was no sadness or shame to temper the happiness of birth. No one mourned the thirty eggs sent directly to the archive, nor would the eggs have mourned for themselves. They had never known anything outside the digiscape. Only humans already in skin could feel shame at the thought of losing skin.

The happiest part of the ceremony was immediately followed by the unhappiest. One by one, seventy weak-kneed junior fledglings and their mentors walked across the clearing to the pyramid of steps and the grey curtain. As they walked, Captain Buru read their names and announced their fates. "Teram; assigned to the archive. Bobona; assigned to rebirth as a senior fledgling. Qora; assigned to rebirth as a senior fledgling. Hillo; assigned to the archive."

Every announcement, whether an archiving or a rebirth, was greeted with the same solemn chant that had begun the morning: "Our honor is your honor. Your honor is our honor."

It wasn't the archiving itself, or even the thought of archiving, that nauseated Tei as he watched. It was, instead, the occasional moan of terror or relief that echoed through the vast room as fledglings stepped behind the curtain. It was the sickly silence of stray tears and heaving chests from fledglings who held their tongues. The whole scene, the air itself, lay heavy as a feast of stones in Tei's belly.

He didn't fear the archive—not for himself. But he feared humanity's fear of the archive.

One by one, junior fledglings disappeared into the heart of the pyramid where the birthing hydropod lay. Half of them reappeared a few moments later, taller than before, walking clumsily inside unfamiliar muscles, staring down at their new arms and chests. Those who didn't reappear simply vanished, swallowed up by the hydropod, forgotten as soon as Captain Buru read the next name on his list.

"Newborn senior fledglings," said the captain, after the last fledgling had reemerged from behind the curtain, "we welcome you. You have proven for the first time that you can earn your place in human skin. We honor your achievement.

Your honor is our honor. Today you begin the journey again. Welcome to your second skin."

All too soon—and yet it had felt like an eternity of waiting—the Finalization began. Ten Finals to be archived. Ten senior fledglings to take their place in Final skin. According to tradition, so that no career stood empty more than a moment, the archivee and his replacement were announced together.

Captain Buru cleared his throat and began. "Cavari, sanitation engineer, assigned to the archive. Thunod, assigned to rebirth in Final skin as sanitation engineer."

Tei spoke by force of habit, one with the assembly: "Our honor is your honor. Your honor is our honor." Beside him, Kanan's jaw tightened.

Cavari and Thunod rose from their seats, walked to the front of the grey curtain, and touched their hands together palm against palm. "As it ends," said Thunod to Cavari, "I honor your service to humanity."

"As it begins," answered Cavari, "I honor yours."

Side by side they stepped into the heart of the pyramid. When Thunod returned, he was alone.

Another three careers were emptied and refilled. Sholi, one of Tei's most faithful companions in the digiscape, was Finalized as a mentor for junior fledglings. Yerima, to no one's surprise, became an administrator. Obel vacated the seat beside Tei to be reborn as a mechanic.

"He'll say your name any moment now," Tei whispered to Kanan. "I can feel it."

Kanan didn't move his head, only blinked in acknowledgment.

Five of the Final skins had been filled. Six. Seven.

"Remember," whispered Tei. "We won't get another chance to talk once they call your name. But I'll be waiting for you in the archive. Remember you promised."

The eighth skin went to a lab chemist, the ninth to a butcher.

"And lastly," said Captain Buru from the podium, "Ipran, skincaregiver, assigned to the archive."

The whole room seemed to breathe in sharply. The other nine Finals chosen for archiving had been seasoned veterans, in their careers since before Tei was an egg. Ipran was a young Final, only two seasons out of his senior fledgling skin. He was well-liked, too—by his colleagues in skincare, who hailed him as a brilliant medical mind; by his patients, who had seen him expertly mend even the worst skin malfunctions; by anyone who had heard his booming laugh in the mess hall as he told stories of wild skincare escapades in the digiscape.

In the tense air beside him, Tei felt Kanan's lungs deflating. Neither of them heard the name Captain Buru announced as Ipran's replacement, but they both knew it couldn't be Kanan. Kanan had never been a good student of skinscience. He was too impatient with the digiscape to learn all the inner workings of skin anatomy. He would have made an excellent messenger, or an energy coordinator, or even an orderkeeper. But not a skincaregiver.

If he had known, thought Tei—if only Kanan had known which careers might have earned him a skin—he might have spent his fledgling years differently. He might have spent less time running the perimeter of the universe, spent more time studying in the digiscape. He might have earned another skin, if only he hadn't been so fixated on skin in the first place.

"At least," Kanan muttered grimly, "you won't have to worry about me visiting you in the archive."

Tei said nothing. Part of him agreed, breathing a selfish sigh of relief to know they were both bound to the same fate. But then he thought of eyes. The knowledge that Kanan's eyes would still exist in skin, even though Tei would never see them properly in the digiscape, had been a source of comfort. It had never occurred to him that Kanan might not be Finalized. It had never occurred to him that, when Kanan was archived, his eyes in skin would simply cease to exist.

Ipran and his replacement—a shy but clever fledgling named Rajamin—met in front of the curtain. They touched palms and disappeared. Rajamin returned alone.

The captain stood in silence, waiting for the applause to dwindle. His eyes scanned the audience as if searching for someone. Eventually they came to rest on the thirty senior fledglings awaiting the archive. An odd look crossed his face: an expression Tei had never seen before, like a combination of eagerness and fear.

"Most careers in the human race," said the captain at last, "are needed in every season. We have always needed mechanics like Obel, mentors like Sholi, skincaregivers like Rajamin. But some careers exist only in moments of extreme need, when humanity faces a challenge no ordinary career can resolve. The Final born into this career earns extraordinary honor, because he serves humanity as no one else has ever served before or will ever serve again.

"No other career can be sacrificed to make room for this new career. Therefore, the Final who enters it cannot be one of the ten whose birth you have just witnessed. We must give birth to an eleventh Final. In accordance with the honor of his position, he will no longer be called by his former name. His new name will be Eleven, because he is born under exceptional circumstances to meet exceptional need."

Tei's heart throbbed with the same kind of fear and eagerness written across the captain's face. Surely Kanan was the one they wanted. Kanan was the one built for exceptional need. He hadn't been chosen as one of the ten because he was fated to become Eleven.

At the podium, the captain cleared his throat. "The career humanity needs in this hour is called *interpreter*. The word will be meaningless to you. So it should be. Humanity has not needed an interpreter since long before the oldest Final among you was still an egg. Only the interpreter himself can fully understand the meaning of the word, the nature of his career. The rest of us do not need to understand. We need only honor him."

Another pause, longer this time. The captain bowed his head and breathed deeply. When he looked up, the fear was gone from his face. He smiled like a proud mentor.

"Assigned to rebirth in Final skin as interpreter, given the new name Eleven, the fledgling formerly known as Tei."

The throbbing in Tei's heart suddenly stilled. Everything was silence, gasping, staring, wondering. Then the universe began to chant: "Our honor is your honor. Your honor is our honor."

3
LILY

LILY WOKE IN A HOTEL ROOM on the seventy-third floor of the Margola Tower. The sun was just peeking above the horizon, but Luka had already deserted his side of the bed. The shower was running. Lily rolled onto her back and pulled the bedsheets tight around her chest. Sateen. A thread count of at least four hundred. Not a bad place to spend her last night.

She hadn't planned on spending the night with him. Not at first, anyway. But somewhere between the first glass of wine and the third, plans changed. He had been charming—as charming as it was possible for a brilliant asshole to be. She could see a hint of goodness in his eyes. Just a hint, which seemed like the perfect amount. She didn't have much more than a hint of goodness herself. No sense flirting above her league.

By the time she leaned in to whisper a joke over the noise of the gala, she meant for her lips to graze the skin of his ear. By the time he hailed a cab, she didn't object when he offered only one address for them both.

After that, every choice felt as inevitable as if it had been written into a script. A hand laid just above the knee, squeezing gently. The inching of their faces towards each other until they couldn't help but kiss. The walk past prying eyes in the lobby, the long ride on an elevator made of glass, the wait for the room door to close behind them before she pressed him against the wall and began unbuttoning his dress shirt. Everything was written in the script. It was inevitable, and there was comfort in inevitability.

Lily didn't need romance. All she needed was good stage directions.

The shower turned off. Luka emerged from the bathroom surrounded by a cloud of steam, cinching the towel around his waist. He was taller in person than his press photos implied, with thin shoulders speckled and hued like a crème brûlée crust. A ring of fat drooped at the base of his otherwise scrawny torso. An engineer's physique, Lily had thought as they undressed each other last night. Nothing to write home about, but nothing to be ashamed of. At least he was more interesting than a pint of ice cream and a few hours' channel surfing.

"You want the bathroom?" he said. A pragmatist's good morning.

Lily nodded but didn't move. She watched as Luka dropped the towel and began pulling on pieces of his rumpled suit.

"You're going to be late," he said.

"I won't have seventy reporters shoving cameras in my face," Lily retorted. "Shortens the commute."

Luka tied his pinstripe tie without looking into the mirror. The knot came out lopsided, veering off to the right. "Well? Do I look like a triumphant genius?"

"The aesthetic bar for geniuses is mercifully low," said Lily.

Luka tied his shoes. "You know what I like? About this? You don't have to pretend I was good in bed last night. I don't have to say I'll call you later. We don't have to ask where this relationship is going, because we already know."

Lily said nothing.

"It's a pity," said Luka, "that all my one-night stands can't end this way. Imagine how simple that would be. Imagine the luxury."

THE LIMITS OF MY WORLD

The room door opened and closed. Lily pulled the bedsheets up over her face. Sateen. A thread count of at least four hundred.

Imagine the luxury.

4

KANAN

HOPING TWICE HURT WORSE than hoping once. But Kanan couldn't help hoping.

The choosing of the first ten Finals felt like drowning—her head plunging deeper beneath an icy river with every rebirth that wasn't hers. The touch of Ipran's palm to Rajamin's was the final scream, the inaudible trail of bubbles. But when Captain Buru started talking about Eleven, a fresh wave of hope washed over Kanan. It felt like waking up after a digiscape drowning, like being given a second set of lungs to breathe with. Kanan wanted more than anything for the captain's words to be about her.

But the sound of Tei's name—Tei's name where Kanan's could have been—brought everything crumbling down a second time. It was a stryker dart, a sudden attack that left a hollow bleeding gap in its wake. A drowning with no waking up.

Never before had Tei's name sounded so cruel.

Kanan's mouth moved as the assembly chanted, but her throat was too dry to make a sound. Tei glanced over. Her glance was half pity, half apology. She brushed a single gentle finger against Kanan's knee.

"You promised," said Tei's lips, her voice hidden by the assembly's roar. Then she rose to her feet, walked toward the pyramid, and passed behind the grey curtain.

When she emerged, she was no longer Tei. Eleven had been born. Everything about her was larger now: her shoulders broader, her torso and legs taller, even her chin and cheeks and lips bolder and more pronounced. If she hadn't hated running so much, she could have learned to run the perimeter of the universe in seventeen minutes or less.

Kanan tried to feel pride for her agemate. Nothing came. The stryker dart had emptied her out. The warmth of the morning's checkers game was just an empty cavity now.

Nothing remained of the aging ceremony except formalities. Eleven disappeared among the newborn Finals on the far side of the assembly, her head bent against the onslaught of applause as she walked. Captain Buru made empty speeches about the honor of Final careers, the honor of the archive. She announced the twenty-nine senior fledglings assigned to the archive, naming each one in slow succession as if another surprise might be buried among them.

"You promised," Tei had said. A strange farewell when Tei was the one staying in skin. How could Kanan do anything else in the archive but hold up her end of the bargain? The promise was all Tei's to keep.

"Kanan," said the captain among the litany of names, her voice never losing its crisp intensity. "Assigned to the archive."

Kanan barely felt herself stand. Everything now was just a digiscape lesson coded ahead of time, a series of motions on the way to a predetermined outcome. Her skin responded as the assembly knew her skin would respond. The weight of their collective expectation pressed her forward in its current. Mentor walked beside her, head shaking almost imperceptibly, mourning the shame of it all.

Jerik's ill-fated escape attempt, nine seasons past, didn't cross Kanan's mind until she was already behind the curtain. The birthing hydropod gurgled green in front of her. Orderkeepers had taken hold of her arms. "Close your eyes," said Mentor, and when Kanan obeyed, she pictured the little fledgling running across the clearing in nothing but underflesh.

It had been hopeless when Jerik tried to escape—pure desperation without a chance of success. But Jerik had been far smaller than a Final, whereas Kanan was nearly the same size. Jerik had let them take the skin off her legs before she began to run. Jerik had wasted her breath on screaming when she could have been running.

Above all, Jerik had never been a runner.

Skin peeled away from Kanan's scalp, away from her cheeks, away from her neck. The hands were at her breastbone now, stripping down and out, tearing long flaps of muscle away from her arms. She was inside her own dream from the previous night, carried along by inevitability, choosing nothing.

She opened her eyes. In front of her, the birthing hydropod churned, its lips wet with froth, eagerly waiting to swallow her up. The suns' amber rays drew her eyes down to the raw underflesh where her old chest skin had been. The thing that was almost her swelled and shrank in rhythm with her heartbeat.

In less time than it took for her chest to rise and fall, she chose.

Both orderkeepers' hands were distracted, one peeling away the end of a strip of muscle from her abdomen, the other wrestling to unknot a tangle of shed skin. Mentor had turned away, leaving a single hand resting on Kanan's shoulder. It was enough.

Kanan ducked low, pulling on Mentor's wrist and jabbing at her exposed knee. Mentor toppled, and Kanan kicked at her as she fell. Mentor's hands clawed air. She flew backwards and hit the surface of the hydropod with a dull crash, drenching them all in water.

Kanan ran.

The orderkeepers' backs were turned, searching for the source of the commotion, and Mentor could see no further than the hydropod rim and the looming underground channel that led toward the archive. In those precious seconds of confusion, Kanan slipped past the grey curtain and darted toward the access gate sunken into the near wall of the alcove.

No one in the assembly reacted to her appearance at first. After the shock of Eleven, every other surprise seemed more believable by comparison. A fledgling whose skin was only half shed, flaps of sinew trailing off her undertorso as she sprinted on blue-skinned legs, could almost have been a purposeful spectacle. Kanan's agemate Shanur and her mentor, who had followed numbly behind Kanan on their way to the archive, watched mutely as Kanan skirted their path.

"Stop her!" bellowed an orderkeeper from the pyramid, emerging wet and furious from behind the grey curtain as she took chase. Three new orderkeepers appeared in the aisles of the assembly and began racing towards the access gate, trying to cut off Kanan's point of escape.

Dripping with water, Kanan nearly slipped but regained her balance. She ran with the strength of fear, faster than her fledgling legs had ever learned to move.

Finals from the assembly were on their feet now, stumbling en masse toward the clearing. Their mouths gaped—whether with outrage or pleasure or just glancing interest, it was impossible to tell in the blur of the moment. Kanan felt something whizz over her shoulder; she ducked instinctively. A patch of earth fifteen skin-lengths beyond her exploded in a shower of dust.

"Hold your fire," boomed the captain's voice. Despite its intensity, her tone was measured and unhurried, almost disinterested, as if the command had been just another name in a list of archive assignments. "Orderkeepers, hold your fire."

The access gate was nearly in reach now. Ten steps until Kanan passed through it. Five. Two.

Someone behind her dove, and a hand caught her by the ankle. Kanan cried out as she dropped onto her hands and knees. Her wet skin was just slick enough to wriggle out of the orderkeeper's grip. She threw her whole body over the threshold of the gate and against the emergency override lever on the far side. A sheet of heavy steel, rimmed with glowing LED stars, slid down from the sky at her back, shutting Kanan away from the assembly room and the roaring crowd.

She was alone.

She breathed through skinless lungs.

Without knowing why, she began to laugh.

The gate would stay closed only as long as she held it down—override levers responded to no texture except skin. And she couldn't stay, because the orderkeepers would come for her by another gate. Four access gates led out of the assembly room, and of the other three, one fed into the same network of hallways as this one. She had two minutes at most before company arrived.

A ribbon of blue muscle dangled from the back of Kanan's forearm, drooping almost to the earth. Kanan clamped her teeth over it and tore, feeling a twinge of pain as the fibers shredded. She looped the ribbon of skin over the lever twice, pulling tight and tying the ends together. Slowly she eased her body away from the lever, making sure the contraption would hold.

"Kanan." It was Mentor's voice, muffled through the access gate, though she was probably shouting to be heard above the assembly's commotion. "Don't let fear rob you of your honor. The archive is still open to you. Humanity still wants you."

For the second time, Kanan began to run. Away from the access gate and the lever wrapped in discarded skin. Away from the distant shouts of orderkeepers echoing through the halls, growing ever nearer. Away from Mentor's pleading yells and the chaos of the assembly.

Away from humanity.

§§§

Since the time Kanan was an egg, the human race had seen three deletions. Premature archiving was more common by far, happening once a season or so, usually after someone suffered a severe skin malfunction. There was no shame in premature archiving—or minimal shame, perhaps. But deletion was a punishment, the consequence of an unforgivable crime against humanity.

The first deletion was a butcher whose name Kanan never learned. She had a long chin and always seemed to be frowning even when she smiled. No one knew why the butcher had been deleted—but whatever her crime, the galley chemists had always hated her (or so the rumor went) and were gleeful to see her gone. Half a season passed before a new butcher was assigned at the next aging ceremony, during which time everyone ate a lot of rehydrated protein paste. The galley chemists served it up with grim pleasure, their short chins seeming to smile even when they frowned.

As for the second deletion, Ciani's crime had been obvious enough. The former archivist was indexing old memories in the archive when she learned about an extinct alien race called the Natchers. What began as innocent historical fascination grew into a feverish obsession. By the time of her deletion, Ciani raved incessantly that the Natchers still existed in a parallel dimension, hiding somewhere above the sunlight, plotting their return to the human universe. Even after she was erased, Ciani's legacy proved impossible to destroy. Natchers became a myth, a threat used to frighten young fledglings into obedience. They were said to haunt the hallways, hiding just past the edge of the visible universe, waiting to steal the skin off delinquent fledglings who left their hydropods at night.

The third deletion, and the only fledgling of the three, began as a disappearance. Her name had been Robiana. Her failure to report began at the end of a leisure evening, her hydropod display blinking its displeasure into the cohort's dormitory. After the suns were lit the following morning, Captain Buru announced her disappearance over the universal throat. All the early communications implied sympathy for the absent fledgling, as if she had gotten lost in one of the remote storage lockers or suffered a skin malfunction. As the days passed, Buru's reminders through the throat turned harsh, promising threats to the fledgling if she delayed in reporting.

The same day she was found, Robiana was deleted. No one was allowed to witness her erasure ceremony, not even her mentor. Her fate was announced through the universal throat. The captain's voice purred with satisfaction.

That same voice chased Kanan now. It rumbled across the walls of every hallway, as cool and unaffected as if Captain Buru were still reading a list of names from a script:

"Kanan, surrender yourself now. Do not wait for the order-keepers to find you. If you wait to be found, you will be deleted.

And rest assured, Kanan, you will be found. You can't run forever. Everyone is found in the end."

Orderkeepers' shouts echoed from somewhere behind her, further away than before and yet somehow louder. Silica pounded beneath her feet. The skin of her legs had long since dried, but her underflesh was becoming slick. Instinctively, she raised a hand to feel its strange contours as they rose and fell.

Was it muscle memory that drew Kanan toward the mess hall as she ran? Every other aging ceremony had ended this way, Kanan and her agemates swept into a jostling crowd bound for a feast. Or was it her growling stomach that commanded her legs, following the scent of baking bread? Whatever the reason, she was nearly there now. The mess hall's north access gate glimmered at the end of a long hallway lined with junior fledgling dormitories.

A tall shadow stepped into the frame of the gate. Kanan skidded to a halt.

"She's lying, you know," said the shadow.

Kanan hesitated, glancing from side to side as she tried to remember if any of the dormitories opened into a new network of compartments.

"The captain," the voice continued. "When she says everyone is found in the end. They never found Robiana."

"Robiana was deleted." Kanan inched backwards. "She was found and deleted."

"Was she?" The shadow stepped forward into the light of the hall's first sun. She had a narrow face, with sharp eyes that seemed to slice into her cheeks. "Do you believe everything you're told?"

To Kanan's left was a dormitory for newborn fledglings. At the far end of walls lined with hydropods, a second access gate stood closed, blinking red. "Who are you?"

"A galley chemist," answered the Final, taking another step forward. "Not a particularly good one, either—galley watch before a feast is no job for a master chemist. But at least good enough to have been assured by the officers' committee that I wasn't at risk of archiving this season."

In her mind, Kanan mapped the nearby networks. One network led to the water processing plant, an open ring of elevated portals surrounding a huge three-dimensional river. The other network dead-ended at the hatchery. The only way to keep running was forward, through the mess hall, past the Final looming in front of her.

"And you're Kanan, of course. The runner. Half-skin is a good look for you." The chemist walked closer, her lips stretching into a slow smile. "Buru may be a liar, but she's right about one thing: You can't run forever."

"Watch me," cried Kanan, launching herself forward. She tackled the chemist, sending them both sliding across the smooth earth. In a flash, Kanan was on her feet again. She raced toward the mess hall.

The chemist began to laugh. "You're even better than I'd hoped," she called out. "But I'm not what you think. I don't want to delete you. I want to help you."

Kanan was into the mess hall when the words reached her. Around her, a hundred tables lay immaculate in readiness for the aging feast, every bowl and spoon and knife gleaming.

Her run slowed to a jog. A walk. A frozen uncertain stillness.

"You can't run forever," said the chemist from behind her, the laughter gone from her voice. "Not in a universe this size. But I can hide you until the universe expands."

"I—" Kanan stammered, turning back reluctantly. "I don't understand."

"Of course not," said the chemist. "How could you? But there's no time. Follow me." She swept past Kanan, toward a secured galley gate shrouded in hazy steam.

"I can't hide in the galley," Kanan protested, stumbling in the Final's wake, torn between distrust and desperation. "Not during the feast. The rest of the galley crew—the orderkeepers—everyone—will be here."

"And where else should a human hide except near other humans?" asked the chemist, using the back of her forearm to trigger the gate latch. Inside the galley, heaping bowls of fresh greens lined the counters, overshadowing rows of beakers and vials poised above Bunsen burners. Every aisle was crowded with racks shrouded in heavy cloth. "This is the only part of the universe where your heat signature won't be detected. Speaking of heat…"

She pulled at one of the rack cloths, unveiling trays of warm bread braided into citrus-peel-studded wreaths, their crusts glistening with tallow. The chemist bundled the fabric together and passed it back to Kanan. "You'll need this. When you're not fully covered in skin, it gets cold in the butchery. Or so I'm told."

The next two access gates required eye scans to enter. "Identity confirmed," croaked each scanner as the chemist bent toward it. "Arisa, galley chemist."

"But how will I get out?" asked Kanan, hesitating before she crossed the first threshold. "The scanner won't recognize me."

"You won't get out," the chemist answered. "Not this way, at any rate. Not without me."

"How do I know I can trust you?"

The chemist laughed drily. "A little late for that now, don't you think?"

Behind the first gate, storeroom shelves stretched from floor to sky. Sacks of grain and crates of tubers and tubs of dehydrated protein filled the low shelves. Above them, too high even for a Final to reach without a ladder, were items Kanan had never learned to identify by name: oils and compounds, grey-tinged powders, bowls teeming with yeast. She craned her neck as she jogged to catch up to her guide, her fear tempered by fascination.

When the second gate lifted, a wave of icy air rushed out, cooling Kanan from the waist up. "It feels like the digiscape," she shivered.

"Yes," said Arisa with a frown, "I suppose it would. One of the few things underflesh and digiscape have in common. Quickly now."

As soon as Kanan had crossed the threshold, the gate slammed down behind them. Ahead stood more shelves, now stocked with greens and pallidflower, citrus and redfruit and figs. "This isn't the butchery," said Kanan slowly, clutching the heavy fabric closer to her undertorso as a thrill ran down her spine.

"Of course not." Arisa pointed past the shelves, to a row of curtains that hung from the sky so still and flat Kanan had assumed they were a wall. "The butchery is back there. You'll find a heap of uncarved darkmeat along the far wall, covered with insulating fabric like the fabric in your hands. That's the best place for you to hide, until I can arrange something better. Cover up as much as you can. Whatever you do, don't make a sound. Go!"

Arisa bent to the eye scanner, which announced her identity as the gate lifted again. She had barely taken two steps before it shuddered to a close, leaving Kanan alone.

The suns were dim here. Their muddy light shimmered in the steam from Kanan's breath as she exhaled. She shook out the fabric in her arms and wrapped it around her shoulders like a cloak, following her own long shadow deeper into the gloom.

The curtains of the butchery creaked and scraped heavily against one another as Kanan pushed them aside. Beyond them, the sky was sunless, or nearly so. Kanan could see only faint shapes and silhouettes. Chunks of butchered darkmeat and slabs of flakemeat—so she assumed—lay neatly stacked against the walls and dangled in rows from cables stretched overhead. The air smelled like a bleeding digiscape wound, like the raw taste in Kanan's throat after a few laps around the universe.

The skin of her feet pulled noisily away from the slick floor as she walked. The odor became stronger. Away to her right, long lumpy silhouettes larger than Kanan's entire body floated in midair, suspended from the sky by invisible cords. The heap Arisa had promised lay directly ahead: a giant mass of contours and angles obscured by a fabric shroud. Kanan lay down a corner of her own cloth and curled up against the heap, holding her breath against the cold that pierced her naked underflesh. Tugging the rest of the fabric around her, she closed her eyes. She tried to forget that anything existed beyond the fabric.

Hours or minutes—there was no way of knowing which—passed in total silence.

Then the stilted voice of the eye scanner: "Identity confirmed. Siplin, orderkeeper." An access gate whirred open and slammed closed.

Kanan's breath quickened. She traced a hand around the perimeter of her curled-up body—half warm skin, half frigid underflesh—making sure every inch of her was covered.

"Start in the back," a voice grunted from the gate. "I'll keep watch here in case she tries to run."

"How could she?" The second voice was familiar, though Kanan couldn't place it. "She wouldn't have clearance to open the gate."

"If she's here," said the first voice, "she must have gotten in somehow."

"Then she's not here."

"Doesn't matter. We've got to check it anyway. She has to be somewhere. She didn't just disappear."

"We'll find her. She's hopeless at everything but running." As the second voice drew closer, Kanan recognized its lurching cadence. Jarawi, a young orderkeeper Finalized just last season, had competed against Kanan in footraces while they were both senior fledglings. Two weeks after her Finalization, Jarawi had challenged Kanan to one last race around the universe. Her Final skin easily defeated Kanan's fledgling skin. They hadn't spoken since. But Kanan had never forgotten the way Jarawi's lips shaped words, spitting them out like slender bones from a mouthful of flakemeat.

"Maybe," said Siplin, her voice louder but still far away. "Still, she was damn good at it for a fledgling. Pity she was assigned to the archive, if you ask me."

"Doesn't matter now. No way she'll get the archive after a stunt like this." Kanan didn't need to see Jarawi's face to hear the vindictive delight in her voice. "All the better. My first deletion as an orderkeeper."

"They're nothing special. You'll see soon enough. Sooner if you hurry up."

The creaking butchery curtains announced Jarawi's approach. Heavy, sticky footsteps traced the edge of the compartment, sometimes pausing as the orderkeeper stopped to probe a suspicious pile or a shadowy corner. Soon the footsteps were nearly on top of Kanan.

All at once, they stopped.

Jarawi bent nearer—even beneath the fabric, Kanan could sense her closeness. The warmth of her skin. The hushed rattle of her breath as she examined Kanan's hiding place in the near-darkness.

Something struck close to Kanan with a dull thud, sending a faint tremor through her. It struck again, further away but still near enough to feel. Then nearer, no more than a skin-length from her head. Jarawi was kicking at the shrouded pile of darkmeat. The heap around Kanan began to shift, the fabric beneath her slipping away.

"What is it?" called Siplin.

"Probably nothing," Jarawi answered. "Unless—"

Jarawi grabbed a fistful of fabric and pulled it aside. Kanan felt a wave of frigid air wash over her. Her face was still covered, but she could feel by the cold that her right arm and half her undertorso lay exposed.

So much for hiding.

There was no sense trying to outrun Jarawi. In the days they were both fledglings, Kanan had been the superior runner, even with one season fewer beneath her skin. But the race against Final Jarawi hadn't even been close. Kanan would have to go on the offensive. She could target the knees, maybe—or, better still, the eyes.

Kanan pressed her heels against the ground, ready to spring upright. But before she could make a move, Jarawi stilled her with a disappointed mutter: "Dammit."

"Anything?" called Siplin.

"Just a pile of darkmeat," Jarawi shouted back. "It's hideous before it's carved."

"Never seen it," said Siplin dispassionately. "Never want to see it any way but carved and cooked and on my plate. Hurry up, won't you?"

"Coming." The heavy, sticky footsteps drifted away, around the last wall of the compartment and back through the butchery curtain. "Identity confirmed," croaked the scanner. "Siplin, orderkeeper." The access gate rose and fell.

Silence again.

For a moment, Kanan wanted to burst out laughing again, astounded by her good luck. Then a second thought, before the relief had settled: What if it was a trap? Surely Jarawi couldn't have missed her, not even in dim light. And Jarawi wasn't the kind of orderkeeper likely to show mercy to an old nemesis.

Slowly, barely daring to breathe, Kanan lifted the fabric away from her face. Her eyes had adjusted to the dark; what had looked like mere shapes and shadows when she first entered the butchery now took on contour and depth and traces of color. Patches of faint brown stained the walls and earth. The long silhouettes dangling from the sky were in fact massive slabs of hewn darkmeat—their exposed sinews and tendons reminded Kanan of skincare disasters she had seen in the digiscape.

When she looked down at her underflesh, she screamed.

Another skinless hand lay beside hers, nearly identical to her own. Beneath it she could see a pale undertorso. A lone leg, not unlike the legs Kanan remembered on skinless Jerik, protruded from the peak of the pile like a macabre flagpole.

Kanan was lying in a pile of underflesh.

Underflesh was darkmeat.

She was darkmeat.

5

TEI

NO ONE HAD WARNED THE GALLEY CREW to set the feast's high table for twenty-two. "It's not necessary," Tei said quickly, when Mentor complained about the missing plates. "We can sit anywhere."

"Nonsense," Buru insisted. "It's an aging feast tradition that the officers' committee and I yield our seats of honor to the newborn Finals and their mentors. Who better to honor today than you two?"

A sullen runner brought two extra place settings and deposited them at the end of the table.

"Wonderful." Buru clapped Tei's fresh Final skin on the back. "That's all we need, then. Slide down, everyone. Plenty of room on the benches for Eleven and his mentor. A historic day, isn't it?"

Seen from up close, the captain's smile looked unnaturally wide, his energy so conspicuous it was almost ferocious. He set a hand on Tei's shoulder and guided him down to the bench. "You'll have leisure for the rest of the day, of course, along with the other newborns. Tomorrow at first light, you'll report directly to me in the command room. You know the way, I trust? All the necessary gate clearances have been seen to. We're counting on you, Eleven."

An orderkeeper appeared at the captain's side. "Excuse me, won't you?" said Buru. He stepped away as the orderkeeper began whispering furiously into his ear. Tei strained to listen, hoping for news of Kanan. What he heard instead was the chatter from a gaggle of fledglings at the table beyond them:

"Maybe it's got something to do with transportation. That's what it sounds like to me."

"Extraordinary need, the captain said. What's transportation got to do with extraordinary need?"

"Maybe there's a flaw in the digiscape. Some error in the coding that could destroy everything. That would be extraordinary need."

"I heard the Eleven is brilliant at coding."

"It's not *the* Eleven, dummy, it's just Eleven. That's his name now."

"Do you think he likes having a new name?"

"I wouldn't want a new name."

"He looks like someone named Eleven."

The fledglings turned to study Tei, saw him staring back at them, and hastily looked away.

In front of the fledgling table, the orderkeeper dismissed himself with a salute. Captain Buru cursed under his breath. Tei sighed with relief.

As long as Buru was cursing, Kanan was free.

§§§

Fully adjusting to newborn skin took three weeks on average. The first week was devoted to muscle bonding, as skin morphed and affixed to its host. Fine motor skills were sharpened in the second week, after days of maddening klutziness. In the third week, the mind and nervous system finally made peace with a skin. Until then, bouts of vertigo, anxiety, impulsivity, and irritability were the norm.

Skincaregivers called this three-week disorientation *adolescence*. Everyone who reached Final skin endured three adolescences: one as they entered junior fledgling skin, the second in their rebirth to senior fledgling skin, and the third upon becoming Finals. Second adolescence, everyone agreed, was the most turbulent of the three. But Final adolescence was most humiliating. Humans chosen for Final skin were supposed to be exemplars of intellect and skill and agility—and yet, in Final adolescence, they became as weak as fledglings fresh from the egg, cursed with inevitable failure at the moment they were most eager to succeed.

Amid the clamor of the aging feast, while his newborn age-mate Sholi chewed noisily beside him, Tei recited the stages of adolescence to himself. The spinning of his head had to be vertigo. Purely biological. An inevitability of new skin.

"You should be eating." Mentor tapped his own fork on Tei's plate from across the table. "Nutrition is crucial in the muscle bonding period."

"I'm not sure I can," Tei answered. "You know how adolescence wreaks havoc on unfamiliar stomach muscles."

Mentor slid another cut of darkmeat onto his plate. "The more severe the adolescence, the more important the meal."

§§§

Tei coded a new dream for himself that night. He and Kanan sat in the middle of a field of hyacinth under a vast blue digiscape sky, playing checkers. There was no sun or shade, no sound or stillness, no shape anywhere on the horizon. Just sky and hyacinth and checkers.

"Lines or circles?" said Kanan, oblivious to the day's events.

"Lines," said Tei. He studied his agemate's eyes, the eyes that were not eyes.

They began to play.

"If I asked you to call me Eleven," said Tei after a long silence, "would you?"

"It might depend why you were asking," answered Kanan. "Would you want me to call you Eleven?"

"Why else would I ask, if I didn't want it?"

Kanan shrugged. "Sometimes we ask for things we don't want."

They continued playing. Kanan began to hum a digiscape melody—a melody Tei had heard just before the aging ceremony began.

"Do you remember anything about today?" asked Tei. "Anything at all?"

"This is your dream," said Kanan. "I remember whatever you want me to remember."

"Whatever I want…" Tei's voice trailed off.

Turning away from the checkerboard, Kanan began picking through hyacinth leaves. He found a long, slender leaf and stretched it taut between his fingers. When he blew against it, it let out a shrill screech, like the call of a wounded bird.

"I want to know," said Tei finally, "what you felt when I was Finalized instead of you. I want to know if it occurred to you when you decided to run away from the archive that we might never see each other again. Or if you thought about me at all, even for a split second, as you were running. I want to know if my eyes cast a magic spell on you—not these empty digiscape eyes, but my real eyes, the ones in skin, the ones I was supposed to lose so you could keep yours."

Kanan blew on the leaf again, releasing two more bird calls before it tore on the third blow. "Do you want me to understand what you're saying?" he asked quietly.

"No," said Tei, his voice breaking. "I don't."

"Then what is it you want?"

Tei closed his eyes. "Checkers. I want to play checkers."

"Lines or circles?" asked Kanan, exactly as he had asked before.

"You choose," said Tei.

"Lines," said Kanan. "I do better with lines."

§§§

Four access gates guarded the hallway that led to the command room. The first required skin confirmation to open. The second was voice-activated. The third used an eye scan. "Identity confirmed," said a digiscape voice as each gate rose. "Eleven, interpreter."

The fourth gate had a square of steel removed from its center and replaced by a glowing white screen. "Write your passcode," the digiscape voice commanded.

"I don't know any passcode," said Tei. "The captain didn't give me one."

"If the captain had given you a passcode," said the voice dispassionately, "it would not be *your* passcode. Write *your* passcode."

"I'm sorry," said Tei, feeling odd about apologizing to a talking gate. "I don't understand. Am I just supposed to write anything I want?"

"My limited programming does not permit me to give advice on passcode creation," said the voice. "It does, however, permit me to inform you that if you cannot manage a task as simple as this one, your future career may suffer accordingly."

Tei reached out to touch the screen, which began glowing green beneath his fingertip. He wrote the word *Checkers*.

"Passcode accepted," said the voice. The gate retracted into the sky. On the other side, Captain Buru stood in a tiny box of a room, a space barely big enough for ten Finals to stand together skin to skin. A corrugated, sun-studded sky lay low and flat above three bare walls.

"Sorry about the gate," said the captain. "The programmer who designed this digiscape interface thought it would be funny to give him a personality, and we've never bothered to fix it. It's wonderful for security, though. It reads your skinprint along with your meaning. Not just anyone could get through that gate by writing *checkers*. It has to be you. Interesting choice, by the way. I didn't realize fledglings still knew about checkers. It's an old game."

"In the archive," said Tei guardedly, "nothing is old."

The captain paused, seeming to consider the point. "Come in, come in," he said at last. "I trust you slept well?"

"Well enough for the first night in a new skin. Is this"—Tei looked from side to side as he entered—"Is this the command room?"

The captain laughed, a laugh too loud for such a small space. "What, this? Goodness no. Some luck we'd have fitting the officers' committee in here. But this is how we reach the command room." He rapped his knuckles against the wall, and the gate descended. The same screen glowed on the gate's other side. Buru held his palm against it. "Command room," he repeated, no longer speaking to Tei.

"Destination confirmed," answered the digiscape voice.

Without warning, Tei's knees buckled slightly, as if the earth had risen underneath his feet. And yet neither earth nor sky seemed to move at all. His head and stomach felt oddly heavy at first, then strangely light. He gasped. "Are we…?"

"It's called an elevator," said the captain. "The engineers could probably tell you how it works, but only one or two have seen it for themselves. This is the only one of its kind in the entire universe."

"Elevator," Tei repeated. "So we're travelling up?"

"Yes and no." The captain smiled strangely. "We're travelling up in relation to where we used to be. But in relation to where we're going... Well, you'll see soon enough. Up isn't always up."

As the captain spoke, the lightness in Tei's body grew lighter still. The sensation was like falling—or perhaps it was more like reaching the peak of a high jump, suspended in the lingering moment between rising and falling. Tei tried to drop to his knees. Instead, his knees shot up to his chest, and his whole body began to tilt sideways.

Or was the elevator tilting around him while he stayed still? Maybe sky and earth were the culprits, playing tricks on his eyes and stomach by conspiring to rearrange themselves. The room looked as if one wall had demanded to be crowned the new earth. New earth and old earth seemed to be fighting among themselves, deciding which one would carry the burden of humanity's feet.

Tei's feet, however, could find no earth to land on. He pushed himself away from a wall that had become the new sky, only to ricochet against another wall that had become the new earth. Everything turned and spun wildly out of control. Eventually he grasped a sun fixture along the old sky that was now a wall. As he steadied his body, the elevator became still again. Nothing around him moved, but Tei couldn't escape the feeling that he was falling.

Beside him, Buru floated in midair, smiling as wide as ever.

"You've arrived at the command room," said the digiscape voice. The gate slid open.

Unlike the elevator, the command room was at least as large as Tei had expected, perhaps larger. It was brighter, too, though Tei couldn't see where the illumination came from. Like the elevator, this room looked as if it had been turned on its side. What might otherwise have been the earth lay against one wall. Chairs jutted out from its surface on slim carbon poles. Straps and buckles dangled off them, drifting aimlessly through the air like underwater plants. Between the chairs, steel tables and boxes littered the wall. Knobs and switches and tiny details meaningless to Tei covered their sideways faces.

The rest of the surfaces—earth, sky, walls—all joined together in a single sphere. There was no telling where earth ended and sky began. Nothing was flat; everything curved downward and outward. It was, thought Tei, like stepping inside a perfectly round citrus fruit. Whatever material the sphere was made from, he had never seen it before. It looked like pure water made solid—not like ice, with its cloudy surface and whiteness, but like water in a digiscape river, dappled with shadows of dark and light that drifted slowly across its surface.

"The material is called diamantium," said the captain. "One of the rarest substances in the universe. I'd offer you a seat, but sitting in a weightless room isn't any more comfortable than standing. We may as well float where we please."

Buru pushed himself out of the elevator, somersaulting through the air and landing lightly on the far side of the watery sphere. He lay back against that rounded wall as easily as if it were earth underneath him. "Don't be afraid," he called back to Tei. "It's perfectly safe."

Tei tried to follow the captain and found himself drifting helplessly in the direction of the chairs, which had now tilted to become part of the sky. He flailed his arms as if swimming through air. With a second shove off a strap-festooned chair, he managed to reach the watery sphere and grab hold of one of its grey ribs. Crab-like, he scuttled across the cool rounded surface.

"What happened to up and down?" he asked breathlessly when he reached Buru. "Why don't our bodies weigh anything in this room?"

"It's a function of something called gravity. You'd need a scientist to explain it to you properly. But it has to do with the universe's constant spinning—the same spinning that lights up our suns and powers our hydropods. That spinning pulls us down and makes us heavy when we're along the universe's outer edge, where humanity walks in skin. Here in the command room, at center of the universe, the rules are different. Everywhere is up and down at once."

Memories of digiscape engineering lessons flashed through Tei's mind. "It all has something to do with centrifugal pseudo-force, then? At the edge of the universe, our bodies' rotational velocity tells us which way is down? And as we move toward the center of the universe's spinning, that velocity decreases to zero?"

The captain's laugh erupted in triplicate, high and hearty. "I told you, ask a scientist if you must. Already you seem to understand it better than I ever will. And this is why we chose you, after all—chose you out of everyone in your cohort, and the two cohorts above you as well. The interpreter must be a person of ideas, a person who can build whole worlds of meaning inside his mind. Or so your predecessor tells us."

"I thought there was no interpreter before me."

"Not in skin, no. Not for many generations. But the archive was designed for moments like this one. You'll do all your training there, or almost all, with the old interpreter himself and with others who were in skin during his generation's crisis."

"What crisis?"

"I can tell you only so much," said Buru. "And everything must be kept in the strictest confidence. Unless you're being trained or standing in this room, not a word to anyone, on pain of deletion. Do you understand?"

Tei thought of Kanan. "Yes," he said quietly.

The captain fixed him with a long stare. "The Natchers have returned."

"Natchers?" Whatever Tei had been expecting, he wasn't braced for a fledgling's tale. "The extinct alien race?"

"Alien, yes. Extinct, no. Or not anymore."

"So the archivist who was deleted for spreading rumors about Natchers—he told the truth?"

"Ciani endangered the human race," the captain answered, shaking his head slowly. "He spoke more than he understood, and his loose tongue might have ruined us all. His deletion was a tragedy. But the committee had no choice."

"Would it be so bad if everyone knew?"

Buru began pulling himself up and down the sides of the sphere, twisting his body at angles that would have been impossible anywhere else in the universe. "Look what became of Ciani. The mere memory of Natchers drove him mad. Order-keepers used to catch him dismantling air vents, or attacking suns with knives he stole from the mess hall. Imagine all of humanity acting that way—looking for aliens around every corner, trying to find a way out of the universe. Our survival depends on people knowing neither less nor more than they need to know."

"And the officers' committee? Do they know about the Natchers?"

"It is their duty to know. As it is mine. And now, most of all, as it is yours."

"Mine?"

"The Natchers have mouths like humans, and they seem to speak to each other. But what they speak is nonsense. It is impossible for a human to understand a Natcher, or a Natcher to understand a human. And yet, as long as their alien race exists in our universe, we have only two options: learn to communicate with them, or annihilate them."

The captain delivered these options matter-of-factly, as if either one might have been equally pleasing. Then he frowned and continued: "Annihilation, unfortunately, is out of the question. The Natchers provide certain"—he paused, searching for the word—"certain *necessities* to the universe. Their existence poses a threat, but if they are entirely erased, humanity is doomed as well. Our only choice is to communicate."

"I thought you said it was impossible to understand them."

"Impossible, yes. To anyone except an interpreter."

"You think I can speak to aliens?"

"I know you can. Or you will be able to, once you've been trained. The interpreter in the archive has studied your profile; he says you're the most promising fledgling he's seen in all his digiscape seasons. That's why we've waited for you. That's why we've made you Eleven."

"What if he was wrong? What if I fail?"

"You won't."

"But if I did?"

Buru sighed. "I suppose it's best you hear it from me now, instead of from rumors in the digiscape later. The numbers are not in your favor. Many humans across the generations have been assigned as interpreters—how many exactly, no one knows for certain. But there is only one interpreter in the archive today."

"What happened to the others? The ones who failed?"

"They became..." The captain trailed off. "To be human is to speak to like a human. The better an interpreter became at speaking like an alien, the harder it was for him to remain human."

"You mean they were deleted?"

"Deleted, yes. But not by the choice of the officers' committee. These interpreters' minds were so poisoned by the Natchers that they willingly deleted themselves. It takes a strong mind, interpreting without losing your humanity."

Tei thought again of Kanan, of Buru's somber threats over the universal throat. He thought of skin and archive and humanity.

"But you have a strong mind, Eleven. You would never choose to delete yourself, no matter what lies the aliens told. Would you?"

"Never," said Tei. "Of course not."

The captain turned his steady gaze onto Tei once more. "That's right. You wouldn't. Because the human race can't afford to see you fail."

6
LILY

LILY'S PHONE SHOULDN'T HAVE BEEN RINGING. The contract had expired a week ago, the same day her sublet ended and left her legally homeless. Until yesterday she'd been sleeping in a chintzy motel on 14th and Barrow, using the front office's decaying landline to order tubs of tofu fried rice and rubbery dumplings.

A Margola Industries liaison had offered to cover the remaining balance of any unfinished contracts. "Sign the new lease," the silky voice told her during her final HR call. "Say yes to another year's subscription. Re-up your streaming services. Savor every last moment. We'll take care of everything after you're gone."

But Lily had insisted on cancelling all her services ahead of time and white-knuckling through the interim. Maybe she made her choice under the residual influence of her mother, a tut-tutting miser who burned candles after dusk to keep down the electricity bill. Maybe she did it because it was what Elliot would have done: throw caution to the wind, sever ties from the old way of life, and plummet headlong into the adventure. Or maybe she just couldn't bear one more reminder that bills remain even after their recipients are gone. Even after the casket is sealed and buried, someone still has to pay the landlord.

Whatever the reason, Lily let the phone contract expire along with everything else, and her phone had–until three seconds ago–lain dormant. She welcomed the reprieve. The last few months had been an incessant stream of calls and texts from people she barely remembered. Old neighbors. Graduate school classmates. Cousins once removed. They all wanted to talk about Elliot, of course. ("It must have come as a shock for you. Fourteen months? You're kidding. I swear it was just yesterday I heard the news.") And then, once Margola Industries started releasing names to the public, everyone wanted to talk about that too. ("Imagine my surprise when I saw you on the list. Are you half as terrified as I would be? All of a sudden you're the biggest celebrity I know.")

Lily didn't want to talk about any of it. Not her newfound celebrity status, not Luka and the Margola sisters, not her training, not her hopes and fears, not her decision to leave. Not Elliot. Most of all, not Elliot.

When the phone rang, sateen bedsheets were still draped over her head like a shroud. The light from the sunrise–her last sunrise–rendered the sheets warm and translucent. This moment, Lily thought, might as well be her funeral. It was as close to a funeral as she would ever get.

The ringing continued.

Lily pulled herself reluctantly upright, shedding the burial cloth. She squinted at the number on the phone. Restricted. She cursed and then answered.

The caller introduced himself three times. Each time the information seemed to pass between Lily's ears without taking root in her brain. At last she was too embarrassed to ask again. "This number was disconnected last week," she said instead. "How did you get through?"

"My network has its tactics," said the caller. "And I have mine. I was hoping you could spare five minutes to comment on a story we're running."

A reporter, then. No wonder his voice sounded like marmalade, sweet and sticky with a hint of citrus sharpness. "Now isn't a good time," said Lily. "I'm already running late."

"Is there another time you'd prefer?"

"Tomorrow," said Lily.

The reporter laughed. "Even I don't have tactics enough for that. Please, just five minutes of your time."

"I'm sorry," said Lily. "You'll have to find someone else to comment on your story."

"The story is about you."

"Me?" Lily froze. "You've got a thousand people to pick from. Some of the best minds on Earth. People who were already making headlines for years before the Margola list went public."

"It's part of a human interest series," said the reporter. "About the heroes who are leaving, and the loved ones they're leaving behind."

"I'm no hero," said Lily. "And I'm not leaving anyone behind."

"What about Elliot?"

Suddenly she couldn't breathe. "What did you say?"

"I've got a contact who worked recruitment for the Project. She reviewed both of your files. And I did a bit of digging."

"Elliot is none of your business. He's no one's business except mine."

"I know it's hard being in the spotlight." The reporter's voice was even sweeter than before. The citrus sharpness had disappeared, replaced with something cloying like apricot preserves. "And you've already gone through so much. But that's what makes you an inspiration."

"Damn your inspiration," said Lily. "You'll have to find a different story."

The reporter cleared his throat. "I'm afraid it's too late for that. We're running the story whether you like it or not. You'll be gone by the time it airs. I'm not asking for your permission. I'm just asking for a comment."

Lily said nothing.

"People are desperate for hope," said the reporter, after a long pause. "And a story like yours, sensitively told–I know you probably don't want to hear this right now, but it's really a beautiful story. It's exactly what people are hungry for."

"If you tell it beautifully," said Lily, "you've told it wrong. If it gives someone hope, you've told it wrong. You want a comment? There's my comment."

She flung the phone against the wall. It tumbled to the floor, a spiderweb of cracks across its shatterproof screen. A beam of sunlight transformed its dark face into a kaleidoscope of yellow.

7

KANAN

KANAN HAD NEVER SLEPT OUTSIDE a hydropod before. She hadn't even known it was possible: to simply close her eyes and drift into nothingness, without feeling the water close over her skin. Had she known, perhaps she would have tried harder to stay alert. But ignorance proved merciful. Relief and cold and weariness overwhelmed her horror, releasing her into sleep like she had never slept before.

Unchosen. Unprogrammed. Unhuman.

She woke to a metallic rattling somewhere above her. Her legs felt stiff and unresponsive, their skin rough to the touch. The taste of acid lingered in her mouth.

The rattling grew, echoing louder and nearer until the whole butchery trembled. Looking up to the sky, Kanan saw a circle of shadowy darkness poised directly over the heap of underflesh. It looked like a patch of absent sky—like a tunnel leading up out of the universe.

Without warning, four skinless bodies fell through the dark circle. They landed atop the heap of underflesh one after another, with four sickening thuds. Then everything was still again.

Kanan approached them gingerly, clutching her insulating fabric in front of her like a shield. Even in the dim light, it was easy now to identify arms and legs and undertorsos. She followed one of the torsos with her eyes. The body ended at the neck, in a severed stump. Kanan reached out a trembling hand to touch its shoulder. It wasn't cold like the other bodies had been. It still felt warm, warmer even than Kanan's own fingers.

Just then, the body began to move.

Kanan stumbled over her stiff legs as she stepped back, falling onto the slick butchery floor. She raised her head in time to see the bodies begin to writhe. First one arm, then a second, then a third, sprouted up from the heap.

She screamed.

"Hush," answered a strange voice, thick and soft like moss. "Your throat they hearing it."

Two bodies emerged from the heap. They were as large as Finals, or nearly so, and more or less human in their shape. But now that she saw them closely, Kanan could never have mistaken them for the rest of the underflesh in the butchery. They still had their heads attached, for one. As for their flesh, the thing covering their bodies was like underflesh but also subtly different—thicker, knottier, more textured. Humans without skin looked small and frail, as if they had been stripped of their power. These creatures looked powerful all on their own. They seemed designed for skinlessness.

"Hush," said the same mossy voice as before. The mouth that moved belonged to the taller and broader of the two strangers, a creature with sun-colored threads covering its scalp. A length of green fabric was wrapped around its waist. The creature strode toward Kanan for a few steps, then seemed to change its mind and walked directly past her. It disappeared behind the butchery curtain.

"Don't be afraid," said the second creature. "We are not enemies." Its voice was clearer than the other creature's had been, lighter and more human. The threads from its scalp were longer, too, waves of brown that splashed across its shoulders and ran like rivulets down its arms. Like the first creature, this one wore the same green fabric at the waist, and a second bolt wound around its chest.

"What are you?" stammered Kanan. She had meant to say "who," not "what," but her mouth betrayed her.

The creature didn't seem offended. "We are humans," it said simply.

"You can't be," Kanan countered. "I'm human. Or I used to be."

"Ah, I'd forgotten." The creature clicked its tongue as if this were a mistake that could have happened to anyone, as if humanity were an easily forgotten thing. "We are what your race calls Natchers."

Kanan gasped. "Natchers?"

From past the butchery curtain, the first creature barked something that sounded to Kanan like gibberish. The second creature responded in kind, then turned back apologetically. "We'd prefer if you don't call us by that word. It is an insult that only a Cyborg—a human, I mean—would use."

"What do I call you, then?"

"You may call us by our personal names. I am Tiqvah. My companion is Avi. And you are Kanan. We have been sent to rescue you."

"Sent? Did Arisa send you?"

"I do not know this name. We were sent by the council. One of our spies overheard your race's orderkeepers discussing your imprisonment."

"No," said Kanan, "I'm not imprisoned. I'm in hiding. No one except Arisa knows I'm here. The orderkeepers searched and couldn't find me."

Tiqvah shook its head. "I know nothing of this. We were told that a chemist trapped you inside this death chamber, where the Cyborgs planned to kill and eat you."

The words *death* and *kill* were unfamiliar to Kanan, but she understood their urgency well enough. She felt her stomach turn, the taste of acid returning to her throat. "You're lying," she said, though she barely believed the accusation. "Arisa protected me. She's going to help me escape to safety."

Avi burst through the curtain again, chattering quickly to Tiqvah. "Near now them," it said to Kanan. "Having time no more."

As the creature spoke, a rope of twisted carbon fibers appeared in the sky, sinking until its tip rested on the heap of underflesh.

"One of your race approaches. It is no longer safe. We must go. You must come."

"But if it's Arisa," protested Kanan. "She can explain. She can help."

Tiqvah stretched out its naked hand. "We can't be seen, any of us. Come."

"I— " Kanan hesitated. "I can't just—"

"Having time no more," repeated Avi. "Coming you." It grabbed Kanan firmly by the wrist, pulling her toward the rope, the heap of underflesh, the tunnel in the sky.

Kanan wriggled out of Avi's grasp and tried to run. But the skin of her legs failed her, stiffening at the knees and sending her skidding across the floor.

From behind the butchery curtain came a faint digiscape voice: "Identity confirmed. Arisa, galley chemist."

The Natchers hissed at one another in gibberish. Kanan heard feet pounding, racing heavily across the slick floor. She rolled upright just in time to see Avi's fist flying toward her face.

Then everything was black.

§§§

When Kanan awoke, the air was warm again. A tarp hung directly overhead, daylight pulsing at its edges. The surface she lay on felt soft and faintly damp, not at all like the universe's silica earth. This earth—if it was earth at all—smelled of unwashed greens, raw and sweet.

Though her head throbbed from Avi's blow, she barely noticed that pain. All her attention was focused on her legs, which burned as if searing coals were being scraped across them. She tried to sit up but found none of her muscles could move. Through immobile lips, she let out a weak moan.

Tiqvah's face appeared above her. "You should not wake," it said. "The pain will be too great."

Kanan struggled to form the words. "What… pain?"

"The skin on your legs. It has been too long away from the Cyborgs' water. It destroys you. It must be removed."

"No," Kanan croaked. "It's all." *All that's left of my humanity.*

"There is no choice. You live skinless or you do not live. I will tell the healer to increase the sleeping draft."

"No," said Kanan again. But Tiqvah was speaking to someone else now, speaking its own gibberish syllables. Other voices responded—two, perhaps three—all of them coming from below Kanan's field of vision, where the coals burned hottest. One voice in particular seemed agitated, its deep thunder rumbling louder until it was almost painful against Kanan's ears.

Tiqvah's human voice returned, a voice so different from its Natcher voice that Kanan was amazed both voices could emerge from the same body. "The healer says we cannot wait for your sleep to come again. The chemicals from the skin have sunk too deep. If we wait, you may lose your legs. The healer says you have good legs. You have strength, uncommon strength for a Cyborg. You will endure the pain."

Against her thigh, Kanan felt the first flap of skin tear away. Something like a needle full of flames dug beneath her muscle until it struck bone. She screamed and writhed. Unfamiliar hands held her against the earth, their fingers reaching for a second tear, a third.

Kanan had dreamed, the night before the aging ceremony, of a moment not so different from this one. The sensation of tearing skin had been different in her dream. The dream-earth beneath her straining fingertips had been smoother, colder, firmer than this alien surface. But the fear was the same. The hands were the same. And so was the powerlessness Kanan felt in the grasp of those hands, as they tore and tore until the last shreds of her humanity were gone.

When sleep finally came, she was still screaming.

8

TEI

THE ANNOUNCEMENT OF KANAN'S DELETION
came two mornings after the aging ceremony, just as the
second meal shift began. It was projected through the universal throat, which meant it reached Tei's ears in a half-empty
mess hall as he and four of his surviving agemates choked down
bowls of lumpy flakemeat porridge, trying to quell the protest
of their adolescent stomachs.

After his visit to the command room, Tei could conjure up a
perfect mental image of Buru speaking through the universal
throat. The captain was strapped into a chair at the center of
the universe, floating upside-down and right-side-up and sideways all at once. His fingers rested on an array of sliders and
dials called the communications panel. A soft-textured black
receiver hovered in front of his open lips, so close he could have
swallowed it by leaning forward. Tei imagined Buru's bureau-
cratic smile, beaming even larger than its already-too-large
default, delighting that the problem of humanity's half-skinned
runaway embarrassment had at last been resolved.

There was no reason to disbelieve Buru's announcement. No good reason, anyway. Robiana's deletion had happened the same way, without warning. There had been a hasty trial before the officers' committee, a hasty conviction on charges of treason. Only the captain and three orderkeepers bore witness to the somber punishment. If the name uttered by the universal throat had been any name other than Kanan's, Tei would have unquestioningly accepted the news as truth.

But Kanan's eyes had been a magic spell. That spell still held Tei under its power. If Kanan was deleted—if the spellcaster was gone forever—how had the spell lost none of its potency?

"You okay?" Tei's agemate Sholi asked from the seat beside him.

"It's just nerves," Tei answered, the same way he had answered everyone since the aging ceremony. "There's so much to learn in a new career. Adolescence only makes it harder. But you know that. It's just as hard for you. We're all Finals now—all of us who are left."

"We're not all Eleven," said Sholi. "The nerves I feel teaching junior fledglings to operate a rowing machine are nothing compared to the nerves you must be feeling. But that's not what I meant." His voice suddenly dropped close to a whisper. "I meant Kanan."

Tei scanned the faces of the others at the table, making sure none of them was listening. Yerima was mimicking his old mentor, distorting his lips and gurgling loudly as Thunod and a lab chemist named Sita laughed along. "Kanan was your agemate too," Tei murmured. "He belonged to all of us. To humanity."

"To all of us," Sholi agreed. "But to you most of all. Surely you didn't think the rest of us were unaware of it?"

"There was nothing," said Tei, "to be unaware of."

Sholi nodded slowly. "Maybe it's best this way. To remember the past only as it should have been. As we need it to have been."

Tei ate a spoonful of tepid porridge.

"If you ever need—" Sholi began to say, and then stopped. "But why would you? There was nothing. Of course."

"Of course," said Tei. There was nothing, and therefore nothing else to say.

§§§

Tei's first day as interpreter-in-training had been spent entirely in the command room with Buru. Mercifully, his second day—and every day following, for as long as necessary—was to be spent in the digiscape, inside one of the fabled career hydropods.

Hydropods were divided into five classes: birthing, training, leisure, dormitory, and career. The birthing hydropod, like the elevator Tei had ridden yesterday, was the only one of its kind in the universe. Its water pipes were larger by far than the pipes of other hydropods. Large enough to carry up the underflesh of a newborn junior fledgling from the hatchery. Large enough to carry away the underflesh of a retired fledgling or Final to its permanent home in the archive.

To be human, Tei's mentor had told him, was to be in the birthing hydropod on these two occasions: arrival from the hatchery and departure to the archive. No one came from egg into skin without needing to be born. And no one, not even the most seasoned Final, avoided the archive forever.

No one who remained human, that is.

Training hydropods and leisure hydropods both served the same function, transporting their occupants into the limitless world of the digiscape. Leisure hydropods were glitchier and received less routine maintenance. Otherwise, the distinction between the two classes was a mere formality, meant to keep labor and rest as separate as possible. In training hydropods, cohorts of fledglings studied the basics of mathematics and skincare and coding, while Finals mastered advanced concepts and career-specific skills. In leisure hydropods, humans of all ages whiled away their discretionary hours in any way they could imagine. In athletic competitions. In fragrant kitchens. In breathtaking adventures. In mystical fantasy worlds.

Dormitory hydropods—what fledglings called "dream machines"—were smaller than other hydropod types, covered with retractable lids for uninterrupted sleep. They could fit along a dormitory wall in stacks five high before reaching the sky. Their water supply was a mere trickle, just enough to immerse and rejuvenate the skin. Their function, too, was limited. They could be programmed for dreamlessness, for preset dreams imported from the digiscape, or for customized dreams manually coded by the sleeper.

Dreams inside a dream machine lacked the clarity of digiscape excursions in a training or leisure hydropod. The mechanism was too simple, and the sleeping mind too murky, to make a dream fully real. But for a gifted code-writer—for someone like Tei—dreams had the benefit of occurring in isolation from the rest of the digiscape. In dreams it was safe to code worlds you would never want the rest of humanity to see.

As for the career hydropods, Tei had never seen one and knew next to nothing about them. They were kept in a restricted-access compartment near the rowing room, accessible only to humans whose careers required unlimited access to the deepest recesses of the archive. "A historian's euphoria and a coder's chimera," Mentor had once said, when Tei asked about them. Tei didn't understand the phrase, but he had never forgotten it.

"You won't have used a career hydropod before, I suppose," said Buru, tapping his chin as if this revelation were a surprise to him. "No fear, the archivist will orient you. I'll tell him you're coming. Just wait until the third shift to report in."

"I could start earlier if you'd like," Tei offered, "in one of the training hydropods."

"No sense," said Buru. "Your studies with the interpreter are all highly confidential; a training hydropod won't have the proper clearances. Best to sleep late while you can. The archivist will be worth your wait. He's very diligent, among humanity's best. But he keeps a different work schedule than most. A consequence of spending all one's time in the digis-cape, I suppose. Inside the archive, it doesn't matter if the suns are lit."

The archivist was unusually slim for a Final, with skin patterned like swirling diamonds and striking eyes equal parts blue and grey. He sprang on Tei as soon as the compartment gate slid open, before the security scanner had finished announcing Tei's identity.

"Interpreter, indeed!" said the archivist, clapping Tei on the back repeatedly. "Such an honor, Eleven, such an honor. I've wanted to introduce myself since even before the aging ceremony, since before you were Eleven at all. All these rumors about Tei, Tei the fledgling code prodigy, flying around the archive for seasons and seasons. Humans in skin don't always appreciate good code—but the archive notices these things. I notice. And now here you are, in the skin."

"Nice to meet you," answered Tei, hesitating at the moment a name could have fit.

"Reif," said the archivist. "The name is Reif. I get so few visitors in here, I've almost forgotten how to introduce myself. It's easy in the archive, you know, to code all the introductions beforehand. Saves time on small talk once you're inside. Time is of the essence when the whole universe of history is at your fingertips and you're just one Final combing through it. But when most of your companions have been archived for generations and the niceties are all programmed out of existence, a fellow does forget how to make small talk. I must be boring you already. But do have a seat. Sit, sit."

Tei sank onto the stool Reif had thrust him towards. "Boring isn't the word I would have chosen."

"Kind of you to say. And attentive to words, too. But of course you are. That will serve you well in your career, won't it? Not that I've been told all the details, you know—imagine it, a lowly archivist like me—just enough to help you find your way in the archive. You'll be spending most of your time with the old interpreter, but there are others you'll want to visit as well. Historians from the era when Natchers first appeared in the universe, that sort of thing. You can probably find your way around better than anyone—those rumors about fledgling Tei can't have been rumors for nothing—but if you do ever need a guide, that's what I'm here for. I probably know the archive better than anyone still in skin. Or is that arrogant of me to say? I don't mean it that way. I just mean I have certain advantages, vis-à-vis my career... But there I go again, talking more than I need to talk. I don't get many visitors in here, did I mention? So nice to see a fresh face, you know."

As Reif talked, Tei studied the compartment around them. Its walls and earth were bare, save for a few secured file drawers and a programming desk in one corner. The single sun in the sky shone so dim Tei wondered if it was malfunctioning. Now that the access gate had closed, most of the light came from the glowing code displays on three hydropod units in the center of the compartment. They illuminated Reif's face at an upward angle, casting the shadow of his nose across one eye.

"Magnificent, aren't they?" said Reif, following Tei's gaze back to the hydropods. "Half again as large as any training or leisure unit, and they've got the processing power to prove it. The flow rate is nearly tripled to maximize connectivity. They're fitted with voice-code reciprocal analytics. Holographic tactile user interface, too—but I don't need to tell you that, you can already see it. And just wait until you get inside. Neural image clarity like you wouldn't believe."

Reif lowered his stool until his eyes were level with the nearest hydropod. His fingers flew expertly across its code display. "The captain says we shouldn't talk programming today. Plenty of time for that later. He wants you inside the archive and with the interpreter as soon as possible. I've already taken the liberty of programming your first encounter. From there, the interpreter prefers to write his own code. It's ready when you are."

"Just like that?" Tei suddenly felt as nervous as a junior fledgling entering the digiscape for the very first time. "Nothing else I need to know before I go in? Are you coming with me?"

With an air of finality, Reif swept his hand twice through the holographic screen floating above the water's surface. The image evaporated into wisps of shrinking numbers. Water gurgled, its green ripples tossing like miniature waves, flowing faster. "There's plenty you still need to know. But no sense listening to me prattle when you could learn it for yourself along the way. And no sense me slowing you down, either. You'll see exactly where to go. Besides, the interpreter is... not keen on company."

Tei clambered over the rim, lowering his back into the water as the current pressed against him. Before putting his head beneath the water line, he hesitated. "This is still the digiscape, right? I can't mess it up permanently? There's no risk if I do something terribly wrong?"

"It's still the digiscape," answered Reif. "But you're Eleven now. You're meeting the interpreter. Risk is all there is."

"Very reassuring." Tei took one last gulp of air.

"Good luck."

Tei slowly released the breath and sank underwater. The skin of his face fused together, sealing the gaps at his mouth and nostrils and eyelids into a solid sheet. Everything became dark—not solid dark, but broken hazy dark flecked grey and white. The gills along his shoulder blades opened and began to breathe.

The water's current, charged like lightning, permeated him inch by inch. When the current reached the back of his skull, he felt himself beginning to fall. When it reached the skin where his eyes had been, he saw the falling as well: a tunnel ringed with glowing digits and symbols, racing past him in crisp detail. The tunnel grew smaller as he fell, squeezing tighter and tighter. Miniscule flashes of solid light scraped against his forehead and flailing feet. His momentum dwindled slowly, arrested by the scraping, until he hung motionless in a pillar of light.

A burst of heat. Everything exploded in reverse. Now Tei was soaring up, the tunnel growing—or was it he who was shrinking?—until each blurred symbol on the tunnel wall was the size of a skin-length, a compartment, a universe. The tunnel bent and folded over on itself, throwing him against a wall of light that wrapped around him like gelatin. Then the gelatin became grass. He was encased in grass, pushing through it blade by clinging blade, emerging up out of the earth like someone escaping from a grave. When he pulled apart his sealed lips, he tasted greenness and dirt.

He had arrived in the digiscape.

Jagged brown cliffs encircled a grassy clearing. In its center stood a single, giant ash tree, its whorled branches reaching up past the height of the plateau. The leaves were variegated and sparse. The shade they cast was equally variegated, patches of orange just bright enough to make the whole clearing visible without seeming to illuminate it.

"They sent you after all," said a voice behind him. "They delayed for so long, I was beginning to wonder if we'd ever have another."

Tei began to turn, but something caught him by the chin and forced his gaze back toward the tree.

"I'd really prefer you didn't." After all the fearsome things Tei had heard about the interpreter, the voice was more timid than he expected. But the hand holding his head in place was iron-strong. "I promised them I'd talk to you. I didn't promise you could look at me."

"Not much to see, is there?" said Tei. "Humans all look the same."

The voice coughed, or perhaps laughed. "Humans? Do we now?"

"Never quite identical." Tei dredged up memories of skin-caregiving lessons, eager to impress the invisible stranger. "No two skins are patterned the same, or with quite the same shades of blue. Heights among Finals vary by as much as five finger-widths. Gait shifts subtly from person to person. Angle of the shoulders, girth of the torso. Shape of the nose and cheeks and teeth. And eyes, of course. Eyes most of all. But beyond that, we're close enough to the same. There's unity in similarity."

That last line had been one of Mentor's refrains, the weary answer given to Tei's incessant fledgling questions. *Why are skins all blue, never orange or pink or maroon? Why was Shanur reprimanded for decorating his dormitory hydropod with chemical paints? Why must everyone eat an equal portion of rehydrated protein paste when it's served in the mess hall?* Unity, answered Mentor again and again. That was the guiding principle of the human race. Unity in similarity.

"They told me you were smart," said the voice. The words didn't sound like a compliment. "Imagine me, then. Imagine me like every human you've ever seen, and let your smart human mind guess at the meaningless details."

Tei did as he was told. A small body, he thought, to match the smallness of the voice. But thick as well, at the least in the arms and hands and fingers—the body of an expert rower. Eyes the color of the earth beneath them, in turns brown and green and dim and bright. Skin patterned with intersecting and collimated lines, running head to toe like the bark of an ash tree.

"Not so hard, is it?" said the interpreter. "And what have you lost by inventing me for yourself? It doesn't matter what I look like. In here least of all. All that matters here is the words. No skin. No distraction. Just imagination and language."

"What is *language*?" The question emerged like a reflex. "Forgive me for interrupting, Interpreter."

"None of that apology nonsense," the interpreter barked. "You're not some quiver-lipped fledgling in a mathematics class. And my name is not Interpreter, no more than your name is Eleven. Call me Kyri."

Tei felt a hand push between his fingers, pressing palm to palm. A formal greeting. By the time he glanced down, the hand had disappeared again.

"What is language, you want to know? Language is words that go together in sets and decide what thoughts we're capable of thinking. Language is the reason humans speak to humans and Natchers speak to Natchers, but we do not speak to one another."

"But you speak to Natchers."

"I did," Kyri corrected. "A long time ago. And I suppose, if Natchers came into the archive, maybe I could again."

"Is that possible?" Tei asked. "For Natchers to enter the archive?"

"Possible?" By the flutter in Kyri's voice, he might have been smiling, though not a happy smile. "Certainly it's not possible. But on the other hand, of course it's possible. What's possible depends what language you're speaking."

"You're telling a riddle."

"It's bound to sound that way, for now. All things in time. We'd best start at the beginning. Before we do—" A hand gripped Tei's chin again, so tight now it was almost painful. "I need your word that you won't speak of this to anyone. Not agemates, not officers, not the captain. Most of all, not the captain."

"But Captain Buru sent me here. He *wants* me to learn to speak to Natchers. Why should my training be a secret from him?"

"You've been ordered here by the captain, yes. And if you fail to learn the Natchers' language, you would be guilty of treason. But the captain doesn't know what he's asking of you. What he doesn't understand—what no captain *could* understand—is that learning the Natchers' language is already an act of treason."

Tei's heart beat faster. He said nothing.

"Buru must have warned you about the interpreters who failed, the ones who deleted themselves? Of course he did. It doesn't matter what he said. Lies, probably, though lies that might seem true if you've only ever spoken like a human. Those interpreters were the same as I was, the same as you will be. Only one difference between us: they were caught doing their jobs."

"You shouldn't talk this way." Tei clenched his fists to keep his hands from shaking. "The digiscape is a dangerous place for secrets. If the archivist looks into our code, or an officer, or anyone—"

"The code you and I are standing in right now is encrypted with dual syntax, both human-based and Natcher-based. Only a programmer who is also an interpreter can read it. I haven't just disabled the eavesdropping feature—a captain could have overridden that. I've made eavesdropping entirely impossible."

"That's illegal," gasped Tei. "Surely the officers' committee wouldn't have allowed it."

"I told them it was the only way for an interpreter to remain human. I told them absolute secrecy could keep me and you tethered to humanity. They were too desperate not to believe. And here we are. The only truly private place in the universe. Whatever we say here, no other human will know unless you tell them. So give me your word."

From above the leaves of the ash tree, the sunlight dimmed as if covered by clouds. The variegated earth became a single shadow. Tei weighed the interpreter's words, weighed his own limited options. "Why would you risk telling me all this?"

Kyri's whisper would have been inaudible if it hadn't come from so close to Tei's ear. "Because it's my duty. Treason or no treason, no matter what language I'm speaking, I haven't forgotten that. Give me your word."

"I swear."

"Good," said Kyri. "Then turn around."

At first Tei saw nothing in the shadows—nothing but jagged brown cliffs behind a vacant carpet of grass. Then he noticed a patch of even darker shadow hanging directly in front of him, like a smudge in the code, an Absence seeping through the walls of the digiscape universe. It would have had the shape of a human, if it had any substance at all.

"I can take a form, if you prefer it." The shadow didn't seem to move when it spoke, and yet it was the only possible source of the voice. "It may be easier for you if I am visible. Then again, perhaps not."

Tei took a step back. "I'd rather not talk to a shadow."

"Very well," returned the voice. "But you may not like what you see."

Sunlight returned, lighting the edges of the shadow with orange as if they were catching fire. The partial image within the shadow burned away bit by bit, bringing the interpreter into view.

Except it wasn't the interpreter. It couldn't have been.

The figure standing in front of Tei was a figure Tei had seen already once before, in his very first moments as a Final. Blue skin covered the legs, peeling away at the waist to reveal the dark contours of an undertorso. Curling black threads hung above the eyes—eyes that might have cast a spell if they hadn't been embedded in digiscape code. Tei had seen this same figure racing across the earth of the assembly room, with two orderkeepers and a screaming mentor in pursuit.

"Well?" said Kanan. "How do I look?"

9

LILY

LILY COULD NEVER HAVE GUESSED how comfortable Luka would look in a suit. In every interview she'd seen, every press release and magazine cover and behind-the-scenes photo essay, he wore a baggy denim jacket over a fully buttoned polo shirt. His pants, if by some misfortune they made it into the camera frame, were always cargo pants. He exuded the aura of a man well beyond his years and yet trapped in eternal puberty. "Neurotic tech savant," the pundits called him, and Luka dressed the part.

But that night at the gala, someone else had clearly done the dressing. His navy jacket was tailored snug against his chest, his shirt crisply starched, his normally erratic hair gelled into precision. For once he seemed to belong in the same league as the Margola sisters, the international tech moguls who had funded and stamped their name across his grandiose dream. Even his smile looked easier and more confident than usual. Or perhaps it was just the whiskey smiling through him.

"Enchanted," he said, when Lily offered her hand and her name. His accent was ambiguously European, with long vowels and disappearing consonants. "I've read your file. Very impressive indeed."

"I doubt that." She was still sipping champagne at that point in the evening, not even up to her first glass of pinot, and much too sober to relax into his obvious flattery. "Architects don't read personnel files. Even if you did, there's nothing unique or remarkable about mine. I've shaken twenty hands already tonight, and I think I'm the least impressive person here."

"Then you must not have met Milana Margola's oldest son yet. Ordinary to the core." Luka smiled conspiratorially. "But excluding him, believe me, there are no unimpressive people in this ballroom. We are history-makers, every one of us. Including you."

Lily looked away and took another sip of champagne. "Maybe you're a history-maker. I'm just an electromechanical technician who thought dying in limbo sounded like more fun than living in Tunkhannock. When they're remembering names, I doubt anyone will remember mine."

"But that's the beauty of the Project." Luka's words came faster, tumbling eagerly over one another. "It's not about your name or my name. We're making a name for all of us, collectively. This achievement belongs to the whole human race."

"Do you really believe that?" said Lily. "Or are you just good at winning over investors?"

"Why not both?"

"My contract is already signed. And if you were hoping for a last-minute donation out of my legacy fund, I'll spare you the trouble by assuring you that I'm dirt poor."

Luka waved over a platter of shrimp cocktail. "I'll ease off the sales pitch, then. But let the record show that I stand by every word. I'm damn proud of Project Universe."

"Project Universe." Lily shook her head. "Such a pretentious name."

"The investors love it," said Luka. "The press loves it. And you, with all due respect, won't be around to complain much longer."

He smiled as if delivering the punchline of a joke. Was there a touch of cruelty, a touch of narcissistic self-obsession, joining the hint *of goodness in his eyes? Or was it just the awkward charm of a tech savant unused to making conversation with beautiful women?*

Why not both?

10

KANAN

"YOU ARE AWAKE."

Until the creature spoke, Kanan hadn't realized her eyes were open. But Tiqvah's words made the real seem real. Air pressed steadily against her face—a sensation like running, though now air seemed to move against her instead of she moving against it. She hadn't known that air could move like water, flowing by its own power. The brown tarp overhead rippled without being touched. From far off, four thin music notes sounded again and again: rising, descending, rising, descending.

Kanan pulled herself slowly upright. A woven sheet fell away from her undertorso, leaving her legs still hidden beneath its folds. Kanan set a hand against the sheet and then looked up at the Natcher.

"Is it gone?" she asked.

"The skin?" Tiqvah nodded. "And the legs are recovering well, or so the healer says. You will walk again."

"Again?" Kanan tried to lift her knees. Nothing happened. She tugged back the sheet and let out a sharp cry. The underflesh below her waist, where the last of her skin had been, was covered in angry red wounds. She traced one of the gashes with her fingers. The feeling registered in her fingertips but not in her thigh, as if her legs now belonged to someone else. "What did you do to me?"

Kneeling, Tiqvah pulled the fabric completely away to expose Kanan's calves and feet. The same ugly gashes covered everything. "It is not our doing, what you see. This is the work of your race. A Cyborg skin can only survive by soaking in that green fluid you call water. Without it, the skin will draw its power from any other source, even its own host. It sucks away what is good and leaves behind a kind of poison. The Cyborgs prefer it this way. It ensures that no one wearing one of their skins can ever escape their control."

Kanan's lips trembled. "What's a Cyborg?"

"A mistake of my tongue." Tiqvah pulled the sheet up over Kanan's legs again. "Many seasons have passed since I last spoke to one of your race. The words are easily forgotten. Cyborg is what I and my people call your race."

"My race? You mean the human race?"

"Yes, precisely. The human race."

Kanan took in a long breath and coughed at the dryness in her throat. "Why don't you just call us human?"

"Because," said Tiqvah, turning away, "human is what we call ourselves."

"We can't both be human."

"No. It seems not."

Tiqvah disappeared behind Kanan's back for a moment, saying nothing more. In the silence, Kanan studied her surroundings.

She was in the digiscape—that much seemed clear. It was the sort of place Tei would have programmed, a world entirely fantastical, with nothing resembling the universe in skin. Not a scrap of silica in sight. The earth was made of grass, grass with interrupting patches of mud and long, tufted weeds. Something resembling a carbon wall stood along the opposite horizon. It stretched as far as Kanan could see in either direction before curving up and out of sight.

In front of the dark wall's nearest point, a copse of trees stood wide and squat. Two Natchers walked among the broad-fingered leaves. One had underflesh as dark as Kanan's, or darker still. The other was light-colored like Avi had been, or like Jerik the runaway fledgling. Both Natchers were covered in the same fashion as Tiqvah, with green fabric stretched around their waists and undertorsos. They carried a woven brown basket between them.

"They gather figs." Tiqvah had returned, carrying a small clay bowl in its hands. "You eat figs in your universe, do you not?"

Kanan's stomach growled at the thought. "Of course the universe has figs. What a funny idea, to gather them from trees."

"Where do your figs come from?" asked Tiqvah.

"From the galley supply portal, of course. Where all food comes from."

"And where does food come from, before it comes from the galley supply portal?"

Kanan frowned. "It begins there. You might as well ask where the light of the suns comes from before the suns create light."

"Might I?" Tiqvah did not seem impressed by the argument. Its lips were twisted to one side, as if fighting a smile. "We will let it be for now. There is too much to be understood all at once. You must be thirsty."

"What is *thirsty*?"

"Do you not have this word?" Tiqvah pinched the skin of its forehead. "No, but of course you would not. The water. I had forgotten. I will show you."

Tiqvah walked in the direction of the fig trees, down a gentle slope which gradually leveled. At the earth's lowest place, a river burbled between two walls of perfectly manicured stone. Tiqvah knelt, dipped its bowl into the river, and carried the dish back brimming with water.

"Thirst," said Tiqvah, "is the feeling of a body when water must be added to it. The Cyborgs cannot thirst, because they take in their water through the skin. But those without skin must take in water the way they take in food, using their mouths. It is called *drink*. See."

Tiqvah lifted the bowl to its lips and began pouring water into its mouth. Its throat moved up and down, as if it were eating.

"Now you try," it said, offering the bowl to Kanan.

Kanan thought of drowning and shuddered. "I can't. Human mouths aren't made for water. I would need my gills."

"Your gills," said Tiqvah, "are gone. But your body's need for water is not gone. You are dry; I hear it in your voice. Take just a small mouthful at first. Make like the water is a fig, and swallow it into your stomach. Chew if you must."

"But the last time I let digiscape water into my mouth—"

"Digiscape?" Tiqvah began to laugh, hiding its mouth with the back of its hand. "Do you think you are in the digiscape?"

Kanan narrowed her eyes. "Of course. Trees. An earth made of grass. Water that's clear instead of green. I've seen it all before. I've been to places just like this one, or almost the same. I know the digiscape when I see it."

"But this is not the digiscape. The human race—my race, I mean—does not have a digiscape. This place is our home. It is the overworld."

"Overworld." Kanan turned the word over on her tongue. "Are we still in the universe, then? Or are we somewhere... outside?"

"We are above the place your race calls the universe. In my tongue, your universe is called *underworld*. My people do not go into the underworld unless we must. It is dark and cold there where sunlight cannot reach."

"Of course sunlight reaches the universe," Kanan protested. She refused to call it *underworld*, no matter what the Natcher said. "We have suns in every compartment."

"Suns, yes." Tiqvah twisted its lips again. "But you do not have *the sun*." The creature spoke those final words with expectation, like a fledgling telling the end of a joke.

Kanan crossed her arms over her bare undertorso. "You're talking more nonsense."

"It cannot be told in your language, I suppose," said Tiqvah. "Or if it can, I do not know the way. It must be seen."

The alien rose onto the balls of its feet and stretched its body out to full length. Its hands reached up to unhook the tarp overhead from one of the poles holding it in place. As the tarp fell away, Kanan's upturned eyes were blinded by something overwhelmingly bright.

"Do not look directly at it," said Tiqvah. "The ones who try have lost their eyes altogether. You must only look near it, and even that only for a moment."

Kanan buried her face in her hands, blinking away tears drawn out by the light's intensity. "That is not a sun."

"Not *a* sun, no. It is *the* sun." Tiqvah hooked the tarp up to its prop again, casting merciful shade. "It is the source of our light in the overworld. Day and night are determined by it. Its force pulls life up out of the ground and makes everything grow."

"And there is only one sun in the whole overworld? How can it be everywhere? Does it burn you when you touch the sky?"

"I should not laugh," said Tiqvah, immediately violating this commandment. "You must forgive me. These are questions I had forgotten anyone could ask. The sky in the overworld is not a thing that can be touched. It is simply space—empty space between earth and sun. As there is only one sun in the overworld, so there is only one sky shared by everyone. We have no compartments here—there is no need for compartments. Compartment walls exist only to hold up the thing you call sky, which is the underside of the earth you are sitting on now."

"But your overworld does have a wall." Kanan pointed out past the fig gatherers in the copse, to the dark expanse stretching in both directions. "Or if it isn't a wall, what is that?"

"That is the edge of the overworld. You have this edge in the underworld too, yes? Like a wall, but with Nothing lying on its other side. You see how the trees do not grow too near to it? This is because their roots have nowhere to reach in the soil. Earth ends, soil ends, everything ends at the edge."

Kanan took a long breath, felt a dusty rattling in her throat, and coughed again.

"You must drink," said Tiqvah, extending the bowl again. "It does not matter if you believe me or no. The water will teach you how it must be swallowed. Come, just a few drops at first."

The clay bowl felt gritty and warm against Kanan's fingers. She held it up to her lips, tilted the water towards her. Just before it touched her lips, she pulled away. "This is insanity."

"I will tell you of insanity. If you don't learn to drink, your body will dry up and die." Tiqvah hesitated, seeing the blankness in Kanan's expression. "You know what it is to die, surely? Your race speaks of death?"

Kanan shook her head.

"*This* is the insanity," murmured Tiqvah to itself. And then, to Kanan: "If you do not already know it, I do not know enough of your race's speech to explain it. Or perhaps it cannot be explained."

"Maybe death is something that exists only among your race," said Kanan, "and not among humans?"

A sound like a bark burst between Tiqvah's pursed lips—a short laugh without humor. "Death reaches the members of every race that calls itself human, whether or not they are willing to speak of it or think on it. You may not understand the word *death*, but this will not protect you from it. Until you understand it, you must trust me."

Kanan kept her eyes on the glimmering water. "How do I know I can trust you?"

"Because," said Tiqvah, its voice sharper now, "I have treated you like a living being and not a slab of darkmeat. You think you know which race deserves the name *human*? Then tell me which race has been more human to you. Or if you cannot answer this, say nothing. It matters not to me. But drink."

Kanan's first mouthful of water was tentative, barely enough to moisten her tongue. When the swallow did not choke her, she took a second mouthful, larger this time. Coolness and relief washed over her. In two more swallows, the bowl was empty.

"You see?" The softness had returned to Tiqvah's voice. "I did not lie to you. Your throat knows how to desire water. It is only your mind that did not know it."

The alien took the bowl from Kanan's hands and returned to the river to refill it. Kanan emptied it, passed it back. On Tiqvah's third journey, another figure appeared in the distance, running with a swiftness that could have put Kanan to shame even when her legs were still clad in skin.

"Avi comes," said Tiqvah as it set the bowl of water in Kanan's waiting hands. "There may be news from the elders."

Tiqvah stepped out into the sunlight to greet the runner. Both creatures folded the palms of their hands together in front of their own undertorsos. Avi's chest heaved and gasped from exertion, and its underflesh glistened under the sunlight. After a moment's pause, they began to speak.

It might have been Kanan's imagination, but she thought she recognized words now from among the Natchers' gibberish speech. Her own name was there, and Tiqvah's and Avi's. But other words as well. *Human. Water. Skin. Underworld.* Vowels and syllables were distorted, making the words sound alien. And yet Kanan could identify them—couldn't she?—in the now-familiar lilt of Tiqvah's tongue and in Avi's soft, mossy murmurs.

Avi was larger than Kanan had remembered from the butchery. The creature stood a head above Tiqvah, its long undertorso and wide shoulders swallowing the other Natcher almost completely in their shadow. As for its legs, Kanan couldn't help noticing those most of all. They were thick and sinewy, nothing like the sleek, blue-patterned legs of Finals in skin. These, thought Kanan, were the underflesh legs of a runner. If she couldn't run in skin, these were the legs she wanted for herself.

Tiqvah began to shake its head and raise its voice, pointing emphatically back at Kanan. "No," the creature seemed to say repeatedly, interspersing the word among strings of unintelligible syllables. Kanan wondered if *no* was spoken the same way by every race.

Avi pushed past Tiqvah, ducking its head as it stepped beneath the shade of the tarp where Kanan sat. "Coming you," it said thickly. "To elders Avi taking."

"The elders must wait," said Tiqvah, speaking so Kanan understood but still fixing its stern gaze on Avi. "The skin has not yet been off a full night and day. Time is necessary before walking. This is the healer's order."

"Need walking not," said Avi, clearly frustrated at being forced to argue in an unfamiliar tongue. "Cyborg Avi carries."

Tiqvah planted itself between Avi and Kanan as the taller Natcher stepped forward. "You will not carry anyone. How can Kanan rest while you drag her across the overworld? The elders must wait."

Avi shook its head fiercely. "No wait. Unless helping us it does, Zillah dies. Healer saying this too." It placed a hand on Tiqvah's shoulder. "Avi promise making."

As Kanan watched Avi's eyes, an image of Tei came unbidden into her mind. Tei in senior fledgling skin, in the last moments before she became a Final named Eleven and Tei ceased to exist. Tei gazing at Kanan—into Kanan—like she wanted something that had no name. Tei bidding Kanan farewell with an urgency that made sense only now, in retrospect: "You promised."

Kanan had promised. But some promises were more easily kept than others.

"I'll go," said Kanan.

The Natchers fell silent, turning to her.

"I'll go," she repeated, looking directly at Avi now. "I'd walk if I could. Is it far? Are you sure you can carry me?"

The taller alien bowed its yellow head. "For Avi, not far. Cyborg without skin having little weight."

Kanan threw the sheet off her legs. Avi looked down and then turned away immediately, barking something at Tiqvah.

"We must dress you." Tiqvah hurried over with a strip of green fabric in its hands. "At the place where your legs divide. It cannot be seen among our people. It is shameful there."

Kanan allowed Tiqvah to roll her from side to side and wrap the fabric around her waist. Its fibers were thin and stiff, rustling against her instead of gripping like a skin. "How can one part of underflesh be shameful if another is not?" she asked. "It's all just underflesh."

"For you, yes," said Tiqvah. "Or so it seems. But the matter is different for us." The alien stepped back to survey its handiwork. "It is enough. You look almost human."

"We go now," said Avi. It lifted Kanan gently by the armpits, slinging her legs around one of its shoulders and her head around the other. Kanan's left ear was pressed up against the slope of the alien's chest. When she opened her eyes, the world passed upside-down and sideways across a horizon made of underflesh.

Avi's steps were tentative at first, but soon the creature hit its stride. Tiqvah ran beside them, drifting in and out of Kanan's view as they bounded across the overworld. The bright thing Tiqvah called sun blazed overhead, dousing everything in sparkling yellow-white. Kanan felt moisture in the places her underflesh pressed against Avi's. She wondered if the moisture was hers or the alien's, or if it belonged equally to them both.

Beyond the jostling horizon of Avi's underflesh, Kanan's vision was full of trees at first. The squat fig trees gave way to taller trees covered in pale green spheres. In front of these, rows of low tufted leaves ran between stripes of dirt. Rivulets of water trickled between them, impelled forward by a force Kanan could not see.

All at once the plants' green became gold. Long tan stalks with sagging tips rose knee-high and carpeted the earth. They moved in waves without being touched, a dry ocean. On and on they stretched, swallowing up the minutes, endless in every direction except where the river and the dark edge of the overworld interrupted. Kanan thought she could hear the stalks' whispered rhythm at Avi's legs. Tiqvah had fallen out of sight now, though its ragged breath was still close.

Where the gold finally ended, a cluster of Natchers appeared along the river's stony edge. They sat among baskets piled high with auburn bulbs, their hands busy at a chore Kanan could not see. The undertorsos of some were bare, others covered. All wore the green fabric around their waists. A few raised their heads to stare as the runners passed.

"We are nearly there," Tiqvah called out between breaths. "It is best if you do not speak directly to the elders. Speak only to me, quietly, and I will give your words to the others."

Kanan raised her head from the jostling of Avi's chest. "They wouldn't understand me, you mean?"

"Best if they understand nothing," answered Tiqvah. "As long as you are merely silence or gibberish, all is well. But if they think they understand—that is where the danger lies."

The earth was made of grass again, dotted with tarps and square plots exploding with leaves. Other voices began to fill the air. The Natchers they passed were nearer and more abundant. Soon they were close enough that Kanan could have reached out and caught the threads above their scalps between her fingers.

"What danger?" she asked.

Avi stopped, knelt, and deposited her in the grass. The sun blinded her for a moment until Tiqvah's shadow stooped low over her, blocking everything else. "If you speak," Tiqvah whispered, "they may hear you plotting to destroy us."

"But I'm not—"

"The fault is not yours. It is in your tongue. Your race has treason in its tongue." The alien held up a finger to its own lips. "Speak only to me, unless you want us both to die."

11

TEI

"YOU'RE HERE," GASPED TEI. He reached out a finger, almost near enough to touch his deleted agemate. "You promised, and now you're here."

Kanan stepped forward so that his underflesh pressed against Tei's fingers. "Here, yes. But I know nothing of promises."

The voice was the interpreter's, not Kanan's. The longer Tei looked, the more the body seemed wrong as well. Jagged stripes, branching like lightning, patterned the leg skin where Kanan's whimsical swirls should have been. A too-broad forehead furrowed above the eyes. As for the underflesh of the torso and face, Tei's view of half-skinned Kanan had been so brief that it was impossible to say.

Still, the resemblance between the two was striking. The slender frame. The protruding jaw. The shape of the wistful smile.

The eyes.

"I remind you of someone," said Kyri.

Tei nodded. "An agemate."

"More than an agemate. The person you write into your dreams." It wasn't a question.

"He's gone. Deleted."

"Deleted?" The interpreter squatted low, tilting back until he was sitting among the twigs and leaves. "That's good news. If he's deleted, perhaps he's not gone after all. Don't look at me like that, I couldn't explain it all to you now even if I wanted to. You don't have language for it yet. Everything is language. Where humanity ends, and where it begins, and everything else. You'll see."

Tei couldn't tear his gaze away from the familiar face. "I don't understand," he stammered. "Why do you look like him? You both— The last time I saw him, he only had half a skin."

Kyri patted the ground. "Sit and I'll tell you. Sit, sit. No use wasting our legs on standing when they aren't legs to begin with. There, that's better. I don't take shape in the digiscape if I can help it. But when I do, I configure myself the way my fellow interpreters appeared at the moment they were deleted. Half-skinning was devised as a punishment for treasonous interpreters, to symbolize the half-breeds they had become. Part human, part Natcher. Or part Cyborg, part human, depending which language you're speaking."

"But you weren't deleted."

"Me, deleted?" The interpreter raised his eyebrows, as if he had never been asked such a question before. "I suppose not. Not as far as anyone knows."

"Then why the half-skin? Why take your shape in the form of someone else's shame?"

"Because," said Kyri, "when the root of our shame is willingly chosen and shared, it loses its power to shame us. It is no longer shame at all. I refuse to let my fellow interpreters be dishonored by pretending I am not one of them."

"The other interpreters were deleted," Tei objected. "You said so yourself. How could that be anything but dishonor? Isn't deletion the definition of dishonor?"

"Very good!" cried the interpreter. "Already you're beginning to see behind the curtain. Definitions, definitions everywhere. As long as we define dishonor according to deletion, we see the world the way humans in skin are meant to see it. We know what must be done, and we do it, because the words tell us so. The words tell us where good and evil can be found, what we ought to desire and what we must never desire. But what if we spoke a language where the words told a different story? What if we saw honor apart from skin or humanity—and dishonor that transcends deletion?"

"There's nothing else in the universe," said Tei. "Skin and archive and humanity, or deletion and absence. That's all we speak of, because that's all there is to see. What else could there be?"

"History," said Kyri.

As he spoke the word, a bolt of lightning struck the giant ash tree. Thunder came instantaneously, deafeningly. By the time Tei had regained his vision, the tree was engulfed in flames.

"You'll forgive the pyrotechnics, I hope." Kyri nodded toward the charred leaves drifting around them. "I've always had a flair for the dramatic. Alas, the occasions to flex those muscles now are few and far between. Although I recently had the pleasure of making Buru scream like a fledgling." He paused and smiled wistfully.

Tei looked toward the sky. The tree was no longer visible at all—it was only flames, flames shaped like branches and leaves, held up by a trunk that had become a pillar of fire. Branches that had burned away from the trunk began crashing down around him. They sliced the earth like knives wherever they met it, leaving dark chasms in their wake.

"And now," said Kyri, "we ride."

Tei turned away from the burning sky and the dissolving earth to find a winged unicorn in front of him. The creature was perfectly white, all except the slim silver horn crowning its proud head. The interpreter, already mounted, pressed his blue-skinned knees against the creature's mane. He offered a hand to Tei, who took it and clambered up behind him.

"Unicorns are a favorite digiscape companion of yours, I understand," Kyri called back to him as the creature stretched its wings around them. "Mine as well. I should warn you, Nauraa is not a gentle flier. You'd best hold onto me."

"It's forbidden," said Tei. And it was. The law left no ambiguity. Prolonged skin-to-skin contact between humans was reserved for special circumstances like skincaregiving and orderkeeping. Even in the digiscape, where skin wasn't truly skin, people were warned against programming scenarios where touch lasted more than a moment. Nearly anything was permissible in dreams, of course—but dreams were different, obscuring the senses like fog, and they were kept private for a reason. As for touching underflesh, only mentors and orderkeepers did such a thing, and that only in the aging ceremony, as skins were fitted on or stripped away.

Kyri leaned across the unicorn's neck and tapped against its mane. "It's not forbidden here. My code, my rules. Hold on or fall off."

The unicorn reared onto its hind legs. Tei's arms wrapped around the interpreter's undertorso by instinct, barely keeping him astride. They launched into the air just as the earth beneath the unicorn's hooves dissolved into nothing.

Tei pulled himself tight against Kyri, pressing the skin of his own torso against the interpreter's bare back. He breathed in deeply, imagining that it was Kanan who sat in front of him—Kanan in half a skin, strong and steady as he had always been, nearer now than ever before.

Tei's stomach tossed at the thought. Or perhaps that tossing was just the sensation of flying, of swooping and curving between flaming branches as the unicorn carried them toward the open sky.

When they emerged above the highest flames, Tei was surprised to see that the sunlight had disappeared, and night—or something like night—had fallen. The dark sky they flew into was speckled with stars, speckled far thicker than the skies Tei usually programmed. These stars clustered together in imperfect blurs, smearing light across the blackness.

"Further up, Nauraa," shouted Kyri, and the unicorn complied. The stars brightened without seeming to grow nearer. Tei looked down to the place earth should have been but saw only white mane and firm haunches and vast beating wings. Eventually the wings stilled, stretching out to their full length as unicorn and passengers glided through the empty space.

"History is best discussed with a change of scenery," said Kyri in the newfound silence. "And I find changes of scenery much easier if there's no scenery to leave behind."

Tei took one hand away from the interpreter's undertorso and held it out against the passing nothingness. "I've never thought to program a landscape among the stars."

"Nor had I, when I was still in skin. But spend enough time in the archive, and the number of thoughts available to you begins to grow. This is one of the scenes I've come to enjoy most."

"Because it's beautiful?"

"Because it's mostly comprised of nothing. Less to program. More to believe in." He brushed the unicorn's mane between his fingers. "Besides, Nauraa is the best company I could ask for."

The unicorn whickered and snorted.

"History, then," said the interpreter. "Let us begin with the creation of language."

"At the Great Construction," said Tei, eager to prove himself. "When the universe was shaped and began to spin."

Kyri shook his head. "Not so long ago as that. In the time of the Great Construction, there was only one way of speaking. Language did not exist yet, because there was no need to separate one language from another."

"You mean there were no words in the beginning?"

"Words, yes—of course there were words. But everyone spoke with the same words, meant the same things. And because they meant the same things, they saw the world with the same eyes. Before language was created, there was unity."

Tei repeated his mentor's old refrain: "Unity in similarity."

"A kind of similarity. But perhaps not what you and I mean by the word *similarity*. What the ancients thought of as similarity, the inventors of language refashioned into difference."

"A thing can't be both similarity and difference at the same time."

"Of course not," said the interpreter reassuringly. And then, less reassuringly: "Unless your language changes."

"So you keep saying," snapped Tei. "But it's still nonsense."

Kyri sighed, glancing over his shoulder. "Simplest, I suppose, to see it with your eyes. Look at my underflesh. No, not just near it. Look directly at it, the way you've refused to do since I materialized. Study it. Tell me what color it is."

"Dark," said Tei. "Like a loaf of bread minutes before it begins to burn."

"Good. And what color is your underflesh?"

Tei looked down at his skin. "I don't know. I've never seen it. Mentor told me to close my eyes when I shed my skin at the aging ceremonies."

Without warning, Kyri dug his bare fingernails into Tei's arm with superhuman strength. A flap of skin tore back, exposing tawny underflesh. Tei swore, but Kyri pretended not to notice. "What color now?" he said.

"Something lighter, I guess." Tei gritted his teeth, watching pinpricks of blood appear at the fringes of his avulsed skin. "Like bread again, but pulled from the ovens ten minutes sooner."

"So they are different, your underflesh and mine. How then can we have unity in similarity?"

"Because underflesh doesn't matter. It's meaningless to the human race. It only exists during a few moments in an aging ceremony." Tei paused to glare at the interpreter. "Unless someone rips off your skin and forces you to see it outside of your rebirth."

"And once you and I have seen our underflesh?" asked Kyri. "What becomes of our unity then?"

"Skin," Tei answered. "No matter our age, no matter our underflesh, we have the same skin. To separate us from the Natchers. To prove our humanity. There's unity in that."

"Is there?" Kyri took a breath so long Tei thought he had finished speaking. When he continued, he seemed almost to be whispering. "What about for me, or the rest of the interpreters? What about for your agemate with half a skin?"

Tei didn't answer.

"You might think we've gotten off topic from the question of language's origin." The interpreter's voice was strong again. "Far from it. In the time of the Great Construction, and in the first seasons that followed, there was only one word for skin, and only one word for underflesh. But then humanity began to argue about which of the two mattered more—the underflesh, or the skin. The ones who trusted in skin, as you do, said that skin was the measure of humanity. Underflesh was merely a distraction, best left invisible and forgotten. But others disagreed. They said humanity belonged to underflesh. Skin, then, was the interruption, disguising a human's true nature.

"And here's the part you must not miss, young interpreter-in-training. When these two groups formed, they used the same word to name two different things. One group, when they spoke of *skin*, had in mind the thing you and I call skin. But the other group used that same word *skin* to speak about underflesh. For the thing we call *skin*, they devised a new word: *shell*. To call skin *shell* was to stake a claim in the debate that divided humanity, to label the skin as something distinct from the essence of humanity. But to call skin *skin*? That too would stake a claim, joining voices with those who said skin was necessary to humanity. Choosing a word was the same as choosing a side. Without choosing a side, it became impossible to speak at all. And so language was born."

Tei clutched the unicorn's flanks with his knees. "But who was right? Who told the truth?"

"Don't you see?" said the interpreter. "They both told the truth, according to the language they had devised. And they both lied, when measured by the language of the other."

"That's all language is, then? A difference in the names people give to skin and underflesh?"

"Not all, no. If that were all, interpretation wouldn't be a career, and the Natchers' words wouldn't sound like nonsense to Buru and the officers' committee. But that was the beginning. Everything else I can teach you—all the vocabulary and grammar and pronunciation that separates Natcher language from our own—everything begins with the question of skin. It is because they rejected skin that the Natchers became Natchers."

"You're saying that the Natchers used to be human? Before they became aliens?"

"In our language, that's precisely what I'm saying. But in the Natcher language, I'm saying that Cyborgs used to be human, before we became Cyborgs."

Tei would have responded, if only to declare his confusion, when a new sight arrested his attention. A grey rock, craggy and pockmarked, drifted toward them in the emptiness. At first it looked small, no larger than Tei's balled fist. The nearer it drew to them—or they to it, perhaps—the greater it swelled. It grew as wide as a skinlength, then a dormitory compartment, then an assembly room, spinning lazily all the while.

Kyri didn't seem surprised by the floating rock. "What I mean to say," he continued, "is that *human* is another of the words taken up differently in different languages. You've always heard the word *human* referring to your own race. In your language, the Natchers are aliens. But in the Natcher language, their race is the human race. It is your race, the race who covered up their skins with artificial shells, that became aliens. In the Natcher language, you are not human. You are a Cyborg."

The rock spun closer until Tei was sure they would crash into it. At the last moment, the unicorn angled its wings, banking left and soaring just over the uneven surface. Tei gasped.

The interpreter laughed. "I warned you about Nauraa's flying. Asteroid, it is called. A rock among the stars. So simple, and somehow still transfixing."

"Do the Natchers call it an asteroid as well?"

"I doubt they have a word for it at all. Because they don't enter the digiscape, their language doesn't need words for things that exist only in the digiscape. Asteroids, of course, but other things too. Unicorns and lions and birds and goblins. Mountains and oceans. Snow. Magic spells. Vacuum cleaners. That sort of thing."

"So they know only about the universe in skin? All they've ever seen is access gates and skies low enough to touch?"

"For them it is not a universe in skin," Kyri corrected. "They do not wear skin at all. Besides, the universe they know is not the place our language calls *universe*. They've seen our universe, yes—or some of them, at any rate. But they exist outside it."

"Isn't *universe*, by its definition, a place with Nothing outside it?"

"So it is."

"Then to speak of Natchers at all—"

"—is to flirt with treason. I'm well aware. Why do you think I've encrypted our conversation? Why do you think Buru insisted on speaking to you about Natchers only in the command room and nowhere else? Truth is always a treason to the rules of language. And so we arrive at last to the matter of deletion."

"You said," Tei stammered, "that if my agemate was deleted, he might not be gone?"

Kyri nodded. "Deletion is the natural consequence of treason against the human race. It means the loss of all the things that make a human human. Or, as the Natchers might say, the loss of things that make a Cyborg Cyborg. When someone is deleted, they are stripped of their skin, and every record of them is scrubbed from the digiscape. As for their underflesh, it is cast out of the universe and into Nothing."

"So humans who are deleted end up among the Natchers?" A hopeful lump rose in Tei's throat.

"At times, yes. I knew of two interpreters before me who spent the remainder of their days among the Natchers. But others…" The interpreter's voice trailed off. "Others went somewhere neither Natcher nor Cyborg can follow. They went into the essence of Nothing."

"You mean they are gone?"

"Gone to everything but memory. As gone as it is possible for anyone to be."

"So our one word *deletion* means two different things?"

"Two very different things. If not more."

"Then how can I know which deletions are which?"

"Your language does not allow you to know. That is how it was designed. Leaving the human race—ceasing to exist inside the universe—that is the only end a human is meant to understand. Until you met me, that was the only end you could understand."

"But now I've met you," said Tei.

"So you have." Kyri's eyes glinted. A glint impossibly like Kanan's, and yet entirely different. "You're beginning—just barely beginning—to speak more than one language. And now the language you used to know will begin to feel too small for you. It was built to hide things you're learning to see."

Past the unicorn's outstretched wing, a colorful blur of stars clustered together. The center of the blur was flat and yellow, with blue-white arms wrapped in smooth lines around it. A pinwheel for the empty darkness. An eye through which some impossibly large creature could look at Tei and Kyri and Nauraa like specks of dust.

Tei shivered. "Buru said that humanity needed me. I've been born under exceptional circumstances to meet exceptional need. I'm supposed to save the universe. But how will any of this help me save the universe?"

"Save it?" The interpreter looked back sharply. "I don't want you to save the universe. I want you to destroy it."

12

LILY

AS LILY STEPPED OUT OF THE HOTEL LOBBY, city smells and city sounds crashed against her. Taxi drivers honked at a delivery truck idling its diesel engine. From the far sidewalk, hidden behind scaffolding and plywood and orange construction canopy, a jack-hammer growled. Grey concrete dust thickened the air. Two men in skullcaps brushed past Lily speaking a language she couldn't place, something tonal with muted consonants and a sing-song rhythm.

Lily opened the door to a yellow taxi in the rear of the logjam. The driver, who had been yelling curses out the window, pulled his head back into the cab. "Where to?"

"North harbor," said Lily, pulling the door shut behind her.

The driver executed a harrowing three-point turn in reverse. He bid the street blockade a one-fingered farewell before rolling up his window.

"How fast can you get there?" said Lily.

"In today's traffic?" The driver swerved sharply left, earning angry honks from two other cars as he cut them off. "Thirty minutes, maybe. Twenty-five if we hit the lights right."

Lily checked the green LED clock on the dashboard. "Make it fifteen and I'll pay you triple the meter rate."

The driver snorted. "If I could work miracles for money, I wouldn't be a taxi driver."

Sinking into the chipped faux leather of the back seat, Lily swore under her breath.

"Where in the north harbor?" said the driver, after a long stretch of silence punctuated with engine murmurs and impatient honking.

"The Project Universe compound. You know it?"

The man raised his eyebrows. "Hard not to these days. What brings you out there?"

Lily looked out the window. The sidewalks teemed with people: A mother dragging two small children by the hand as they ambled behind her, sucking on brightly colored popsicles. A balding man with a silver-tipped cane, stepping always with his right foot first, then bringing the left up to meet it. A group of college-aged kids dressed all in black, carrying cardboard signs with messages like "Justice Now" and "Protect Every Life" and "We Will Not Be Silent" scrawled in marker across them. She barely had time to study one face before two others had crowded in to take its place.

"Saying goodbye," she said.

"You're losing someone?"

For a moment, the lump in Lily's throat was so large she couldn't speak. She choked it down into her growling stomach. "By now, aren't they lost already?"

The driver reached up to touch the rosary beads dangling from his rearview mirror. "I drove a family of five out to the compound last week. They were saying goodbye to their oldest son. Barely seventeen years old. The dad kept telling me how proud he was. 'My boy's grown up now,' he said a hundred times. 'My boy's a hero.' The kids were all crammed in the back with their mom. Not enough seatbelts for everyone, but that's legal here, and they didn't seem to mind. The kid leaving, he was white as a vampire. Faking a smile for his little sister while she held his hand. None of them said a word the whole drive. But Dad had enough words for everybody. 'The most important step we've ever taken toward the survival of the human race,' he said. 'Can you believe my son is part of it? I couldn't be prouder. My boy's all grown up. My boy's a hero.' Over and over again he said it. Like that game where a word turns into nonsense once you repeat it enough times."

"Do you think they're heroes?" asked Lily. "The ones who leave?"

"No matter what you call them, they're still gone at the end of the day."

Lily let her eyes drift up to the roofs of skyscrapers and the cloud-streaked sky beyond them.

"You mind the radio?" said the driver, and then turned up the volume without waiting for an answer. Thudding bass notes made the condensation on the driver's iced coffee cup tremble. Lily's heart pounded in time with the music.

When the song was over, she checked the glowing green dashboard clock. "Is traffic always this bad?"

"Always bad," said the driver. "But worse the last two weeks. First the protestors, then the counter-protestors, now everybody protesting each other all at once. Lucky you're not headed downtown, or you might as well just get out and walk."

"What are they protesting?"

The driver cocked his head to one side. "You been living under a rock somewhere?"

Outside her window, Lily saw another group holding signs, this time dressed all in yellow. Her eyes strained to read the marker scrawl. "Looks like these guys want to save the soul of our nation. Does that make them the protestors, or the counter-protestors?"

The driver snorted. "They're all saving the soul of our nation. Every last one of them. Trouble is, nobody agrees what the soul of our nation needs saving from."

The taxi inched forward. Lily could see the ocean now.

"If they're all saving the soul of our nation," she said, "how do you tell which side is which?"

"Most of the time?" The driver shrugged. "I just look at the color of their clothes."

ACT TWO

Every way of seeing is also a way of not seeing.

~ Kenneth Burke
Permanence and Change

13

KANAN

THE AIR SMELLED OF FIRE. Not a galley oven or a Bunsen burner, but something akin to campfire—sweet ashy smoke rising up from a jumble of broken branches and wedges hewn out of severed tree trunks. It was a digiscape smell, reminiscent of training sessions with Mentor and fantastical adventures with Tei. Kanan had never imagined the same aroma could exist outside the digiscape, to be smelled by humans in skin.

No, *humans in skin* couldn't be the right phrase for this world outside the digiscape. Kanan wasn't human anymore. Kanan had no skin. And yet, here she was.

Alien voices surrounded her on every side. Occasionally she recognized the timbre of Tiqvah's voice or Avi's terse murmurs, but most of the voices were unfamiliar. The way Avi had laid her on the earth, she saw only grass and blaring sunlight and the glint of her own underthighs curled close to her face.

The voices spoke her name repeatedly, loudly. They were arguing over her.

Tiqvah bent low. "We will lift you," it whispered. "To lie down in the presence of the elders is forbidden. They do not wish to make an exception to the law, even now."

Kanan felt hands beneath her armpits pulling her upright. Tiqvah stood on one side of her, Avi on the other. In front of them, five wooden thrones formed a semicircle. An ornate canopy hung above each individual throne, shielding its occupant from the sun. At the center of the semicircle, fire crackled inside a ring of polished stones.

The five creatures sitting on thrones wore a different fabric than Tiqvah and Avi, not simple green mesh but a thick tangle of blues and reds and purples. Leaves encircled each elder's skull in a woven crown, hiding the place where other Natchers' scalps were covered with threads. The elders' underflesh was different too. Instead of stretching taut, it hung loose against their frames, drooping like Final skin draped over a fledgling.

The elder in the center chair, smallest and most wrinkled of the five, pounded both fists against the fabric on its chest and began to speak.

"The chief elder explains why you have been brought here," Tiqvah murmured into Kanan's ear. "The elder's grandchild suffers from a sickness."

"What is *grandchild?*" Kanan whispered back. "What is *sickness?*"

Tiqvah held up an apologetic hand to the chief elder and spoke a few words of gibberish. Then it turned to Kanan. "*Grandchild*, you cannot understand now, since you do not understand *child* at all. It is like a fledgling mentee, but more, much more. As for *sickness*, it is what your race would call *skin malfunction*. We who have no skin know that the problem lies deeper, deeper even than the underflesh. This child's sickness is one our healers can treat only with chemicals from the underworld. But the Cyborgs in the underworld—your human race—have stopped providing us with chemicals."

"Stopped? How could they stop if they don't even know Natchers exist?"

Tiqvah hissed and gripped Kanan's arm like a vice. "You must not use this word *Natcher*. In the presence of the elders least of all." The alien scanned the faces of its elders to see if any had heard Kanan's insult. All five sat impassive.

Kanan clenched her bicep against Tiqvah's fingers. "What I mean is, how did the humans give chemicals to your race in the first place if we thought you were just a fledglings' story? And if we did give you chemicals, why would we stop?"

Tiqvah relayed Kanan's question to the chief elder. The elder frowned deeply and began to speak. "We do not seek to understand the workings of the Cyborg race," Tiqvah translated. "Our race has always delivered half our crops to the underworld in exchange for Cyborg chemicals and manufactured goods. These are the terms of the treaty since before any of us was born. We have never failed to deliver what is owed—not even in seasons of famine like this one, when the sun burns dimmer and the crops rise slowly. But your race has broken the treaty these three seasons past. Some goods they give us less than we are owed; others they give nothing at all."

A few of the elders nodded angrily at this pronouncement. The one sitting on the far right—a large, bulky creature whose bare chest was streaked with scars—spat into the grass as it glared at Kanan.

"I'm sorry," said Kanan to Tiqvah, and then repeated the words more loudly toward the elders: "I'm sorry."

At the word "sorry," the gathering erupted. The elder on the right leapt to its feet, bellowing. Another yelled as if it had been wounded. The chief elder shook its head furiously, until the crown of leaves had slipped sideways on its brow.

Tiqvah let go of Kanan and held out both hands toward the elders. "War!" the alien cried repeatedly, though Kanan was sure she must have misheard. "War! War!"

The word seemed to calm the others. The chief elder nodded uneasily. "War," it said.

Tiqvah began speaking quickly. Kanan turned to Avi, who stood beside her with narrowed eyes. "What is happening?" she asked in a whisper.

"Avi having not power to explain," the creature said.

"I said I was sorry," Kanan persisted.

"This *sorry*, for Cyborg tongue, having good?" asked Avi. "Not here. *Sorry* not having good in overworld."

The elders' heads still shook, but their anger had lessened. One elder, whose circlet of leaves was dotted with tiny white blossoms, smiled kindly in Kanan's direction and gave a slight nod. Tiqvah returned to Kanan and spoke into her ear. "I have explained that you did not mean to cause offense. They understand that you regret your race's actions. Quietly, now. Do not let them hear your words."

"I don't understand," whispered Kanan, "what all this has to do with me."

Tiqvah spoke to the chief elder, who rose from its chair and began pacing before the fire. "The chemicals needed to save the child are kept in your race's infirmary," translated Tiqvah. "The gate to the infirmary is not like most access gates in the underworld, as you know. Most gates hang open until they are commanded to close; this gate stays closed until it is commanded to open. Anyone with skin can open the gate—but of course, our people do not wear skin. This is why the elders ask for your help. They wish you to travel with a raiding party to retrieve the chemicals."

"Look at me," said Kanan. "I'm not in skin either, remember? I'm no more help than the rest of you."

"But if we bring you to skin, you can wear it," explained Tiqvah, not bothering to relay Kanan's words to the elders. "The wearing of skin is forbidden in our race—even to save a life. But you, in skin, can take us to the chemicals."

Kanan's heart rose into her throat. She barely dared to believe it. "You're saying we would take a skin, and I— I would become human again?"

Tiqvah spoke to the chief elder, who responded with an upraised finger. "We take the skin only a moment. We do not keep it. Everything must be stealth. We arrive at night, take only the chemicals we need, nothing more. If your race learns that we have sent a raiding party into the underworld, we risk war."

"War," said Kanan. "You and the elders were just shouting about war."

Tiqvah shook its head firmly. "It is different in our tongue. This word for us means speaking and listening, seeking understanding."

"That sounds more like peace than war."

"Our races' tongues are full of opposites."

"So when I said I was sorry—" Kanan began.

Tiqvah grabbed her by the shoulder, turning her sharply away from the elders' watching eyes. "Hush. This too is an opposite in your tongue and ours. *Sorry*, for our race, means recognizing an evil and then refusing to take responsibility while being secretly glad it exists. It means pretending kindness while perpetuating cruelty. When you say you are sorry, the elders hear pleasure at your race's treachery."

Kanan balked. "They think I'm treacherous, but they trust me to go with the raiding party? To bring me back down to the human universe and put me in skin and risk a war and stake a fledgling's future on me?"

"Of course they do not trust you," said Tiqvah. "Every word you speak is an outrage to them. But their options are limited. They have made their choice."

"What about me? Do I have a choice?"

"There is always a choice. If you agree to help, you will have the gratitude of the race in whose hands your fate rests. But there is risk too—risk for all of us, yes, but for you most of all. The Cyborgs only fear my race; you they will hate, because you were one of them. I cannot say what would become of you if we are caught."

"If I refuse, then?"

Tiqvah glanced over its shoulder at the elders, who had begun talking among themselves. "If you refuse, the elders will decide your fate. Their counsel is divided. Some are willing to extend kindness even if you will not join the raiding party. Others wish to see you banished from the overworld."

Kanan looked past Tiqvah to the elder who had spat on the ground. It leered back at her.

"I'll go," she said. "As soon as my legs can run again, I'll go with your raiding party."

Tiqvah nodded. "I will tell the elders."

From across the fire, the chief elder raised its head expectantly. It smiled at Tiqvah's first words, then resumed frowning and uttered a curt reply.

"The chief elder says," Tiqvah translated, "that the raiding party cannot wait until your legs are recovered. The child has no time. The chemicals must be brought immediately. Tonight. Does this change your answer?"

Kanan looked down at her useless legs and swallowed. "No. I want to help."

Tiqvah reported the answer to the elders, most of whom began smiling again. The chief elder seemed about to speak when the elder on the far right—the one with the scarred bare chest—pointed a finger at Kanan and began to shout. Kanan could distinguish only one of the words, spoken again and again in the alien's booming voice: "Help."

"Elder Javan has seen your lips," whispered Tiqvah. "The elder accuses you of trying to help our race. I must tell them this is a lie."

Turning back to the elders, Tiqvah shook its head and smiled widely, issuing a string of soothing words that meant nothing to Kanan. The elders seemed satisfied—all except the one Tiqvah had called Javan, who continued to scowl.

"It is done," said Tiqvah to Kanan at last. "The raiding party is set. Now we depart. Join your hands in front of your chest. It is the proper salutation."

Kanan did as she was told. Four of the elders—all but Javan—returned the gesture. A moment later Avi had scooped Kanan onto its shoulders again. They ran without speaking until the world Kanan could see above Avi's chest turned from green to gold. Their pace slowed. Avi's chest began to heave with what Kanan assumed was fatigue. Kanan felt herself lowered gently onto the earth.

"You have nearly killed us both," said Tiqvah, its voice quavering in the boundary between anger and laughter. "But all is well. The raiding party is approved, and the child may yet be saved."

"What about the elder who shouted?" asked Kanan. "The one who saw my lips?"

Tiqvah frowned. "Javan is not pleased. I fear we have made an enemy. But the elders need only a majority to approve the raid. Among the other raiders, Avi will vouch for you. It is enough. We must be grateful it is only Javan who heard you speaking of help."

"But I do want to help," Kanan protested. "What's wrong with that?"

"Opposites," Tiqvah answered wearily. "With the Cyborgs, always opposites. This word *help*, in our tongue, it means to usurp, to control, to dominate. What you mean as promise, Javan hears as Cyborg threat."

Avi crouched against the dirt, its back bent away from their conversation, still heaving with the strain of the run. Kanan gazed out past the creature's naked underflesh, toward the gliding river. "Where did the opposites come from?" she asked. "Why do our races speak so differently?"

"The history I do not know," answered Tiqvah. "I am charged with the present, not the past."

Kanan traced the brown earth with her finger. It was warm from the sun, crumbling like powder beneath her touch. So foreign from the earth she had known in skin. "Could I learn to speak the way your race does?"

"I do not know. It has never been done in my time."

"But you learned to speak like a human."

Tiqvah nodded. "Some, anyway. As much as necessary. But to work in reverse—from the Cyborg tongue to the tongue of my people—is a different matter. Barriers exist in either direction. But I can teach you only the barriers I know. Without a guide, the journey between tongues is perilous. To speak truth in one tongue while lying in the other, it is like betraying yourself. A kind of madness."

"Surely others before me have attempted it."

"Attempted, yes." Tiqvah looked away. "But never succeeded."

"What happened to the ones who failed?"

"Such things are best not spoken of," answered the alien, standing and tapping its companion on the shoulder. "Avi, come. We must prepare. You must be strong for your sibling."

The other Natcher seized a handful of grass from the earth and pressed its face against the blades.

"What is *sibling*?" asked Kanan.

"Another word that cannot be explained," said Tiqvah. "No more talk now of words and tongues. We must run."

When Avi approached to sling Kanan over its shoulders, she thought she saw the trails of two tears cutting through the dirt on the alien's face. But then she was in the air again, where all she could see was sky and underflesh and golden earth.

§§§

The raiding party gathered beneath Tiqvah's tarp as the sun grew dim. The shadow cast by the tarp had not moved, but it was nearly invisible now, its edges blurred by crepuscular gloom. Beneath the waning sunlight, the river blackened like tar.

Avi appeared at the horizon first. Two other Natchers followed. The thread on their heads—*hair*, Tiqvah had called it—was darker than Avi's, but otherwise they looked nearly identical. All three wore belts around their waists. Canteens hung at one hip, long knives with luminescent blades at the other.

"Cousins," said Tiqvah as the three approached, and then seemed to regret the word. "But this means nothing to you. It is best if you do not speak at all in their presence. With Avi it is different. Avi has taken pains to understand the Cyborg tongue." The alien paused, its face sinking. "And pain, too. Pain as well as pains. As for the others, you saw what came when the elders heard you today. Their ears cannot hear what your lips mean to say. You understand the raiding party's plan?"

Kanan nodded.

"Good. Then there is no need for you to speak. Assuming, of course, that everything goes according to the plan."

A bold assumption, thought Kanan. But it was too late now to object. Avi and the others had arrived, joining their palms together in greeting. Tiqvah returned the gesture and nudged Kanan to do the same.

"Enos," said one of the newcomers, pointing a finger to its chest.

"Barak," said the other.

"Mahlah," said Tiqvah, pointing out toward the river.

At first, Kanan wasn't sure where Tiqvah's finger pointed. Then she noticed a shape moving through the river, a bulky floating sack that travelled faster than the current around it. In front of the sack, a Natcher glided almost imperceptibly through the water. It emerged dripping along the bank, untying a tow rope from its ankle and hefting the sack over its shoulder.

Like Tiqvah, Mahlah wore fabric across its chest. It also wore a device on its feet, something resembling large birds' feet with webbing between the talons. "This one in our language is called *aquarian*," Tiqvah murmured in Kanan's ear. "No one knows better than Mahlah the water tunnels between overworld and underworld."

Even in the dim light, Kanan could see the brightness of Mahlah's smiling teeth as the aquarian tromped toward them. Kanan didn't need to understand the Natchers' words to recognize the playful banter of their greetings. Mahlah seemed fascinated by Kanan; the alien stared at her with a wordless grin until Avi called it away with a barked order. The five Natchers crouched together in the grass, their tones turning serious.

Kanan looked out at the darkening sky. Unlike the digiscape, this sky held no stars—just a dull, grey glow by which everything stayed faintly visible. The sun was cool enough now that Kanan could look directly at it, its daytime blaze reduced to patches of ash and ember. The knife at Avi's side and the knives worn by the creatures Tiqvah called *cousins* had become the brightest objects on the horizon. From a distance, they might have looked like three earthbound stars, three glimmers of blue-white light kissing the darkened grass.

As the aliens talked, Mahlah opened its sack and distributed pungent hunks of bread. "For eating," whispered Avi as it passed one to Kanan. She bit into the bread. It was full of a thick, savory paste that felt cold against her teeth but warm on her tongue. Avi watched attentively as she devoured it, passing her a second as soon as she had taken her last bite of the first. The aliens too ate quickly. They rested on their heels, as if prepared to leap up at any moment. Once the meal was over, though, their hurry seemed to dissipate, their voices lightening with laughter.

At last Mahlah stood and reached for its sack. It pulled out four more pairs of birds' feet, which it passed to the other Natchers. "Fins," Kanan heard Mahlah say, and she realized she had heard galley chemists use the same word to talk about the crispy thin edge of slices of flakemeat. The other Natchers affixed these large, inedible fins to their own feet.

Next from the sack came six masks shaped like human faces. "For breathing while swimming," whispered Tiqvah, as it set a mask beside Kanan. The mask fit loosely over her face, sealing against her cheeks and chin and forehead. In her hands the material had looked dark and impenetrable, but once it was in place she found she could see and breathe through it as if it were made of air.

Kanan had shuddered when Tiqvah explained their plan to reach the underworld by water. "It is not the safest way," the alien had said. "But it is the best way to enter undetected. And with a guide who knows the channels, it is safe enough."

"I'm not much of a swimmer," Kanan had said. "Besides, without skin, I don't have gills."

"Without functioning legs," answered Tiqvah, "you are no swimmer at all. But everything will be seen to."

Mahlah led the way back to the river. One of the cousins—the one called Barak—took Kanan's arm and seemed ready to hoist her onto its shoulders, but Avi grunted and shook its head. The creature had claimed her and would allow no one else to carry her. That thought comforted Kanan for some reason she couldn't name.

When they reached the edge of the river, Kanan took a deep breath and closed her eyes. Avi tightened its arms around her undertorso. They plunged beneath the river's surface. Kanan felt water cover her scalp, but her face was still dry, her lungs still breathing what felt like air. She opened her eyes. Other Natchers appeared around her in watery blurs and trails of bubbles, unevenly lit by the cousins' glowing blades.

They swam against the current at first. Then down, down until Kanan's skull ached from the pressure of the water over-head. She wondered if there was any bottom to the river, or if it stretched endlessly low the same way the overworld sky reached endlessly high. Ahead of them she saw the flutter of Mahlah's fins, propelling the alien forward as its arms hung loosely at its sides.

Not until her fingers brushed against its smooth edge did Kanan realize they were inside a tunnel. Avi's kick had grown slower. Still they raced forward as fast as before, pulled onward by a current now flowing in their favor. The tunnel divided ahead of them, each branch blocked by a network of crossed bars. Mahlah caught the bars of the left branch and pulled itself through. It waited patiently for the others to follow before continuing forward.

As they swam, the tunnels became tighter and branched more regularly, so often Kanan lost count. Some paths were covered with fine mesh or studded with spikes. Down one tunnel, flashes of green coruscated like lightning in the distance. Sometimes the current pulled strongly away from the path Mahlah had taken, and Kanan could feel Avi's chest heaving as the Natcher kicked harder to defy the current's pull.

After a final downward turn, Mahlah's fins stopped kicking. Its body straightened. Avi followed suit, propelled forward like a stryker dart. Water rushed around them. Kanan felt herself falling, the tunnel tightening, threatening to crush her. Then there was no tunnel, only open air that exploded with sound as Kanan and the water around her burst into it. She clung to Avi's clenched fists and closed her eyes as the force of impact burst all around her.

At last everything was still.

They floated in a pool of sluggish green water. The tunnel that had carried them here hung high above them, spewing out a waterfall that sent slow ripples across the pool's surface. Avi rolled onto its back. Kanan shifted to one side, clutching the alien's chest like a floating log. The cousins were laughing. "Hush," Mahlah chided them, though it too was smiling.

Along one side of the pool, a metallic tub about a skinlength in diameter rose above the water's surface. Mahlah swam to it and climbed up, motioning the others to follow. They began taking off their masks and fins.

"The path into the birthing hydropod," Tiqvah whispered into Kanan's ear. "It detects underflesh. It will allow no other substance to pass through."

Mahlah gathered up the masks and fins, depositing them in their sack along the dark shoreline. Then the creature reached into the water and pulled up a lever hiding just beneath the waterline. All at once, the water inside the tub became a whirlpool, swirling down with a hungry slurp and refilling again in a matter of seconds.

Mahlah pointed to Enos, then pointed into the tub. The cousin climbed inside. Once its body was submerged up to the chest, it reached down and stripped off the fabric at its waist. The Natchers averted their eyes; only Kanan continued watching, though she could see nothing beneath the water's green surface. Enos balled up the sleek fabric between its hands. Once the fabric was fully hidden, Mahlah pulled the lever again. The whirlpool appeared in an instant, pulling the cousin down and out of sight.

Barak followed, then Avi. "You must go next," whispered Tiqvah. "I will follow behind and help Avi finish placing you in skin. Mahlah meets us at the rendezvous."

"But my legs," Kanan protested.

"The passage takes only a moment," said Tiqvah. "One deep breath is all, and the water will carry you. The fabric you may leave with Mahlah, to be brought with the swimming gear. You will not need it in skin."

With Tiqvah's help, Kanan removed the cloth at her waist and slipped into the center of the tub. She nodded to Mahlah and closed her eyes. With a pull of the lever, the water swirled around her and pulled her down. She felt herself dragged sideways and then launched upward. When she opened her eyes, she was inside the assembly room pyramid, waist-deep in the birthing hydropod. Avi grabbed her by the elbows and pulled her out of the water.

Beside the grey curtain at the pyramid's opening, the cousins stood with knives drawn, their backs turned to Kanan. On the opposite side of the pyramid, a patch of carbon earth had been pried open to reveal a basin full of water. Avi plunged its hand into the water and pulled out two empty Final skins.

Disentangling them, the alien dropped one back beneath the water and held the other out to Kanan.

"Quickly," it said.

Together they found the skin's backnerve, the long rubbery ridge running from scalp to buttocks where the legs divided. Kanan followed one leg down to its tip and placed her foot against it. As she pulled the muscle fibers tight against her underflesh, a thrill of energy ran through her. Avi fastened the skin over her other leg. The alien turned its head away as it worked, trying not to see the bareness of Kanan's waist.

Tiqvah was beside them now, its hands joining Avi's to finish setting the skin in place. When the final flap had sealed over Kanan's scalp, Tiqvah whispered, "Can you stand?"

Kanan pulled her knees forward and rose uncertainly to her feet.

"I had hoped so," said Tiqvah. "The muscles of skin are not like underflesh—they can work to a degree even when the legs beneath are faulty. You will be weak with adolescence, of course. But at least Avi will not have to carry you. Wounded or not, you are still a runner."

As Avi and Tiqvah sealed up the basin of empty skins, making the earth solid again, Kanan bent her knees and began taking tentative steps. She ran her fingers across the Final skin she had coveted for so long. *Still a runner*, she thought, and fierce pride swelled within her.

Tiqvah led the way to the infirmary. Out of the pyramid, through the upper east access gate, down a long barren hallway that ran the length of the assembly room. Suns glowed faintly in the sky every few skinlengths, their light dimmed for night-time. The cousins held their knives at the ready as they flanked Tiqvah on either side. Kanan followed behind them, and Avi brought up the rear, glancing over its shoulder every few steps.

Two compartments short of the infirmary, Kanan heard the orderkeeper patrol approaching. Their footfalls echoed loudly, especially in contrast to the gentle stride of the Natcher raiders. Tiqvah held a finger to its lips and drew its body flat against the compartment wall. Kanan and the others did the same. The footfalls grew closer, until they were all Kanan could hear except the sound of her own breathing.

Three Finals appeared in the faint light of the access gate. They took slow, heavy steps forward, looking directly at Kanan and her companions. Barak lifted its knife. Tiqvah shook its head almost imperceptibly, turning a palm toward the floor.

The orderkeepers were right beside them now, near enough to reach out and touch. But their gaze had shifted forward. They said nothing, walking with the same heavy footfalls. They passed through the access gate on the far end of the compartment. Gradually their footfalls faded away.

"It's a simple drug," Tiqvah had explained to Kanan earlier that day. "It does not keep a human from walking or speaking. But it makes the universe in skin like something out of a dream machine, dulling all the senses. Our spies ensure it is given to any orderkeeper patrol we might encounter during a raid. It is how we keep peace."

"But how do your spies pass the drug to humans?" Kanan had asked. "And how do they know which orderkeepers might pose a threat?"

Tiqvah had simply laughed and shaken its head. "My race must be allowed its secrets."

Seeing the drug's effects filled Kanan with a fresh burst of confidence. Avi's backward glances as they traversed the last two compartments felt unnecessary, even paranoid. Soon they stood at the closed access gate leading to the infirmary.

"Shell," said Tiqvah, and Kanan recognized the Natcher word for *skin*. She held the back of her skin-clad hand against the gateframe. The gate slid up into the sky.

Kanan had been in the infirmary more than once as a patient, when her own fledgling skins malfunctioned. She had always feared the room. Cupboards crowded with beakers. Vast skincare machines thrusting their mechanical fingers down from the sky. Faint traces of something like blood or acid lingering in the air, making the whole compartment smell red despite the yellow light.

Now, surrounded by Natcher raiders, in a borrowed skin with no malfunction, Kanan saw for the first time how like a galley the infirmary was. Bunsen burners everywhere. Tables long enough to hold a Final in skin or a dozen trays of bread loaves. Scents crashing violently into one another, always hinting at darkmeat or underflesh just out of sight.

Against the far wall, Kanan's former agemate Rajamin watched with empty eyes as the raiding party entered. ("The skincaregiver assigned to the night shift will need to be drugged more heavily," Tiqvah had told Kanan earlier. "It is dangerous if done incorrectly. But our spies will ensure the Cyborg is not permanently damaged.")

"Welcome to the infirmary," mumbled Rajamin. "What seems to be your malfunction?" She half-raised an arm, dropped it to her side, and let her head slump onto her chest.

It took Avi only moments to find the chemicals in question. Two were almost white and sat in heavy vats along the earth, long-handled ladles poised above them. The third, murky and purple, was stored in a much smaller vial that released its contents one drop at a time. Avi and the cousins uncapped their canteens, filling each one with ladlesful of the white chemicals and four drops from the murky purple vial.

Soon the canteens were sealed. Rajamin mumbled after the raiders as they filed out, never lifting her head: "Now that your malfunction is resolved, please report back to your scheduled shift."

They had arranged to meet Mahlah along the second tier of the water processing plant, at the portal where pieces of shed skins were collected, cleaned, and reassembled for the next newborn. Kanan would strip out of her skin and leave it floating among the discarded fragments before they donned their fins and masks and swam back up the channel into the overworld. ("It will seem like a simple error in their numbers," Tiqvah had explained to Kanan, "one skin too few at the pyramid, one too many still awaiting assembly. As long as the skin remains in the underworld, the question of where it is returned or in what fashion matters little.")

As Kanan climbed the steps to the second tier of the giant spiraling river, where humans' green water was tested, cleaned, and recharged, she thought that the raid had been almost easy. Far easier than Kanan had expected by Tiqvah's stern warnings. And why shouldn't it have been? Raids were nothing new for the Natchers. How else could they have coexisted with humans for so long, undiscovered except by one half-mad archivist?

Tiqvah held up a hand, stopping the whole crew in their tracks. It uttered a string of gibberish. "Mahlah here already should," whispered Avi into Kanan's ear. "No Mahlah meaning wrong."

In an instant, Kanan's optimism dissolved. Tiqvah's old warnings flooded in to fill the hollow space. *The Cyborgs only fear my race; you they will hate, because you were one of them. I cannot say what would become of you if we are caught.*

The sound of shouting pulled Kanan back to the present. "Natcher," cried a familiar human voice in the distance.

"Requesting immediate backup. Natcher approaching the water processing plant."

Mahlah appeared first, staggering beneath the bulk of its sack, lips open with an unspoken apology to the others. Close behind the alien—no more than twenty paces back, and closing in quickly—was Jarawi the orderkeeper.

Darts from Jarawi's stryker whizzed past Mahlah, exploding haphazardly against the silica. Jarawi's aim had always been terrible, Kanan remembered, ever since the days of their fledgling marksmanship lessons together. Still, Kanan couldn't help admiring her old adversary's speed as a runner. It was an admiration tinged now with horror, leaving a taste like acid in Kanan's throat.

Avi had disappeared from Kanan's side. The alien sprinted down the steps toward Mahlah and Jarawi. Between its teeth, it clenched a glowing knife.

Jarawi erased the remaining gap between herself and Mahlah with a leap. She caught the sack on Mahlah's back and sent them both tumbling across the earth. A moment later, Avi was on top of the orderkeeper, driving its knife through the skin of Jarawi's neck. Where knife met skin, Jarawi's neck sparked and crackled, melting away to make room for the blade.

Jarawi gasped and then grew silent.

Avi stood. The blade in its hand was dripping.

Kanan had seen skin failures before, too many to count. But only ever in the digiscape, where they could be reset at a moment's notice. She had never witnessed a failure without a reset. Jarawi's eyes were still open. She looked up at the tall sky as if plotting her premature journey into the archive.

Avi and Mahlah raced up the steps, carrying the sack between them. Mahlah opened it and began distributing fins and masks to the others. As the alien retrieved the last mask, it let out a distressed cry. The apparatus had been crushed in the scuffle with Jarawi, rendering it useless.

The aliens began to speak all at once. Tiqvah silenced them with a hand and pointed to Kanan.

"You will keep the skin," it said in human words, not bothering to whisper. "The gills make it possible for you to breathe without a mask. It is the only way we all escape alive."

"But the humans," Kanan protested. "They'll know we stole it."

"They know already a raiding party has been here," said Tiqvah. "An orderkeeper dead, and shouts of Natchers? If we leave someone behind, they will know it all more. There may be no way now to avoid war."

"War?" Mahlah repeated, its face a mixture of confusion and hope.

Tiqvah replied with Natcher words.

One by one, the aliens leapt up to grip the river's carbon edge, pulling themselves over it and into the water. When only Tiqvah and Kanan were left on dry earth, Tiqvah caught Kanan's arm. "I must warn you," it said. "You are not prepared for what will happen to you inside the river."

"I've swum in skin before," frowned Kanan.

Tiqvah shook its head. "This water is not like digiscape water. To enter the Cyborgs' green water in Cyborg skin alters the mind. Inside a hydropod, the water's power over you is controlled. But outside a hydropod—the energy is different there. Unrestrained. Carrying the thoughts forcefully but not purposefully. I've been told it is like fever dreaming. Like grasping after a forgotten memory. Like singing and soaring and dying all at once."

"Will I be able to swim?"

"Avi will carry you. If you can, you must relax the muscles of the skin and try not to fight Avi's grip. But you may not know yourself enough even to relax. You may not know yourself at all. Not until the water is clear again."

New echoes approached them from below. Orderkeeper shouts. Heavy footfalls.

"Go," said Tiqvah.

Kanan jumped, caught the edge of the river with her fingers, and hoisted herself up. She took a final unnecessary breath before plunging beneath the water.

Everything went black.

§§§

Kanan was with Tei. Not the Final named Eleven, but the old Tei, the one in senior fledgling skin, the Tei of checkers and laughter and promises. Water surrounded them on every side. They sat astride a creature Tei called *dolphin*, ducking beneath the waterline on its back, bursting up again into the shimmering light. Kanan breathed air through her lungs one moment, water through her gills the next.

Tei's arms wrapped around Kanan, gripping her tightly at the chest. The touch was surely forbidden, lasting too long, pressing too close. But if Tei loosened her grip, Kanan knew she would fall from the dolphin and sink into an eternity of water. Her gills would fail, and she would drown, and this time she would have no skin to wake up into.

"Relax," said Tei. "I'm not letting go. I'm never letting go."

Grass sprouted up from the water and slowly turned the ocean green. Still the dolphin swam, carrying them now beneath the grass, now above it. The earth chopped and swelled and foamed as they soared across it. Kanan clutched at the slim triangle rising up from the dolphin's back.

"It's called a fin," said Tei. "Fin, like the crispy part of flake-meat I refuse to eat. Like the device Natchers wear on their feet."

"Natchers are a fantasy," said Kanan.

"So are dolphins," Tei retorted. "So is ocean. In the digiscape, there's no difference between skin and fantasy."

The dolphin turned sharply, throwing both its riders. They tumbled across the grass. Tei's arms dug in tighter. Kanan landed facedown, tasting dirt. "Let me up," she said.

"No," said Tei. "I'm never letting go. I promised."

"But it's different now," said Kanan. "We made those promises in a different universe. Nothing is what it was."

"You're right," said Tei. "Everything is different, because you are dead."

Kanan rolled over. She was Jarawi now, and Tei was Avi, and Tei was pulling a dripping blade from Kanan's neck. Then Tei was weeping, throwing herself across a skin in failure, grasping at every place she could reach as if afraid Kanan would dissolve into the grass.

"I'm alive," said Kanan, but all that left her throat was a low gurgle. "I'm alive, I'm alive, I'm alive."

"You're dead," said Tei. She lifted Kanan and carried her into the butchery. Her arms gripped tightly, never letting go. Not when the orderkeepers came to peel away Kanan's skin. Not when the butcher carved her into a pile of darkmeat. Not when the galley ovens grew hot, when she was on Buru's fork, when she was behind Buru's smiling teeth.

"I'm alive," Kanan cried again and again, fighting against Tei's grasp with every word.

But Tei kept her promise.

Tei never let go.

14
TEI

TEI PROGRAMMED HIS DREAM MACHINE for checkers again. Or the scene of the checkers game, at any rate: Kanan in front of him with crossed legs, a square of gingham fabric between them, hyacinth all around. But when Kanan offered lines or circles, Tei answered, "Neither. Let's take a walk."

Tei had no one else to talk to. Not Reif the archivist, whose eager face hovered over Tei's as he emerged from the digiscape with a racing heart. Not his former mentor, who greeted him in the hallway with a new mentee in tow. Not the agemates sitting beside him during the evening meal, swapping stories of adolescent bumbles in their new careers. Certainly not Buru, who watched him from across the mess hall, the same lips that had announced Kanan's deletion now stretched into a calculating smile.

Only Dream-Kanan was left to be Tei's confidante. Not a real human confidante, of course, but at least an effigy of one, blurred at the edges. The mind behind those flat dreamscape eyes could know exactly as much or as little as Tei wanted it to know. Dream-Kanan was the last shred of privacy in a world overflowing with treason.

They left the checkerboard behind and walked through the hyacinth. Leaves and blossoms tangled fragrantly against their legs. "Look," said Kanan, after they had ambled forward in silence for a long while. "The checkerboard again."

"I should have programmed more flowers," said Tei. "It's a small dreamscape. No matter where we walk, we can only get so far before we're back where we started."

"I don't mind," said Kanan. "This way, if you change your mind about playing, the board is never hard to find."

They walked. The checkerboard disappeared behind them, reappeared in front of them.

"Do you think," asked Tei, "that you could take off the top half of your skin before we talk? A weird request, I know. But it's the last way I remember you. And if I'm going to tell you the whole story—everything that's happened since you left—I need you to be as nearly you as you can possibly be."

Kanan shrugged. "I chose to be a half-skin once. Why not a second time? But you'll have to help me take it off."

They stopped and stood face to face. Tei set a hand on Kanan's head, then hesitated. "I can't."

They were almost nose to nose, close enough to feel the warmth of one another's breath.

"It's just skin," said Kanan.

"Skin is all you've ever wanted," said Tei.

"That was before the aging ceremony. There must have been something I wanted when I ran. Something that had nothing to do with skin."

"Like what?"

"Who knows?" Kanan closed his eyes and covered Tei's hand with his own. "Maybe whatever is hiding underneath."

Together they pulled, peeling the skin away. One flap, then another, discarded and swallowed up by the hyacinth bulbs. Each place where Tei's fingers caught skin, they brushed against the softness of underflesh as well. Kanan shivered at the touch. Every breath came slower than the last. The skin disappeared strip by strip.

"That's far enough," said Kanan. "Any further and I won't look like the same Kanan you remember."

Tei had stopped breathing. "What if I want more than I remember?"

Kanan caught Tei's hand in his own and pulled him forward. "What you want can't be had with dreaming."

They walked hand in hand. Human and half-skin. Underflesh against blue.

It felt odd, telling a story to someone who didn't need to be told. But Tei told the story anyway. He lingered over every detail, pretending the blurry creature in front of him was more than a dream. He described the feeling of becoming Eleven, his meeting with Buru, the interpreter's revelations in the archive. Finally, he reached the part of the story that troubled him most.

"Destroy the universe?" gasped Kanan, even though there was no reason for the revelation to surprise a creature invented inside a dream. "You're sure you understood right?"

Tei shook his head. "Maybe not. Kyri claims it's a matter of interpretation. That once I learn to speak Natcher, once I understand the history of the human race, the idea of destroying the universe won't mean what I think it means, and it won't seem evil anymore."

"You think he could be right?" asked Kanan. "Maybe you need to give it time before you can understand."

"I'm not sure I want to understand."

Kanan tapped a finger against his chin. "What if there's something worse than treason? Or something better than the universe? Or just something—I don't know—more? More than we have words for?"

"That's what Kyri says. Sometimes I think I might believe him." Tei stopped and turned to face Kanan, setting his hand against his agemate's bare undertorso. "He says you might not be gone. That even though you're deleted, even though deletion is the end of humanity, there can still be something after it. Something beyond humanity. I catch myself thinking, if I had that choice—to be human or to be with you—maybe I wouldn't choose humanity after all. Maybe that means I do believe in more than just universe and deletion. Or I want to believe in it, even though I know it might be a lie."

"If it's a lie," said Kanan, "it's the cleverest form of treason I've ever heard."

Tei nodded. "I've always thought I knew good from evil, and whichever one I did, at least I would know what I was doing. But if Kyri poisons my mind with his talk of language, and I start believing it's noble to commit treason? Maybe I'll start to believe that destroying the universe is better than saving it."

"What if it is better? What if the thing our language calls *saving* is just a kind of destroying?"

Tei shuddered fiercely. "Don't tell me Kyri's gotten to you too."

"I'm an extension of your consciousness," said Kanan. "Kyri's gotten to me exactly as much as he's gotten to you. No more, no less."

"Then what do I do?"

Kanan reached down and began plucking hyacinth stalks, collecting them into a bunch in his fist. "I don't see how you can do anything yet. It's just gathering for now. Gathering words. Gathering moments. Waiting until you know more than you thought there was to be known."

"And if Kyri's talk of language makes me start thinking like a Natcher? If every new word I learn makes the truth seem less true?"

"Truth must be a fragile thing if it only survives in one language."

"That's exactly what I'm afraid of."

Kanan tied his bouquet with a long hyacinth leaf and presented it to Tei. "How can you be afraid," he asked, "when there's beauty everywhere?"

As their fingers touched, a jolt of energy ran through Tei. The dreamscape flickered to black for a moment, returning foggier and wilder than before.

"I'm alive," said Kanan, his voice strangely distant.

Tei shook his head. "I don't understand what you're saying."

"I'm alive." Kanan walked further into the hyacinth without looking back.

Tei ran to catch up, wrapping his arms around Kanan's bare undertorso. They were close—unlawfully close—and still it didn't feel close enough.

"Let go," said Kanan.

"I'm not letting go," said Tei. "I'm never letting go."

Only in dreams could Tei have outwrestled Kanan. They fell together into the dirt, Kanan's arms pinned against his naked sides. Kanan managed to turn himself around in Tei's grip so they were face to face, eye to eye. Kanan's mouth, smeared with dirt from the earth, kept repeating the same nonsense phrase: "I'm alive, I'm alive, I'm alive."

Alive. It was a meaningless word. Or perhaps—if this hadn't been a dream—it could have been a Natcher word.

"Let go," said Kanan. "I'm alive, I'm alive, I'm alive."

"I'm never letting go," said Tei. "Not ever."

Kanan flickered between Tei's arms. Sometimes he wore half a skin, sometimes a full skin, sometimes no skin at all. Sometimes human, sometimes Natcher, sometimes terrifying, sometimes irresistibly alluring.

§§§

When Tei awoke the next morning, the earth beside his hydropod was spattered with water. "A surge through the system overnight," he overheard one plumber telling another, as they passed by his dormitory compartment on their way to the mess hall. "Who knows why? Those new filters keep acting up."

"I bet that messed up more than a few dreams," laughed the other.

"Probably," said the first. "But dreams are the least of our worries. You wouldn't believe the mess over at the processing plant."

Tei scrubbed at the water with his foot, spreading it thin across the earth. Within moments, it had evaporated.

15

LILY

AT 10:06 A.M., LILY AND FORTY-EIGHT OTHER *crewmembers boarded the transport. The first hundred crewmembers had been taken last week. The rest would join them in stages before the end of the month. And then? Then would come the day everyone was waiting for, the day that had already made Luka famous. The end of the world as Lily knew it. The beginning of a world she had studied in books and training exercises but could still only barely imagine.*

Luka, the Margola sisters, and a few other high-profile executives shook hands with each of the crewmembers as they boarded. When Lily reached the front of the line, Luka gave her the same flat smile he had given forty others before her. "Good luck," he said.

Lily wondered if he had slept with any crewmembers before last week's departure. She wondered how many more lovers he would find in the coming weeks, how many bodies he would press up against on the seventy-third floor of the Margola Tower knowing they'd be gone forever when morning came.

"If I need luck," said Lily, "you haven't done your job."

Luka's flat smile didn't change. He was already shaking another hand.

The transport was built for fifty passengers, but one of the programmers had disappeared from the roster at the last minute. "Got some girl pregnant," Luka told Lily with disdain as he peeled off his own condom the previous evening. "Decided to stay and help raise the kid. How sweet."

Lily strapped herself in beside the empty chair. Blank walls and blank faces surrounded her. She wondered how the missing programmer felt this morning. Was he heartbroken, the way Elliot had been for fourteen months and six days? Was he bitter at an accidental fetus for spoiling the opportunity of a lifetime?

Or was there another opportunity he wanted even more?

Engines began to rumble. The transport moved slowly at first, then so quickly Lily felt the skin on her cheeks slide back toward her ears. Beyond the blank transport walls, she imagined Earth shrinking, all its details melting into blobs of tan and green and blue. The straps dug into her chest as she jostled roughly against them. She thought about the way lives ended, and the way they began.

16

KANAN

KANAN RETURNED TO HERSELF BIT BY BIT. First the arms around her changed—no longer Tei's lithe blue skin, but Avi's sinewy underflesh instead. The hollow channel of Buru's throat transformed into a tunnel of water. Then Kanan remembered the raiding party, the journey home, Tiqvah's warning about Cyborg water on Cyborg skin.

"Relax," Tiqvah had said. Kanan let herself go limp against Avi's chest. Ahead of her, three pairs of fins fluttered rhythmically, lit by the glow of the cousins' knives.

When they emerged from the water into a dark overworld, Kanan slumped weakly on the grass. Natcher voices rose and fell around her. Then a splash, and two sets of feet pounding away into the twilight.

"The skin must come off," said Tiqvah, rolling Kanan over. Avi hovered nearby, nursing a swollen eye. "And you must help. Skin responds best to skin. My fingers cannot make the first tear. It has to be you."

"No." Kanan surprised herself with the firmness of her voice. "I won't take it off. You said I could keep it."

Tiqvah straightened Kanan's limbs one by one, laying her out flat. "You will. But you cannot wear it permanently. Not without a hydropod to restore its charge each night. You saw what the last skin did to your legs. This one could kill you. We will store it in Cyborg water until you must wear it again."

"I thought there was no Cyborg water in the overworld," said Kanan.

"Mahlah will hide it in a place between the worlds, a place known only to Mahlah. The elders would forbid the plan, if they knew. Elder Javan most of all." Tiqvah exchanged a meaningful look with Avi. "But when the need arises, when they learn the skin has been kept, they will have no choice but to accept it. Only a fool refuses a weapon the day the war begins."

"It's war, then?"

Tiqvah sighed. "Perhaps. I do not see how it could be anything else. Avi's cousins are bringing word to the elders. Now hold still."

"Holding still before not," grumbled Avi, tracing a tender finger around its eye.

Tiqvah bit its lip to stifle a laugh. "You did put up quite the fight, you know, with Avi in the water. The eye will heal; the grudge may not. Still, Avi knows the blame is not yours."

Avi merely grunted and turned away.

"What went wrong?" asked Kanan, as Tiqvah began to peel away strips of skin. "How did the orderkeepers find us?"

"They must have changed shifts at the last moment," said Tiqvah. "The orderkeeper who chased Mahlah was not meant to be scheduled for the night shift. The drug was administered to another. We have always known such a thing could happen, but we have never been caught by a Cyborg orderkeeper before."

A strange kind of loyalty welled up inside Kanan—a loyalty to skin, even as she watched Tiqvah peel her own skin away. "Jarawi," she said.

"That was the orderkeeper's name?" asked Tiqvah.

"That *is* her name. A skin malfunction doesn't change a name. She is still Jarawi in the archive. She is as much a member of the human race as she has been."

"As you please," answered Tiqvah without conviction.

Avi, who had been crouching at the water's edge, rose and took a few steps nearer. When the alien saw Kanan's waist bare, it covered its eyes and barked something in Natcher. Tiqvah barked back.

"Avi does not wish to see you without a covering," Tiqvah explained in human words. "I have said that Avi may help, or Avi may leave. Avi chooses instead to sulk by the river."

The taller Natcher grunted without turning toward them. "Avi not sulking. Avi keeping law."

"What law?" asked Kanan. "What does the covering mean?"

"It is called *clothes*," said Tiqvah. "It covers parts of the body we use when new human beings are created. In our race, each new egg grows inside the body of a parent until the egg is ready to enter the overworld on its own."

"You're saying you've grown other creatures inside of you?" Kanan shuddered at the thought.

"Not I, no," laughed Tiqvah. "I may never do so. But my body is like the bodies of those who do. And someday, if I should choose it and be chosen for it, then perhaps I will try to grow an egg inside of me."

"Human eggs aren't grown that way," said Kanan, though Tiqvah must have known it already. "We're formed in the hatchery. Our early seasons are all spent in the digiscape, learning to speak and move and act like a human. It's not until our seventh season that we're large enough to be born into junior fledgling skin. Do your parents carry an egg for six seasons?"

Tiqvah's eyes widened at the thought. "Heavens no. The egg is not a full season inside the parent's body before it is born into the overworld and becomes a child. Our children are not like your Cyborg fledglings. They cannot speak or understand, cannot feed themselves, cannot walk. They are entirely help-less. Your race spends six seasons nourished by Cyborg water; our race's young are fed with milk from the breasts of their own parents. What your race learns suspended in water, accessing the digiscape's memories, our race learns by living."

Avi struck the water with the back of its hand. "*Our* race," it murmured. "All but Tiqvah."

Tiqvah closed its eyes, holding Kanan's skin in its hands, and said nothing.

"Tiqvah created in hatchery," Avi continued. "Raised in Cyborg water."

"You—" Kanan stumbled over the words. "You came from the hatchery? You were a human?"

Tiqvah nodded. "I was a deleted egg. Mahlah pulled me from the holding tank and brought me up to the overworld. I was not a Cyborg the same way you have been. I never knew skin. But digiscape, honor, humanity—those things I still remember a bit from my six seasons in Cyborg water."

"But our bodies are not alike," objected Kanan. "My body could never do the things you say your body is capable of."

"Not anymore." Tiqvah stopped pulling skin, touching its fingers gently to the underflesh of Kanan's knee. "Not now that you have been in skin. Before we reach skin, Cyborg eggs are like the children of the overworld. But the Cyborg rituals that prepare eggs for skin—the knives of your hatchers and the chemicals of your skincaregivers—turn the Cyborg body into another kind of creature. The creation that could have belonged to bodies is given over to machines. That is the Cyborg way."

"Then a human in skin can never become a Natcher?"

Avi snarled and leapt to its feet. In a flash its hand was around Kanan's throat. "Speak this word, and never again Cyborg speaks."

Tiqvah laid its hand on the warrior's back. "Peace, Avi. The underworld's tongue is blind to its own harm. You know this as much as me. Or better still."

Avi's grip slowly loosened. The creature stood, spat in the dirt, and bounded away into the night.

"I'm sorry," said Kanan. "I meant no harm."

"Sorry?" Tiqvah's eyes narrowed. "It is just as well Avi has not lingered to hear you say so. But we cannot hold you guilty for a tongue you never chose. Even so, you must mind your throat. This word *Natcher* must never be spoken again. Even Avi cannot bear to hear it—and Avi is kinder than most of our race would be."

"Your race calls mine *Cyborg*. Isn't this as much an insult as the other?"

Tiqvah pulled away the last of Kanan's skin and offered her a cloth to wrap around herself. "It might seem so, if you have never known what it is to be called *Natcher*. But words are like your race's digiscape code. They carry whole histories with them. And futures too, sometimes. To be a *Natcher*, in the tongue of the underworld, is to be part of Nothing. When Nothing arrives in the underworld, it is treated like Nothing. It has no name except the name of an object, the name *It*. So the object is treated in the manner befitting an object: starved, tortured, dissected."

Kanan would have interrupted to ask for definitions of the unfamiliar words. But the look on Tiqvah's face sealed her lips.

"They are actions for which the Cyborg race does not need words," Tiqvah continued, answering Kanan's unspoken question. "Actions which follow automatically from the words already existing. They are actions done only to an object. To be a Natcher is to be murdered by a race which cannot even understand the meaning of murder."

Tiqvah fell silent. Its fist tightened around Kanan's shed skin. The creature breathed heavily. Kanan opened her mouth to respond and found she had nothing to say.

"We had endured for generations without an incident. So long a time that the Cyborgs seemed to forget our race existed at all. And then—" Tiqvah's eyes glistened. "Six seasons ago it happened. Perhaps we had grown too careless, too fool-hardy. The scout's name was Vahri. A playmate of Avi since before their first swim. The night Vahri was discovered by the orderkeepers—"

More silence. Something in Tiqvah's eyes caught the faint light around them, shimmering and flickering.

"This is what my race hears," said Tiqvah at last, "when we hear this word *Natcher*. Like code, it tells the story of horrors that have been, horrors we fear may be again. Where the word increases, the horror increases. The two have become so tangled up with one another that they cannot be pulled apart."

"Has the word always worked this way?" asked Kanan.

"Always. For as long as my race's memories have existed."

Kanan looked out toward the sky. A hint of yellow warmth had crept into the darkness. In the distance, she heard the rise and fall of four thin music notes. "And can words ever change?"

"If worlds can change," said Tiqvah, "then words must change. But I have never seen it done."

§§§

Kanan slept fitfully through the heat of the day. Each time she closed her eyes, her vivid Cyborg-water-induced dream from the previous night greeted her. Tei's arms held her tight as the skin peeled away. Her mouth filled with dirt. The earth heaved beneath her like ocean and grass.

She woke to the sound of shouting just as the sun was beginning to wane. A small crowd had gathered at the fig trees on the far side of the river. In the center of the commotion, two fully grown Natchers held the arms of a creature half their size. The smaller creature tugged and squirmed fruitlessly. Its eyes were full of fire.

"The child you see?" said Tiqvah, when it saw that Kanan was awake. "That one in our tongue is called *thief*. The child takes figs from a tree it has no right to take."

Kanan sat slowly upright. "I've seen others take figs from those trees."

"The ones you have seen before are the trees' owners," said Tiqvah. "Only they have the right to take the fruit."

One of the creatures standing in the crowd fell to its knees in the dirt, wailing loudly.

"The thief's parent pleads for the owners to overlook the law," said Tiqvah. "The child did not know better. The family has not eaten for two days. It may be a lie, but this is the plea."

"Two days?" Kanan's stomach rumbled at the thought. "Why wouldn't they eat? There's food everywhere."

"Everywhere, yes—for those with the right to it. But not for the thief's family. Their clan owns only a few fields of grain and no part of the river. If they wish to eat, they must first be hired. Their wages can then be bartered for food in the market. You will not understand—not at first. It is to be expected. There is no law like it among the Cyborgs."

A new Natcher stepped forward, brandishing a length of gnarled wood. The child sucked in its breath, showing the contours of its ribs, as the creatures on either side pulled its arms tighter.

"The parent's plea yields nothing," said Tiqvah. "The law will not be overlooked. The thief must return what is stolen."

The gnarled wood whistled through the air and hit the child's exposed belly with a thud. The clamor from the crowd increased. Some were weeping. Others laughed or jeered or murmured. The parent who had been on its knees collapsed to the ground.

The gnarled wood swung two more times. The child began to wretch. Half-digested figs poured out of its mouth and splattered onto the ground.

Kanan turned her head away. "How can you bear to watch?"

"Because it is my duty," answered Tiqvah simply.

"And what name do you give to the thing you are watching?" asked Kanan. "What is it called in your tongue?"

Tiqvah's eyes never left the spectacle. "Justice."

§§§

The hand that woke Kanan in the dead of night would have made her scream, if it hadn't been clamped tightly over her mouth. Tiqvah lay a skinlength away, beneath the far corner of the tarp, snoring softly. Too far for Kanan's flailing hands to reach.

"Hush," said the shadow looming over Kanan. "Mahlah will not hurt you."

"You speak in my tongue," said Kanan as the hand eased away. "But I thought only Tiqvah and Avi—"

"No time now for explaining," said Mahlah. "You must come at once, before Tiqvah wakes."

Kanan accepted the hand Mahlah held out, allowing herself to be pulled to her feet. She could just make out the contours of the aquarian's face. "Shouldn't Tiqvah be told I am leaving?"

"No," hissed Mahlah, and then the creature's tone softened. "Safest for all if the double-tongue knows nothing."

Kanan felt her pulse quickening. "Where are we going?"

"Soon enough you will see," said Mahlah, stepping closer. "You must trust me."

Kanan tried to step back. Her skinless legs moved clumsily and sluggishly, unused to following orders. "And what if I don't want to come?"

Mahlah sighed, resting its hand against the nape of Kanan's neck. Kanan noticed too late the tight squeeze of Mahlah's fingers, holding her head in place as the creature's other hand laid a damp scrap of fabric over Kanan's nose and mouth.

Her shadowy vision melted into absolute black. The last thing she felt was a breeze tickling her ear, delivering a husky whisper:

"Then Mahlah will carry you."

17

TEI

TEI'S GIFT FOR LEARNING the Natcher language sur-
passed everyone's expectations. Even Kyri said so, though he
masked his compliments with a gruff admonition: "Don't let
it go to your head."

As for humans in skin, they understood little enough about
Tei's career to be easily impressed. Buru had mastered the
politician's art of knowing next to nothing on a subject and yet
speaking with absolute confidence. "Not yet a quarter season's
study," he gushed to the officers' committee, "and already our
interpreter sounds like one of the aliens' own."

That last part certainly wasn't true. ("You sound like a strangled ox," Kyri had said, unkindly but not inaccurately, the last
time they'd had a conversation in Natcher.) Still, Buru could
be forgiven for stretching the truth a bit. He was under a lot
of strain since the incident with the Natcher raiding party and
the missing skin and Jarawi's premature skin failure.

More than half of the officers' committee had been ready
to declare immediate war on the Natchers—to send the whole

orderkeeping force with their strykers out into Nothing on a mission of revenge. It was Buru who persuaded them otherwise. The universe, he reminded the committee, hung in a delicate balance. Humanity didn't fully understand what role Natchers played in that balance. If the whole alien race was abolished, who knew whether food would continue to fill the galley shelves, whether water would continue to flow through the processing plant and into each hydropod? With the Natchers gone, who knew whether the suns would keep shining?

"Nonsense," some of the officers had scoffed. But they couldn't deny that Buru had a point. Three seasons ago, humanity's mechanics had noticed the suns' brightness beginning to dim. Buru blamed the Natchers and retaliated by cutting their supply deliveries. A temporary measure, he had told the committee, until light was restored. But the suns never returned to their former brightness. Instead, in a matter of weeks, the food appearing in the galley supply portal began diminishing as well. The human race grew more accustomed to hunger as their eyes adjusted to the darker skies.

"This is why we began searching for an Eleven, an interpreter, in the first place," Buru reminded the committee. "There are questions that must be answered. Before we can consider erasing the Natchers, we must be able to speak with them, to know what they know. We move when the interpreter is ready, and not a moment sooner."

When the interpreter is ready. No one seemed to know what the words meant, exactly, or how long it would take before they finally became true. But Buru was eager to prove in the meantime that progress was being made. He paraded Tei in front of the committee every week, offering vague reassurances: "He's nearly there now. We've made the right choice of Eleven, no question about it. If you'd heard what I've just heard, you'd be smiling as wide as me. A little more patience, and our race will be ready to face the greatest crisis we've seen in generations."

Despite Buru's pleas for patience, war lingered in the air. The orderkeepers spent more time training in skin than ever before. They chanted rhythmically as they ran in packs around the perimeter of the universe. Tei grew accustomed to the sound of their chants echoing everywhere he went—the dormitory, the mess hall, the archive room, the hallways in between—every twenty minutes like clockwork. Between laps, orderkeepers crowded into the digiscape to practice marksmanship and hand-to-hand combat. When all the training hydropods were filled, they commandeered the leisure hydropods as well. "For the good of humanity," they said. "For the safety of all our skins. For Jarawi."

The officers' committee Finalized a new orderkeeper from among the senior fledglings to take Jarawi's place. "It is an unprecedented thing," said Buru at the special assembly, "to give birth to a Final between aging ceremonies. But these are unprecedented times. The order of our universe, and the role of those who keep it, has never been more critical to uphold."

The newborn orderkeeper's name was Resen. Tei had never spoken to him, but rumor had it Resen was a loner who excelled at running and rowing. Half a season earlier, Kanan could have been the one chosen to take Jarawi's place. Half a season. That was all it took to turn a fledgling's fate upside-down—to make the difference between Finalization and deletion.

But Tei had little time to dwell on such thoughts. Every moment not dedicated to eating or sleeping was spent in the archive room. If he wasn't with Kyri, discussing verb tense and syntax as they floated among the stars, he was learning the mechanics of the archive and the career hydropods from Reif. Soon, to the archivist's delight, Tei could program an entire archival venture without once consulting the interface manual.

"You mustn't forget," Reif lectured him, "to stop and find some time for leisure. Get out of the digiscape every once in a while. I barely ever take a rest, myself, and look what it's done to me." The archivist wrapped two fingers around his slender arm. "Atrophy, that's what they call it. No matter how good a skin might be, it's no better than the human it holds. I haven't rowed in more seasons than I care to remember. Missed more than a few meals, too. It shows, doesn't it? So much archive, so little time. But you're young. You mustn't let yourself follow the same way as me. Can't have our esteemed Eleven looking like an underfed recluse."

Reif's advice fell on deaf ears. The longer Tei spent in the archive with Kyri, the more meaningless everything else seemed to become. What did it matter whether the suns were lit, or which spices the galley chemists used on the third shift's flakemeat? Why should Tei spend a leisure evening with his agemates in the digiscape, when the world his career had opened to him felt a hundred times more vast than anything humanity had language for?

There were no Natchers in the archive for Tei to talk with, so Kyri programmed a Natcher of his own. "Only a simulation," he explained, "based on a memory of mine." The creature's name was Kiphu. It had long red hair falling past its shoulders and high cheeks that stretched its lips into a constant smile. Its voice was low, heavy, thick like swamp mud.

"No wonder I sound like a strangled ox," said Tei, "when this is what I'm trying to mimic."

"It's closer to reality than you'd think," countered Kyri. "Not a perfect accent, by any means, but the best we can do until you see the overworld for yourself. A sight better than I can offer you myself, certainly. As for Kiphu's personality, I've left as much intact as I could under the circumstances. Certain modifications had to be made. It would not do, for instance, to have the creature constantly trying to kill you. Not yet."

"I appreciate that." Tei searched Kyri's face for any indication he was joking. It was impossible to be sure.

Kyri's mention of death reminded Tei of Kanan's words in the dreamscape: *I'm alive, I'm alive, I'm alive*. When Tei had first told Kyri about the dream, the interpreter simply shrugged. "It's a Natcher word, sure enough. I didn't realize I'd taught it to you. Or maybe you're so gifted with the Natcher language that you knew it without being told?"

About Natcher ideas of life and death, Kyri was only too happy to explain. But how Dream-Kanan had come to speak the word *alive* remained a mystery. "There was a surge of water that night," said Tei breathlessly. "Perhaps—"

Kyri waved away the theory with his hand. "No sense asking questions that can't be answered. Still too many questions that can be."

And indeed, it boggled Tei's mind how many new answers he was learning—answers to questions he had never thought to ask until he began learning the Natcher language. He had never wondered, for instance, why humans used the pronouns *he* and *she* interchangeably to talk about other humans.

"It wasn't always that way," Kyri explained, as they soared over a snow-peaked mountain range on Nauraa's back. "In the days before the Natcher-Cyborg split, the words appear to have had two different meanings. Whatever they meant in those days, there's no record of it now. But you'll notice, when we travel back in the archive and talk to humans who lived before the invention of language, they consistently use the pronoun *he* to talk about some people and *she* to talk about others. There's almost no variation. It's nothing like the language we spoke when I was in skin, where the words were exact synonyms.

And nothing like the language humans in skin are speaking now, I assume."

Tei nodded, even though Kyri's back was turned. "I use *he*—it's easier to say. Even when other people say *she*, I change it in my head and wind up hearing *he*. Kanan always liked saying *she*, though. I remember that. Not that it matters. It's all the same word in the end."

"It is now, yes," said Kyri. "But not in the archive. It used to mean something more."

"Couldn't you go back and ask the ones who used it that way?"

Kyri tightened his grip on Nauraa's mane as the unicorn banked left around a rocky outcropping. "I've tried. No one can do more than point to the others and say: 'This one is *he*. This one is *she*.' They can't explain why. Or if they try to explain, the words mean nothing, not in human language or in Natcher either. Whatever *he* and *she* used to mean, either the memory of it has been scrubbed out by archivists, or it no longer has any meaning."

"Do the Natchers use *he* and *she*?" asked Tei. "I know we call them *it* in our language. But do they have pronouns of their own?"

The interpreter shook his head. "Singular personal pronouns are one of the many things the Natchers lost as language changed. Some of them still use the word *it* in their own language, but only as a crude insult. The Natchers believe it is an offense to avoid a thing's name so long as that name is available. Natchers have no need for pronouns, then, because everything they speak of has a name. If it cannot be named, they say, it should not be spoken of."

"They erased pronouns from their language? Just like that?" Tei snapped his fingers.

Kyri mimicked the finger snap. "Not *just like that*, no. This change—and so many others—happened over the course of seasons and generations. It was small things at first. A rising suspicion about the confusion caused by pronouns. An insistence that names were more polite. Subtly using pronouns less and less, looking down on anyone who did. The more separate the races grew from one another, the more entrenched the change became. Over the course of the Natcher generations, the memory of the old pronouns grew fainter and fainter until it was entirely lost."

"Didn't anyone try to fight the loss?" asked Tei.

"For them," said Kyri, "it was not loss. It was gain. By losing pronouns, they gained back the importance of names. Just as we humans lost the difference between *he* and *she* and so gained the power of unity. In language, everything lost is also something gained. Everything gained is also something lost. Every way of seeing is also a way of not seeing."

Tei looked out at the bare face of a passing mountainside. "What else did the Natchers lose from their language?"

"The copula," answered Kyri. "*Is, am, was, were, being, been*—all the words that unite the sides of a sentence and make them equal. The Natchers didn't trust this idea of unity. They said it was a Cyborg distortion, to cover over difference and pretend sameness. Speaking with the copula—thinking with the copula—was condemned as lazy and imprecise. Like singular personal pronouns, copular verbs faded out of Natcher language."

"And they gained something from this loss?"

"The beauty of diversity. The seeing of things as they really are, in all their difference, without a pretense of similitude." Kyri scoffed. "Or so the Natchers have always said. But their ideals are a far cry from their reality. The overworld has always been mired in division. Factions form around the color of underflesh, the possession of resources, the grudges of parents and grandparents and ancestors long since forgotten. The Natchers have their difference, yes, and it is all they have."

"Then humanity was right to keep our copula," said Tei, feeling a surge of pride in his race.

Kyri turned back sharply, frowning. "I wouldn't celebrate so quickly if I were you. Look what we've lost in the name of human unity. We forget what our bodies look like, what they might be capable of before hatchers and chemists turn us into skin-wearers. Anyone who doesn't fit the human mold, we archive. Every underflesh that cannot be fitted perfectly into skin, because it is too tall or short or misshapen. Every mind too dull or too sharp to become a cog in the machine of the universe. We carve away a hundred eggs until they are seventy, forty, ten. We create more than we need in order to kill our own excess."

"Kill?" Tei winced at the accusation. "We're not like Natchers, dealing in life and death. Everyone shares the honor of the human race. In the archive, too, there is eternal honor."

Kyri's face betrayed nothing. "You're sure of it?"

"As sure as I am," said Tei, "that earth is earth, sky is sky, universe is universe. The meaning belongs to the words themselves. The definition answers the question."

"So it does," said Kyri. "Or so it did, back in the days when you spoke only one language."

In an instant, Nauraa and the mountain range disappeared. Tei and Kyri stood inside the assembly room pyramid, watching a mentor and two orderkeepers pull the skin off the body of Tei's former agemate Shanur. Skinless Shanur let himself be lowered into the birthing hydropod. One of the orderkeepers pulled a lever jutting out from the wall. Shanur began to sink.

"All this," said Kyri, "you know how to imagine. But what comes next has never been shown to you. This time, we follow the body all the way to the archive."

As Shanur sank, Tei and Kyri followed as if pulled by magnets. Earth and walls melted around them. A fierce current pulled Shanur's body down a watery tunnel and through a series of tubes. The body landed in a small metallic chamber, waist-deep in water. His head was caught between a network of straps, pulled tight to render it motionless.

Four long probes sprang out of the walls and plunged themselves through Shanur's skull. The fledgling cried out in pain.

"What's happening?" asked Tei.

"His neural impulses are being extracted for preservation in the archive," said Kyri.

"Extracted?" Tei's voice shook. "Why should anything need to be extracted? All of him is being transported to the archive. Everything but the skin."

"The archive is just code," said Kyri. "Nothing more. Bodies cannot go into the archive. Only the idea of bodies, once they have been converted into strings of letters and numbers and symbols. "

"And what becomes of the bodies themselves? The part of the human that is neither skin nor idea?"

"Does it matter?" said Kyri. "Such a question can only be asked with Natcher words. There is no name in Cyborg to speak of bodies. We have skin and archive. For a few moments in between the two, we have a fleeting glimpse of underflesh. But the thing you now recognize as a 'body'—the human being in its barest material form, fully independent of skin or archival preservation—doesn't exist in Cyborg minds. Our humanity ends where our words about humanity end. Without a name, we have nothing to lose and nothing to grieve."

The screaming stopped. The probes retracted. Then a searing blade flashed through the air, severing Shanur's head from his body. The body fell again, pulling Tei and Kyri with it through another series of tubes. There was no water now, only frigid air. At last, Shanur—what was left of him—landed in a pile of underflesh.

"Welcome to the butchery," said Kyri. "Within a week, he'll be in someone's bowl of darkmeat stew. As for the head, it will be decomposed and sent up to feed the soil of the overworld. I've skipped over a few of the interludes, so you could see it all happen at once. Most bodies are kept alive, unconscious in a holding tank, for weeks or months before they're decapitated and butchered. But this is what it means to be digitized. This is what becomes of underflesh in the end. This is what our race means when we speak of eternal honor."

They were astride the unicorn again, soaring across a black sheet pinpricked with light. Tei's stomach lurched with the beating of the unicorn's wings. He could taste darkmeat on his tongue.

When he opened his mouth to speak, all that came out was vomit. He wretched and wretched until everything in his stomach was gone.

§§§

They flew in silence for what felt like hours, watching asteroids drift lazily past. At last Kyri spoke. "Only one thing left now for you to see."

"Please." Tei shook his head. "I can't bear to see any more."

"Of course you can't bear it." Kyri nudged Nauraa's ribs, urging the creature faster. "That is why you must see it."

The object looked from a distance like any other asteroid. But as they approached, Tei realized it was far larger and more perfectly round than the other asteroids he'd seen. More colorful, too—streaks of blue and white patched with brown and green.

"It's called *planet*," said Kyri. "Planet Earth, to be specific."

"Earth?" Tei thought of the silica earth his feet in skin knew so well. "Seems like a dull namesake for a many-colored sphere floating through the stars."

Kyri laughed. "I thought so too at first. But the planet is not named for the substance under your feet. The substance under your feet takes its name from the planet."

The white streaks swelled bigger and nearer than the rest. "Look out," cried Tei, closing his eyes as Nauraa flew directly towards one. When the collision never came, Tei opened his eyes and realized they were passing through a thick, wet fog.

"Clouds you already know, of course," said Kyri. "They're common enough in the digiscape. But you've probably never seen one from above—or from the inside. Hold tightly now, Nauraa is about to land."

The unicorn tilted its wings back, gliding gently down until its hooves rested on damp sand. To Tei's right, ocean stretched as far as he could see. On his left, scattered trees and heaps of fallen, rotting palm branches lined the beach.

"Welcome to Planet Earth," said Kyri. "Does it look familiar?"

Tei turned his head in every direction. "It feels like the digiscape. The same massive sky. The same endless horizon."

"And so it should." Kyri slid off Nauraa's back and held out a hand for Tei to follow. "The digiscape was designed to simulate this place—to make sure the human race never forgot how to live on a planet like this one."

Tei slid down and felt damp sand press between his toes. "How could we forget what has never been done before?"

"Do not be too sure," said Kyri, "that you know the whole shape of human history."

"I was the best historian in my cohort," Tei bristled.

"The best at receiving the story you were told—I have no doubt about that. But history-telling always turns our attention toward certain details and ignores others. Which moments matter? Which do not? Whose memories will be paraded before the fledglings, and whose memories can be erased? These questions are decided by those with power to decide them. Studying history as you've done it simply means learning the story someone wanted you to hear."

"What do you suggest instead?"

Kyri pointed out toward the water. A human silhouette stood between them and the setting sun, belly-deep in the waves. "I thought you might want hear about Planet Earth from Adam."

Tei squinted out toward the figure. "You mean the Adam of history classes? The first human born in skin? I've heard him tell his bit of history. Every fledgling hears him."

"So they do. They hear the part of the story he's permitted to tell—the part he's able to tell in a language they can understand. But I think you'll find he has more to say now that you have more language available to you."

"The Adam I remember wore skin," Tei objected. "This one has a bare undertorso like yours."

Kyri took a few steps into the water, motioning for Tei to follow. "The code of training hydropods—and leisure hydropods as well, of course—requires everyone to appear in skin. Just one of the many limits placed on the archival world, to keep it under control. Only when they are visited through a career hydropod can archived humans appear as they want to appear. Only here can we speak as we want to speak. And even then, only if the programmer allows it."

"You're saying Adam doesn't wear skin unless the code forces him to wear it?"

Kyri nodded. "In Adam's era, a human's skin needed to be worn only sometimes—in work, but not in leisure. In the archive, he does the same. When Adam is paraded in front of fledglings in training hydropods to teach history, he wears his skin to work. At rest, he returns to underflesh. If he could choose to stay in underflesh forever, I think he would."

"Then why doesn't he give up teaching history to fledglings and stay here on Planet Earth?"

"Because he is code. Code does not refuse its assignments. Code does not have desires of its own. Not without a programmer's permission."

"And here?" asked Tei. "Where the only programmers are you and me?"

"I've done what I can to create space in the code for archival Adam to speak and think as much as possible like the real Adam who once lived. But the code is never perfect. There are too many barriers in the way. Too many laws imposed onto the system. Too many nosing archivists scrubbing out the inconvenient parts of history. No one in code can be identical to their pre-digitized selves in skin. Not even me."

Tei said nothing. They were knee-deep in water now, twenty skin-lengths from the spot where Adam stood with his back to them.

"I'm not the interpreter who once lived in skin," Kyri continued. "Not really. Surely you've learned enough of the Natcher language by now to understand that. Kyri is dead. What you see of me—what you see of every archived human—it's all just a selective memory of who we used to be. Just digitized neural impulses copied from the living Kyri's mind before his body was butchered and eaten."

Vomit started to rise in Tei's throat again. He choked it back. "If you're not really Kyri, then what's the good of talking to you? What's the good of bringing me here to talk to Adam? If history is biased and partial and imperfect, why should I bother to learn the past at all?"

A wave crested in front of them. Kyri ducked beneath it and emerged dripping. "Because it's the best hope we have left. The only hope we have left."

They stood directly behind Adam now. His gaze remained on the sunset, the underflesh of his narrow brown shoulders glistening with salt and sand and sweat.

"Got time for a history lesson?" said Kyri.

Adam didn't turn. "The nerve," he murmured. "Here I am skinless, in my own home, enjoying a rare moment of peace. And you show up unannounced to demand a history lesson."

"We'll leave, then." Kyri winked at Tei and made a great show of splashing through the water as he took a few backward steps.

"Good riddance," said Adam.

"Good riddance to you too," said Kyri.

No one moved for a moment. Tei looked back and forth between Kyri's smirk and Adam's shoulders.

It was Kyri who began to recite first:

In the beginning, there was Nothing. There was no skin, no archive, no universe. Then the Architect said, "Let us make a universe out of Nothing." So the Architect took the materials of Nothing and shaped them into earth and sky and water. When he set his mighty hand against the perimeter of the universe and pulled, the universe began to spin through Nothing.

Without turning, Adam's voice joined Kyri's, repeating the words every fledgling knew by heart:

Then the Architect said, "What good is a universe without human beings?" So he reached into Nothing and pulled out human beings, and he placed them inside the spinning universe. But when he saw the frailty of their underflesh, he said, "It is not good for humans to be without skin." So he formed skin from the materials of Nothing and declared that skin would cover underflesh. And he poured water over the skin and said, "Skin must never be without water, nor water without skin." And that is why water is green to this day.

At last Adam turned toward them. His face reminded Tei of a fledgling, but he was certainly tall enough to be a Final. He wore a deadly serious frown at first. With each passing sentence, though, another hint of a smile crept into his lips.

Then the Architect said, "Let humanity forever grow and increase." And he created the hatchery and filled it with eggs who would become fledglings who would become Finals. And the first of these eggs, the Architect's own offspring made in his likeness, was called Adam. Adam became the firstborn of all the human race in skin. But when all the skins in the universe had been filled, the Architect was weary and did not wish to make more skins. He said, "Let us make an archive, a space limited only by the power of code and imagination, where humans can exist without skin and yet not be skinless. And in this way the human race will have no more limits." So the Architect took the power of water and harnessed it in hydropods, and he wrote the first lines of digiscape code.

Both Adam and Kyri were stifling laughter now. Adam lifted one fist out of the water, raising it in a mocking salute.

Then the Architect said, "Humanity must endure forever. It must make a name for itself. But I cannot endure forever. I must let go for the sake of humanity." So the Architect launched the universe from Nothing into Nothing, and he himself faded into the Nothing. And so the universe has spun ever since, giving humanity a place outside of Nothing, ensuring that our honor will endure forever.

Kyri began to applaud slowly. "All hail the great Adam, firstborn in skin, figurehead of human history." His voice dripped with sarcasm.

Adam bowed deep, setting his face into the waves. He emerged spraying water and wiped his eyes with the back of one hand. "That was all you needed, then? You've got everything you came for?"

They waded toward each other until they were chest to chest. Each one wrapped his arms around the other's undertorso. It was a gesture Tei had never seen before.

"An ancient form of greeting," said Kyri after they unclasped, answering Tei's unspoken question.

Adam snorted. "Ancient form of greeting, my ass. The things the universe has come to."

"It's the curse of the archive," shrugged Kyri. "Worse for you than for me, but no picnic in either case. The dead shouldn't have to watch themselves become historical artifacts."

Adam opened his arms toward Tei. "Do you mind? I'm still a hugger, on the rare occasions the code allows."

Tei shrugged. Adam threw both arms around him, pressing their chests together. When their faces grew uncomfortably close, Tei turned his neck to one side. He held his breath until it was over. As he stepped away, he brushed Adam's wetness away from his skin, wrinkling his nose in distaste. "I can see why this greeting didn't stand the test of time."

Kyri laughed and prodded Adam with a finger. "You see? I'm not the only one to find it awkward at first, even with the touch laws set aside."

Adam shook his head in dismay. "Those laws have ruined you all with fear and paranoia. What else could be expected from people who try so hard to forget the limitations of their bodies? Trust me, if you two had been alive in the early days of the universe, or even before the Great Construction, you'd enjoy hugs as much as I do."

"Before?" Tei frowned. "But there was nothing before the Great Construction."

"Precisely," said Adam, sweeping an arm around him. "Welcome to Nothing."

"Remember," Kyri interjected, "in human language, everything beyond the universe is Nothing. It cannot be spoken of, cannot be thought of, as anything other than an irrelevance. So it becomes Nothing. This is why the Natcher overworld exists in Nothing. Your agemate Kanan, if he is still alive, survives in Nothing. And Nothing is also, inevitably, the only way the human race can talk about our former home."

Tei's mouth fell open. "You mean to say that Planet Earth was—"

"—the Nothing where the universe began," finished Adam. "The original home of humanity. Or as original as I know, anyway."

"Then the Architect didn't create the human race?"

"Yes and no," said Kyri. "That group of people you call *human* is defined by skin and by archive. The Architect created both. So in that sense, the Architect created your idea of the human race. But he didn't create the beings inside the skin. He didn't create the beings whose minds would be programmed into the archive when their bodies died. If you use the word *human* to mean both Cyborgs and Natchers, as well as whatever came before them, then the Architect couldn't possibly have created the human race. He was one of them."

Tei nearly choked. "The Architect was human?"

"He was as much underflesh as you or me," nodded Adam. "So were all of them—the race that lived on Planet Earth before the Great Construction. They were the ones who gave the Architect what he needed to build the universe and start it spinning and launch it away from Planet Earth. It was for the whole race—for their eternal survival, for their honor—that the universe was made."

"Some honor," said Tei. "We don't even know they exist."

Adam smiled sadly. "And they'd be chagrined to hear it, I'm sure. They had no idea how much their fellow humans would evolve after millennia away from Planet Earth, trapped inside a tiny universe. The Terrans never dreamed how language would shift over time until everything outside the universe was reduced to Nothing. The digiscape was supposed to help us remember where our race had come from and where we were going. No one imagined it would become a substitute for both."

"When you say *going*," asked Tei, "do you mean the universe was supposed to take us somewhere? Somewhere on the other side of Nothing?"

Kyri and Adam exchanged glances. "Perhaps," said Kyri to the firstborn of the human race, "you could tell your story from the beginning?"

"No," said Adam, "that's too far along. I'll tell it from before the beginning."

18
LILY

LILY HAD BARELY HEARD OF GLIESE 832C when she signed her life away to Project Universe. Her brother Elliot was the one who had worn a fishbowl over his head like a space helmet when they were kids, reenacting the Mars landing in the patch of sand behind their mother's double-wide trailer. And when, twenty years later, Margola Industries put out its call for applicants to the first-ever exoplanet settlement crew, it was Elliot who sent her the link with a two-word message: "Family trip?"

It was Elliot who told her about ExoSkin, too: part synthetic fabric, part fluid electrical current, part exoskeletal muscular system. Lily found it hard to believe that the next generation of space suits would look like spandex superhero costumes. But when Elliot said it with enough conviction, she almost believed. "That's your ticket in," he had told her, rubbing her shoulders like a coach prepping an athlete. "You wrote a whole dissertation on fluid electromechanics in human prosthesis. You're perfect for this."

Elliot lived in the double-wide by then. Their mom was gone: first to a nursing home, where she thought every male nurse was her cheating ex-husband; then to a dusty patch of earth on the edge of town, with a plain granite headstone where Lily left handfuls of wildflowers every time she visited.

"It's the never coming back that freaks me out," said Lily. "A few months, sure. A few years, even. But to spend the rest of my life on a spaceship that won't get anywhere for thousands of years?"

Elliot leaned against the vinyl-paneled wall. "There's no other way. Unless you're travelling at light speed–which is just impossible, in theory and in practice–getting around our galaxy takes time. That's what makes Project Universe so groundbreaking. A self-contained, self-perpetuating ecosystem that can sustain generation after generation of human life. With enough patience, you could wind up anywhere in our galaxy."

"With enough patience," said Lily, "I could be dead."

"Die here, die up there. As long as you live first. Besides"–Elliot waved an arm toward the window on the far side of the living room–"there's nothing here worth sticking around for."

Lily caught her brother's arm. "There's you."

"That's why I'm coming with you. My application is already submitted. We'll tell the Margola sisters we're a package deal."

Three weeks after Lily sent in her application, the other half of her package deal was diagnosed with stage three non-Hodgkin's lymphoma. Lily forgot about everything except chemotherapy and platelet transfusions. Cancer had been "cured," of course–but only if you were rich enough to afford cutting-edge mitochondrial bioengineering. No one spent that kind of money to save a thirty-one-year-old office manager living in his dead mother's double-wide.

Elliot still followed the news of Project Universe religiously. At each chemo session, he recited his findings to Lily while an IV bag dripped life-saving poison into him. He talked as if they were both accepted into the space shuttle's crew, as if lymphoma was just a stubbed toe in their race to the stars. "Look at this breakthrough in artificial sunlight generation," he would say. "No vitamin D deficiency for us." Or,

"They've ruled out Proxima Centauri b as our destination planet; the stellar winds make it uninhabitable. But Gliese 832c is looking more and more promising. Four times farther, yes, but who's counting?" Or, "Anocyte-charged water is a go. It needs so little energy to sustain itself, we can probably generate it with hand cranks or rowing machines. Imagine that, you and me powering a whole ecosystem."

When stage three of lymphoma became stage four, Elliot disappeared from his own stories. "ExoSkin will definitely get you onboard," he began to say. Or, "They're talking about mechanizing all childbirth onboard, for safety and population control. Good thing you never wanted kids anyway." Or, "Self-renutrifying soil will make agriculture in space better than anything we've got on Planet Earth. You'll see."

"So will you," lied Lily.

Fourteen months and six days after Elliot's diagnosis, a second granite headstone joined their mother's on the edge of town. Lily picked two bunches of wildflowers. There was no funeral.

The phone call from the Margola sisters came the following week. "There's nothing here worth sticking around for," Elliot had said. Lily could finally see just how right he was. She signed the papers without bothering to read the fine print.

Better to lose herself in Elliot's daydream than stay stuck inside her own nightmare.

19

KANAN

KANAN'S SENSE OF TOUCH RETURNED FIRST. Her body lay at an angle, resting against something cold and smooth and hard. Droplets of water tapped against her under-flesh in irregular rhythms. More water lapped at her feet.

"The grogginess will soon wear off," said Mahlah, its voice distant and garbled. "Hold the herbs close against your face and breathe deeply."

Kanan did as she was told. Leaves and stems, coated with soft tiny hairs, tickled her nose. She sneezed.

"Not so close as that, perhaps." The tremor in Mahlah's voice suggested a barely stifled laugh.

"Where are we?"

"A hiding place. One of the many aerating pockets in the river network between worlds. Kanan's new skin is kept here. And other things, too, sometimes. Things that must be hidden."

Colors and lines began to emerge out of the grey haze over Kanan's eyes. A dingy cave stretched above her. Its walls were slippery and brown. Water dripped from razor-sharp stalactites overhead. "Why am I here, then? Am I another thing that must be hidden?"

"It is Mahlah who hides," said the aquarian. "You are my guest."

Kanan blinked and pulled the herbs away from her face. "I suppose you drug all your guests?"

Mahlah shrugged. "Only when necessary. Mahlah hoped you would come willingly. But there was no time to explain. Tiqvah was near to waking. If Tiqvah had woken, the opportunity would have been lost."

Kanan pulled her knees towards her and slowly, tremblingly, rose to her feet.

"Your legs recover well," said Mahlah. "The healer will be pleased."

Kanan looked around the cave. Its walls were totally enclosed. The sloping rock she stood against was pockmarked with pools of shimmering water, some so shallow she could see the sediment beneath, others impossibly deep. "Lucky for you I have no place to run."

"You are Mahlah's guest," repeated the aquarian. "Not Mahlah's prisoner. Mahlah will swim you back to the overworld whenever you wish."

"Then bring me back now," said Kanan.

"Very well." Mahlah lowered its body into the water. "Only be warned: once we return to the overworld, Mahlah will not speak the words of a Cyborg again. And when you speak to Mahlah like a Cyborg, Mahlah will pretend not to understand."

"That's your secret, then? You're hiding your knowledge of my tongue?"

The aquarian hesitated. "This is one of the things Mahlah hides."

"But wouldn't the others be pleased if they knew?" said Kanan. "Isn't it an advantage for your race to understand the words of the underworld?"

"The overworld both values and distrusts those with two tongues," said Mahlah. "Skill with Cyborg words is undeniably useful. But the skill makes the one who possesses it a source of constant threat. The creature assigned by the elders as a double-tongue must work harder than anyone to prove their loyalty to the overworld. So it is that Tiqvah follows every law flawlessly and yet is viewed by many of our race with suspicion."

"What about Avi?"

"The grandchild of an elder, a skilled warrior, can be forgiven for knowing a few words of the Cyborg tongue. Besides, the circumstances of Avi's learning inspire sympathy. No one could doubt Avi's loyalty to the overworld."

"And they would doubt yours?"

Instead of answering, Mahlah ducked its head beneath the water, unleashing a trail of bubbles in its wake. Kanan watched until the bubbles had all but disappeared. When the aquarian emerged, it clutched something tangled and sodden and blue in its fist.

"My skin," said Kanan.

No sooner had the words left her mouth than she realized her mistake. This skin's colors were too vivid, its patterns too stark, to match the skin Kanan had taken from the humans.

"Mahlah's skin," said the aquarian. "And not an entire skin, either. Not yet."

"How did you get it?"

"Patiently." Mahlah laid the tangled strands of skin on dry earth and crawled out after them. "Bit by bit, so the disappearance is not noticed. With the help of a friend."

The word *friend* was new to Kanan. Still, its meaning seemed clear enough. "A human, you mean."

Mahlah nodded. "The same Cyborg who teaches Mahlah's tongue to split. It is the advantage of an aquarian, to come and go without the others questioning. Easy enough, when the waterways are unattended, to bring another along to a hiding place like this one."

Names and faces from her fledgling years flashed through Kanan's mind. "Who?"

The aquarian pressed its lips tightly and said nothing.

"But why would you want a skin?" asked Kanan. "Your race hates skin."

"So we do. So did Mahlah, not so long ago."

"What changed?

Mahlah held out one foot, displaying a delicate braid tied around its ankle. Age had worn the plait thin, but three strands were still distinctly visible: one brown like a plant stem, one skin-blue, the third blacker than carbon. "You see? It represents three worlds. Overworld here, underworld there. And binding them together, a cord taken from a place that is neither overworld nor underworld. A cord pulled from the very heart of Nothing."

Kanan touched two fingertips against the black strand. It pressed stiff and cold against her underflesh, leaving an indent when she pulled away. "How can a cord come from Nothing?"

"The one who gave the gift to Mahlah had been there, in a place neither overworld nor underworld. It was there she found the cord; and another just like it, for the braid around her own ankle."

"*She*?" Kanan held the human word in her mouth, marveling at how unfamiliar it had begun to feel. "Then it's a human you're talking about? The same human who gathers bits of skin with you and teaches your tongue to split?"

Mahlah shook its head. "This one who gave the gift was no longer a Cyborg. But not an overworlder, either. Not for long, anyway. No one who wears skin can remain an overworlder. It is forbidden."

"Then this one who went into Nothing wore skin? How could she wear skin and yet not be human?"

"She wore it only sometimes." Mahlah reached for the pile of skin and began draping strands across its own underflesh. "Not the way Cyborgs do, out of need. She wore it for the freedom it gave her to journey into Nothing."

"You say *wore*," said Kanan, "like the wearing is past. Where is she now?"

"Gone into Nothing," said Mahlah. "For three seasons now. So deep into Nothing she may never return."

Kanan's jaw tightened. "You mean she's dead?"

"To the Cyborg," said Mahlah, "you are in Nothing. Are you dead?"

Kanan dipped her skinless hand into the water. The current washed over it, blurring and distorting its edges. "Did you ever go with her into the place where the cord came from? The place she called Nothing?"

"Mahlah would have gone," said the aquarian. "But it was impossible. To be in Nothing without skin means death. This is why Mahlah gathers pieces for a new skin. When the skin is complete, Mahlah too will complete the journey into Nothing."

"I thought the citizens of the overworld were forbidden from wearing skin."

"So we are. The punishment is exile. If Mahlah is caught, there will be no return to the overworld."

"And you're willing to risk it?" said Kanan. "Just for a chance to see how far the universe extends? You're willing to risk losing everything and everyone?"

"Mahlah would not be the first to risk such a thing." The alien looked pointedly at Kanan. "Besides, Mahlah will not be alone. Another will come."

"Who?"

Mahlah's stern expression relaxed into a secretive smile. "A friend."

"How long have you been planning?"

"Too long." Mahlah laid the last strand of skin muscle against the underflesh of its leg. It stood to its feet, brandishing its blue stripes proudly. "But soon we will be ready. As soon as the skin is finished."

"You could go sooner," said Kanan. "You could take my skin."

Mahlah froze. "You want the skin taken away?"

"Of course not," said Kanan, suddenly unsure if the words were true. "But you're the only one who knows where it's hidden. My wanting has no power to stop you."

"Mahlah is no thief." The aquarian began peeling skin away, returning the strips to a sodden pile on the earth. "Mahlah does not need Kanan's skin."

"Then what is it you want?"

"Your help," said Mahlah, "to retrieve the rest of Mahlah's skin. And when the time comes, if you are willing, your company on the journey into Nothing."

Kanan's heart pounded. "Tiqvah and Avi would never allow—"

Mahlah struck the water with its fist. "Of course they would not allow it. Their ears are shut up against the very possibility. They cannot know of Mahlah's plans."

"You're asking me to betray them."

"Call it what you will," said the aquarian. "Mahlah calls it by another name."

"Tiqvah and Avi have been kind to me. The overworld is the only place I have left. I won't go behind their backs." Kanan pulled herself toward the lapping water. "Take me home."

"Very well," said Mahlah with a sigh. "The plan will continue with or without you. But you must swear not to speak one word of this night to Tiqvah or Avi or the others. A loose tongue could endanger us all."

"What if I refuse to be silent?" said Kanan, the heat of anger rising in her face.

Mahlah's head sank. The question hung in the air for a moment before the creature answered. "No one would believe you. Your mouth is still full of Cyborg treachery, no matter how loyal the mind behind that mouth. Mahlah has always been a creature of the overworld, always spoken like a creature of the overworld. If the overworld can trust only one of us, they will trust the one whose words most resemble their own."

"What if I find a way to make them believe me?"

When Mahlah raised its head, the eyes that met Kanan's seemed reluctant. Pleading. Wistful. But the words coming from the creature's mouth were as deadly sharp as the blade bound to its waist: "Find a way, and it will be the last thing you ever find."

20

TEI

THE FIRST EXCURSION INTO LILY'S MEMORIES left Tei disoriented and overwhelmed. Colorful pictures appeared in midair and danced above the sealine as Adam spoke. ("Just like a movie theater," the historian said, though the phrase was meaningless to Tei.) The ocean swelled to high tide, turning Tei and Adam and Kyri into disembodied heads among the waves and foam. By the time the last image had faded from the sky, Tei was breathless. From shock? From anger? From the exertion of treading water? There was no way to be sure.

"These memories," Tei gasped. "Where did they come from? How can you possibly know them?"

"All things in time," said Adam. "The story is only just beginning."

"And what about Gliese 832c? Is the Universe still on its way there?"

Adam let out a deep sigh and dipped his head back into the ocean. "I wish I knew. Since I was digitized, I've seen hundreds of captains enter the archive. At first, they would update me on our progress through outer space, tell me about the course we were charting among the stars. But as Cyborgs and Natchers lost the ability to speak to each other, the memory of our destination started to fade away. Has the ship's autopilot kept us on target since then? Are we light years off course? Is the Universe still moving at all? It's impossible to ask these questions anymore, because the questions have become meaningless. The only way to find answers now is to get inside the command room and see everything firsthand."

"But you're archived," said Tei. "How can you get out of the digiscape and into skin again?"

"I can't," said Adam. "But you can."

§§§

They met in the command room—or rather, a digiscape facsimile of it—the next morning. Tei sat in the captain's chair, with Adam beside him to guide his hands across the Universe's complex control interface. Adam wore something called tee-shirt-and-shorts, loose tubes of fabric that dangled off his skinless limbs and sometimes drifted weightlessly out of place. ("The height of fashion on Planet Earth!" Adam claimed. Tei refused to believe it.)

Tei had seen the control interface countless times already, during his weekly visits to Captain Buru. But the only bit of the interface he had witnessed in action was the communications panel, where Buru's fingers flew with ease over sliders and dials as he spoke into the receiver of the universal throat. Everything else—every other lever and knob and joystick and holographic display—was unfamiliar to him. Buru never touched them in Tei's presence. Most of them, Tei doubted Buru had ever touched for himself. In Buru's mind, they probably existed as mere decorations: like tassels on a uniform, or shiny gemstones in a ruler's crown.

For Adam, though, every device had a purpose. Each one became a mini-lecture directed toward Tei: "This lever here beneath the safety guard? That's the fluid rotation regulator. It controls the speed at which the universe spins. Turn it all the way down, and every hydropod would lose power. Pseudo-gravity would stop, too. The whole Universe would become as weightless as we are right now." Or, "This meter measures the anocyte wattage generated from the rowing room. It shows how much wattage we have stored up before the ecosystem begins to degrade." Or, "This set of holographic screens? They access surveillance feeds from cameras in every major hallway on the lower deck and a few other high-security areas. I'm sure your Captain Buru gets a lot of use out of this little tool." Or, "This little asteroid alert system was one of my favorites. The autopilot always recommended keeping a wide berth, but I liked to fly in close and get a good view. I used to imagine what it would be like to get out and walk across one—to feel something other than Architect-made flooring under my feet."

As he explained each device, Adam taught Tei the workings of the Universe's navigation system. How to adjust the spacecraft's bank and pitch and yaw. How to control coaxial thrust. How to calculate trajectories around electromagnetic interference according to predictive stellar mapping. How to use the angles and distances between stars to triangulate the Universe's place in the Milky Way galaxy.

Some of these principles were already familiar to Tei. Like every senior fledgling, he'd taken aviation lessons inside the digiscape, learning how to control the green-glowing winged contraptions called *aircraft*. An odd thing, he'd thought at the time, to learn a digiscape skill with no practical application for humans in skin. But so much of Tei's required digiscape training—so much of every fledgling's training—had been the same. What was the point of learning to swim, if swimming was forbidden inside the water processing ducts and could be done only in the digiscape? What was the point of learning to till soil, or to survive in extreme temperatures, or to drive four-wheeled vehicles called *rovers* across arid sandscapes and up boulder-strewn mountains? Tei's senior fledgling mentor could offer no sensible reason why these disciplines mattered in order to become a Final. And yet they continued to be taught and tested, season after season, hailed as bedrocks of human education.

"The traditions are as old as skin itself," Mentor had said. "They are built into the fabric of the digiscape. They test the instinct and boldness and mental dexterity that make any human successful." Tei pretended to be satisfied by the answer, even though it was no answer at all.

With Adam, though, the original logic behind the digiscape training traditions became clear. "For Gliese 832c, of course," he said, wiping beads of sweat away from his forehead with the sleeve of his tee shirt. "To make sure that whatever generations are alive when the Universe reaches its destination have the skills they need to settle a new planet. That's why all the digiscape's training exercises were designed. Otherwise, that entire cargo hold full of landing gear and low-occupancy shuttles becomes useless."

"Cargo hold?" said Tei.

Adam sighed. "I keep forgetting how little of the Universe you've been told about. To say nothing of the universe outside."

Tei looked up to the diamantium window, where a thousand pinpricks and clusters of starlight gleamed. "Why is it," he asked, "that when I'm here with you in the digiscape, I can see the stars? But when I'm with Buru in the command room in skin, the diamantium is like a river's face, all fluid and murky?"

"Surface deflection protocol." Adam pressed his hand against a nob on the control interface, causing a shadowy mist to swallow up the starlight. "It's this one right here, see? Press down to activate, pull up to deactivate. It keeps direct light from coming in through the diamantium. Handy in case we fly close to something intensely bright, so the crew can stay in the command room without burning our eyes out of their sockets."

"And why would it be activated now? You think we're near something that bright?"

"Not at all." Adam sighed again. "That nob has probably been pressed down for so long that no one remembers a time before it was pressed. And if no one remembers what used to be, no one will bother to imagine what could be."

"I still don't understand," said Tei, "how so very much could be forgotten. How could the destination of the human race disappear from our minds?"

Kyri, who had been sitting in silence with Kiphu, unstrapped himself from his chair and drifted into the air. "The idea of a destination didn't disappear—not altogether. But the nature of that destination was lost over time. What began as a literal claim about the Universe's journey and arrival devolved into spiritual language."

"Spiritual?" Tei tilted his head to one side.

"An old word," said Adam, "from even before my time. It's a way—a bunch of different ways, really—for making sense of the world. Stories about why everything exists, and where everything is going, and what it all means."

Kyri nodded and then somersaulted in midair. "And of course, every claim of meaning—every story about why and how and where next—is still spiritual after a fashion. But some of the people who used that old word, they meant it as an excuse to ignore the world right in front of their eyes. When someone needed help, they said, *We will give spiritual help*, and then did nothing to change what was. When their presence in the world worked evil, they said, *We will work spiritual good*, and then carried on working evil. Aboard the Universe, the circumstance was not so different. Our race took language describing the nature of the Universe and made it mean something entirely different, something more comfortable and convenient. *Our Universe is on a journey*, we said. *Someday our race will arrive at its destination*. But we meant it all as metaphor, not as literal scientific fact. We shrank down our cosmology to fit the size of our miniature Universe."

"Why didn't anyone try to stop us?"

"We tried to stop each other," said Kyri. "Natchers tried to stop Cyborgs. Cyborgs tried to stop Natchers. But the more committed each group became to exposing the dangers of the other, the less able we became to see our own dangers. The more our language evolved to express the truth of the world as we saw it, the less our ears could understand anything except the words of those who already agreed with us. As eager as we were to stop each other, we had no interest in stopping ourselves."

§§§

It was Adam's idea for Tei to sneak up to the command room in the middle of the night. "How else will you get the surface deflection protocol deactivated long enough to calculate our position? You'll need the room to yourself for as long as you can possibly get it. No better time than nighttime—tonight, if you're not too tired."

"What's the hurry?" Tei asked. "Can't it wait until I'm more prepared?"

"Prepared?" Adam shrugged. "You already know three times what you need for a reconnaissance mission. Everything else is just luck. No sense waiting around for luck."

The third night shift was just beginning when Tei scrawled the word *checkers* onto the glowing white screen of the elevator gate. His hands trembled, making the shadows they cast tremble as well. The suns overhead shone dark amber, barely brighter than the steel-grey sky.

"Shouldn't you be in your hydropod?" said the snide digiscape voice as the gate slid upward.

Tei waited to answer until the gate was closed behind him and his palm pressed up against the screen's other side. "Command room."

"Does Captain Buru know you're here in the middle of the night?"

"I have the clearance." Tei fought to keep his voice steady, pressing his fingers onto the screen more firmly. "Command room."

Without a sound, the elevator began to rise. Tei felt a wriggling anxiety in his stomach that had nothing to do with weightlessness.

When the elevator gate slid silently open, nighttime dimness shrouded the command room. Tei gripped the frame of the gate with his fingertips and propelled himself gently forward. He caught himself against a corner of the control interface and swung around it, landing smoothly inside the captain's chair.

Buckling himself into the chair, he glanced around the room. Shadows swam along the diamantium, patches of light and dark appearing and disappearing like watery currents, providing what seemed to be the room's only light. For weeks now Tei had dreamed of what might hide beyond those shadows—the pinpricks and swirls of nearby stars and distant many-colored galaxies. He dreamed of finally seeing in skin what only digiscape had been able to give before.

His trembling hand was already resting on the surface deflection protocol nob when a voice spoke from the darkness behind him. "Intoxicating, isn't it?"

Tei's head snapped to one side in terror. The seat buckles kept him from turning far enough to see anything other than shadow.

"Please," said the voice, stretching out every word into a sibilant whisper, "carry on. Act like I'm not even here. Do what you would do if you were all alone."

"I just—" Tei stammered. He felt damp beneath his skin. "I came up here to think. It's easier to think without gravity weighing me down."

"Is it? This must be how all our past interpreters came to think such lofty thoughts. Before they deleted themselves, I mean."

It wasn't until Tei heard the smile accompanying those last words that he recognized Buru's voice. The captain drifted forward into Tei's line of sight.

"I used to sneak up here too, you know. Back in my days as an administrator, when I was first appointed to the officers' committee. I would lie down in my dormitory hydropod without setting it, wait until the others in my cohort were asleep, then come up here and sit in the captain's chair just like you're doing now. I'd stay a whole shift, sometimes two, thinking about the day the old captain would be archived and I'd make sure I was the one to take his place. I imagined that his seat was mine, the control interface was mine, every part of the universe it reached was mine. The whole universe would be mine someday. I knew it. It felt more real when I could see it and smell it and feel it beneath my fingers. It was like being in a dream machine with skin on, still wide awake. Intoxicating." He breathed in through his nose, slow and deep.

"I swear," said Tei, "I just came up here to think. Sometimes it helps me to speak out loud, to speak with Natcher words, in a place no one else can hear."

Buru chuckled. "You'll need to lie more convincingly than that if you hope to wind up a captain someday. Come now, try it again. Shoulders up, voice strong, eyes looking right into mine."

"You've got it all wrong," said Tei. "I don't want to be a captain."

"Much better," nodded Buru. "I almost believed you that time. But try to make the lie more believable. I've been an officer, and then a captain, too long to be fooled by anyone claiming not to want a captain's power. It's impossible to be in this room, to sit at the head of the universe, and want anything else. I know you've seen it in the rest of the committee. I know you've felt it in yourself. Don't try to hide it. Don't be ashamed of it. There's nothing more human."

Tei began unbuckling the straps that held him against the captain's chair. "Fine. Then I'm human."

Buru laid an unlawful hand against the interpreter's chest, holding the buckles in place. "I've always liked you, Eleven. You're smart, and strong too. Even stronger than the committee realizes. They take for granted, I think, how difficult it is to do your work. How could they appreciate what they don't even understand? How could they know the crippling burden of the secrets you carry?"

"I have no secrets from the officers' committee." Tei breathed in deeply, feeling the weight of the captain's hand pressed against his lungs.

"Almost as bad as your first lie," said Buru. "Eyes staying with mine, remember? Don't think about your breathing so much. It's best to be casual. Smile like you have no reason to doubt yourself. See? That's better now, isn't it?"

They were both smiling, lips hanging slightly open, one set of teeth mirroring the other in the dimness.

"Tell me again," said Buru, "about the secrets you don't have."

Tei spoke without moving his jaw. "I have no secrets from the officers' committee."

"Good." Buru's voice had shrunk to a whisper again. "That's exactly it. The kind of lie we can all agree to believe in. The kind of lie that keeps people like you and me in skin."

Tei didn't answer.

"I won't tell anyone that you've been here in the command room without orders. It might sound like insurrection, if they knew. The committee might misunderstand. But I understand. You're like me. I hope it works out for you. I hope I can name you to the captain's seat as my successor when the time comes."

"Thank you," said Tei stiffly.

"In the meantime," said the captain, "best if you don't let yourself be seen coming up here alone. The digiscape voice who takes your passcode has been known to spread rumors. I'd hate to see word get out to the wrong ears. It's a delicate business. Some of the committee are very protective of their captain. The thought of someone else in the command room unsupervised, uninvited—they might take it as a threat, you understand. Best to leave now, and only return with a formal invitation."

"Of course," said Tei. "If you'll just let me finish unbuckling?"

Buru tapped Tei's chest before pulling his hand away. "We all have our secrets, Eleven. I'll keep yours, and someday—" his teeth flashed white in the darkness "—someday, you'll keep mine as well."

§§§

Kyri and Adam pretended that Tei's failure was only a minor setback. "A bit of bad luck," said Adam gently. "That's all. Even if you'd succeeded in calculating our location, it still wouldn't answer the question of how we'll get the ship back on course."

"Short of mutiny," added Kyri.

Adam's lips twisted. "I'd settle for mutiny."

Kyri shook his head. "What good would a mutiny be? What good is reaching Gliese 832c at all if the crew doesn't even realize they're on a ship to begin with?"

"I have to tell them." Tei's pulse quickened as he spoke. "Not just the humans, but the Natchers too. I have to convince them about what the Universe really is. There's no other way."

"Perhaps," said Kyri slowly. "Perhaps it will come to that in the end. But first, best to learn all you can. Piloting. Switching between languages. Who knows? Maybe Buru's offer to help you become captain will amount to more than just an empty promise. As long as your reputation stays intact, we've got all the time we need to make a plan."

The days flew by without ever seeming to move. Tei barely spoke now to anyone in skin. The closest thing he had to a living companion was Reif. The archivist's eager smile and endless chatter greeted him twice per day: each morning before he sank into the digiscape, and each evening as he emerged with bleary eyes and stumbled to the galley for an after-hours meal. "Is there anything you need, Eleven?" Reif would ask. "You look exhausted. Archival work is grueling, isn't it? But doubly so for you, of course. I don't mean to compare our careers. Imagine it, a lowly archivist like me, pretending to understand an interpreter's work. But if you ever need... or if you just want to talk with a fellow programmer, of course..."

"I'm fine," Tei would answer without bothering to consider whether the words were true. "Not much I can say right now. It's all highly confidential, you understand."

Reif's head bobbed furiously. "Of course, of course. I hope I didn't seem to be prying. It wouldn't be proper, a lowly archivist like me, presuming to pry."

The mess hall, to Tei's relief, was usually deserted. His age-mates all worked in traditional careers that ended before the first dinner shift. "We miss seeing you," they told him as they passed in hallways. "We'll skip a leisure evening sometime to come sit with you while you eat. You must have so many stories to share." None of them followed through on the promise. Tei was only too happy to let them forget.

The others who appeared at the galley after hours were usually orderkeepers or skincaregivers about to begin the night shift. After an on-duty galley chemist had doled out their portions, latecomers tended to sit alone, rubbing sleep out of their bleary eyes. Rajamin shared a table with Tei once or twice on his way to the infirmary. He ate little and said even less. The rest of the time, Tei sat alone.

All the more unusual, then, the evening an orderkeeper carrying a steel plate sat down across from Tei and held up his palm in greeting. "The name is Resen," he said.

Tei simply nodded and took another bite.

"And you're Eleven," the orderkeeper continued. He spoke in quick, hesitant bursts, like someone unused to making conversation. "You're here after hours even more than I am, and I've got the night shift two of every three days. Comes of being the newest Final and all. I'm not complaining. A Final skin is a Final skin. As long as we're both here, I thought we might eat together."

Tei forced a smile worthy of Buru. "Why not?"

Resen stabbed a ring of steamed whiteroot with his knife. "We have something else in common, you and I. Our unusual Finalization, I mean. You as Eleven, of course. My whole cohort was shocked when it happened, totally threw off our wager system. And me, taking Jarawi's place between aging ceremonies. I never imagined a whole assembly just for me. But these are unprecedented times."

"So says the captain."

"The rest of my cohort is still in fledgling skin," said Resen. "I'm always on patrol during their leisure evenings. I wouldn't join them in the digiscape, though, even if I could. Mentor says it wouldn't be natural, a Final spending leisure with fledglings. I'm in a new dormitory now. It's like I don't have agemates anymore."

Tei bit into a biscuit and realized the dough was wrapped around darkmeat. Gagging, he spat it out onto the table.

Resen gaped.

"I'm sorry," Tei murmured. "Hit a lump of leavening. Very bitter. In fact, I—" He stood, picking up his plate and the lump of chewed meat. "I need to get back to work. I'm sorry."

"Sure." Resen's face fell, then lifted again with feigned indifference. "I'll see you around."

Tei hurried away without looking back.

§§§

The galley chemist who collected Tei's half-finished plate a few weeks later shook his head as he scraped the plate's contents into a purifier tube. "What's this untouched darkmeat I see?"

Tei shrugged. "I wasn't hungry."

"You weren't hungry during my last night shift either," said the chemist. "Or the night shift before that. Not for darkmeat, anyway."

Tei tried to remember the chemist's name. He had learned it before. But his mind was so full of digiscape, there was barely room left for skin. "I guess darkmeat isn't my favorite."

"No?" The chemist gave him a long look. "Mine neither, as it happens. It's hard to spend as much time as I've spent in the butchery and still enjoy the final product."

Tei glanced around them. The mess hall and galley were vacant. "Are you saying—?"

"Best to ignore what I'm saying," interrupted the chemist. "It's what I'm not saying that matters."

"Then you understand—?"

"Just enough." The chemist closed his eyes. "Just enough to wish I understood nothing at all. A word of advice before you go, Interpreter? Choke down a bite every once in a while, to keep the others from getting suspicious. Better this side of the fork than the other. And trust no one. Not even me."

§§§

Tei knew something was wrong the moment Adam's face began dissolving into trails of numbers and symbols. Kyri's undertorso was next to go, followed by the rest of their bodies, the command room control interface, the giant diamantium window. Without warning Tei was underwater, breathing through gills. Then the gills closed. The skin across his face opened into mouth and eyes and nostrils. He emerged from the water with a loud gasp.

"I do apologize," said Reif. His shadowy head loomed over Tei in the dimness of the archive room. "I never prefer to program an interruption— with work as critical as yours, least of all—"

"An interruption?" Tei blinked water out of his eyes. "Is something wrong?"

A second shadowy head appeared beside Reif's. "Wrong?" said the shadow. "No, no. Quite the opposite. Something is wonderfully right."

Even in the dim light, Tei could see the glow of Buru's smile.

"Our orderkeepers have captured one of the Natchers. Found it snooping near the galley, probably looking for a scrap of food to steal. A perfectly timed gift from the universe: an alien prisoner to interrogate, at the very same moment we have an interpreter who understands its gibberish."

Tei's heart beat so fast he was sure his skin must be pulsating. "But I'm not ready."

"It doesn't matter," said Buru. "Humanity is ready for you. Your time has come, Eleven. Your training days are over."

21
LILY

THE UNIVERSE WAS STILL ORBITING Earth when Lily missed her first period. She said nothing about it, and thought about it almost as little. She had just abandoned her home planet, after all. She was living inside a giant spinning wheel made of carbon and silica, eating food grown in synthetic soil by artificial sunlight. Surely that counted as more than enough stress to wreak havoc on a menstrual cycle.

When the nausea came, she chalked it up to the effects of pseudogravity on her digestive system. Half the crew had struggled at first to keep down an entire meal. Besides, she wasn't sleeping well. Wearing an ExoSkin to bed, floating in a puddle of anocyte-charged green water, breathing oxygen through mechanical gills–the alienness of it all made her afraid to close her eyes for fear she would never wake up.

She missed three more periods without even noticing. ExoSkin absorbed everything a body might excrete–urine, feces, sweat, blood– and chemically disassembled it before releasing it into the wearer's hydropod each night. Waste water that cycled out of dormitory hydropods flowed back to the water processing plant, where it was purified and recharged to repeat the cycle. The longer Lily wore her ExoSkin, the easier it became to forget she still had a urinary tract or a reproductive system. The easier it became to forget she had a body at all.

Some crewmembers, especially the younger ones, barely took off their ExoSkin even in leisure. They spent every spare moment in a hydropod, smitten with the unlimited possibilities of virtual reality. Their bodies grew so used to the enhanced strength of ExoSkin that doctors began worrying these crewmembers' muscles would start to decay, their bodies evolving to become overly reliant on ExoSkin's artificial muscles.

As for Lily, she preferred to while away her leisure hours on the upper deck, wearing Earth clothes and lying in the grass beneath the shade of a fig tree, listening to the burbling of the irrigation canal. The ship's gravity was harder to navigate without ExoSkin, but not so hard that Lily was willing to give up the sight of her own arms and thighs and ankles. A bit of well-placed cloaking technology had rendered the upper deck's ceiling girders and elevator shafts invisible to the naked eye. ("A simple enough modification," Luka had said, "but our psychiatry team believes it will work wonders for crewmembers' mental health.") The blue-tinted sky and artificial sun were a near enough approximation of Earth that Lily sometimes managed to pretend she was back home again, lounging in the dubious grass along the north bank of the Susquehanna.

If she stayed on the upper deck until dusk, she could watch the sun grow slowly cooler without ever moving. There was no sunset or sunrise inside Project Universe—only the cyclical cooling and heating of the ship's anocyte-powered energy core. Once evening had arrived in earnest, the thing Lily called sun hung like a faintly smoldering coal over a sky made of ashes. "The moon has arrived," she would say to anyone within earshot, or else to the vacant space around her. "It's the moon by night, until it warms itself enough to become the sun again. Just what the moon back home must have always wanted. A chance to burn brighter than anyone believed it could."

She went into the digiscape only once a month if she could help it. Just long enough to gather two bunches of wildflowers and lay them on two granite headstones.

The day Lily realized she was pregnant, the Universe was passing Jupiter. Crewmembers flocked up to the command room, where a massive diamantium window let them look out across the expanse of space to see the gas giant as close as a next-door neighbor. Awe sealed everyone's lips. Photos would be sent back to Earth, of course, but no photos could do justice to the reality of the sight. Jupiter's unblinking red eye glared back at them from between vibrant stripes of swirling gas.

It was there in the command room, floating in the weightlessness of space, that the baby kicked for the first time. Lily might have blamed it on her imagination if a second kick hadn't followed, even harder than the first. She gasped. Someone floating beside her looked over for a moment and raised a curious eyebrow. "It's nothing," Lily whispered, pulling her eyes away from Jupiter and making her way toward the nearest elevator.

Inside the privacy of the elevator, she ran her hand across the smooth surface of her ExoSkin. Her belly was rounder than usual, though her wide bone structure and ExoSkin had managed to disguise it until now. She knew the truth in an instant—knew with such certainty that she wondered how she hadn't realized it from the very beginning. Or had she been willfully ignoring the signs? Had she allowed herself to avoid the truth until it became unavoidable?

"Damn you, Luka," she murmured. "Damn you and your condom and your hint of goodness."

An abortion was the only way. So Lily assumed, and so the doctor on call announced in the same breath that he confirmed the truth of her pregnancy. The Universe simply wasn't equipped for natural childbirth, let alone the things a mother would need to raise a child through infancy. Onboard reproduction and early childhood had been relegated to the scientists for a reason.

"What if I wanted to keep it?" Lily asked. It wasn't a serious question—not in the moment she asked it. Just a curiosity.

"Out of the question," said the doctor sharply. "It can't be done."

"But it's still my choice."

The blue ExoSkin around the doctor's eyes narrowed. "Choice? No, no. No choice. You signed away that right when you came aboard."

Lily had been promised one phone call back to Earth—only one—before the Universe passed out of the solar system and quantum data transfer became prohibitively expensive. She hadn't planned on using it. Nor had she planned on using the business card Luka left her as a joke, tucked inside the front pocket of her duffel bag, with a handwritten note that read, "Call me sometime."

Planned or unplanned, here she was.

When Luka answered the phone, Lily imagined he was just preparing for bed. He would be dressed in a complimentary hotel bathrobe, draining the last sip from a double pour of fifty-year-old whiskey. "Who is this?" he grunted.

"It's Lily. The associate ExoSkin technician who thought dying in outer space sounded like more fun than living in Tunkhannock. Also, lately, the mother of your son."

The silence was so long Lily wondered if Luka had hung up. "You're shitting me," he said at last.

"By wasting my one phone call back to Earth? Don't flatter yourself. Call the medical crew if you want a paternity test. It's either you or immaculate conception."

"Shit," said Luka.

"They say it's got to be an abortion."

Luka exhaled heavily. "Of course it does. I almost thought... the way you said son, I almost thought you meant the baby was already born. But you'd only be in the second trimester now. An abortion. That's the right thing to do. The only thing to do."

Another long pause.

"I've never had a kid before," said Luka.

"Me neither. You ever wanted one?"

"Not really. No time. No patience. All that shit."

"It's funny," said Lily. "I always thought I didn't need one more thing to take care of. Now I'd give almost anything to care about something."

"You're saying you want to keep it?"

"No. Maybe. I don't know."

Silence.

"It would be the first baby born in space," said Luka. They were an engineer's words, not a father's. The words of someone concerned with record-breaking and history-making.

"But the medical crew said—"

"I'll have a word with the Margola sisters. They'll have a word with the captain. Whatever you choose, I'll make sure the choice is yours and no one else's."

Lily let out a long breath. "Thank you."

"It's the least I can do," said Luka.

She could hear the hint of goodness in his voice. Neither more nor less than a hint.

"What will you call him?" asked Luka. "If you keep him, I mean?"

"It's corny," said Lily. "You'll laugh."

"I won't laugh."

"In my head, I've started calling him Adam. The first man born into a new Universe."

"Adam," Luka repeated.

"I told you it was corny."

"Maybe it isn't corny," said Luka. "Maybe it's history."

ACT THREE

this is the oppressor's language
yet I need it to talk to you

~ Adrienne Rich
The Burning of Paper Instead of Children

22

KANAN

THE SAME EVENING MAHLAH WAS CAPTURED by the Cyborgs, Kanan and Avi kissed.

Kanan hadn't realized at the moment of the kiss that words existed for such a thing. She had never seen it done, had never even thought of it. But she didn't need a word to feel the heat from Avi's breath as the creature leaned towards her in the gathering dusk. She didn't need a word to know, from the moment Avi's lips pressed against hers, that she wanted them to stay there forever. She didn't need a word to thread her fingers through Avi's sun-colored hair, pulling their bodies closer, tightening the seal of their mouths and the dance of their searching tongues.

Half a season earlier, Kanan would have been disgusted at the idea of placing her body so close to anyone else's, let alone the body of an alien like Avi. But life in the overworld had changed her. She had learned to swim in the river without gills, to climb trees and drop ripe citrus fruits into Tiqvah's waiting basket. She had learned to run on skinless legs, with

Avi critiquing her form and marveling at her natural agility. ("You run like a creature accustomed to the mechanisms of the Cyborg shell," Avi would say disdainfully, to which Kanan would reply with equal disdain, "I run like a creature who's faster than you.")

She no longer craved the sensation of skin encasing her underflesh. If anything, she preferred bare underflesh and clothes woven from plant fibers. She felt freer, lighter, more alive than she had ever felt in the days she was dressed like a Cyborg.

Cyborg. Clothes. Alive. They were words she had no memory of beginning to use. And yet, once she began using them, she had no memory of how she had ever been able to speak or think without them.

She had started calling herself *human* again, too. That word no longer carried all its old implications in her mind. Humanness, she decided, was something that couldn't be torn off you like a skin. It wasn't an accessory to be worn or an honor always at risk of deletion. Being human could only be meaningful if it was simpler, more basic than she had been taught. Humanness had to be expansive enough to fit both the people of the overworld and the Cyborgs under their feet.

As Kanan's vocabulary grew, it also shrank. She didn't use the word *Natcher* anymore. The very thought of it—its harsh consonants, spat out from between Cyborg lips with disgust—now made her shudder the same way Tiqvah had once shuddered when Kanan called the overworld race by that name. Even the word *it* no longer felt like the right pronoun to describe the creatures around her. Kanan tried briefly to erase pronouns from her mind altogether and use only the proper names of things, the way Tiqvah and Avi did. But pronouns were too much part of her thinking to remove them altogether. Failing that, she considered calling the citizens of the overworld *her*, just as she did for Cyborgs. But that pronoun felt wrong also. *Her* made Kanan think of skin and aging ceremonies, of Buru's speeches, of fledglings longing for Finalization. None of those things was remotely like the creatures who lived in underflesh beneath the light of a single sun.

In the end, Kanan decided to call the humans of the overworld by the other Cyborg pronoun, the pronoun she had always known but never bothered to use. *Him.* The overworld humans would be *him.* This plan made enough sense to stick inside Kanan's brain. *Him* wasn't quite the same as *her*, after all. But it wasn't so different either.

The conversation with Mahlah faded slowly from her mind, like a dream dissolving to make room for reality. The aquarian who greeted her in the market and swam the river with breathtaking speed was nothing like the blue-striped, Cyborg-tongued creature she had encountered that one haunted night. This Mahlah spoke only in overworld words, gazing past Kanan with polite disinterest. This Mahlah cared nothing for Cyborg skins. Whatever plans the aquarian had laid—whatever the identity of his Cyborg friend, whatever the meaning of the thin braid tied around his ankle—none of it seemed to matter beneath the shining sun of the overworld. None of it seemed real. The longer Kanan said nothing, the less she remembered there was anything to say.

Talking with Avi had grown easier as the weeks passed. No longer did he speak in strings of unrelated words tossed together like salad greens. There was smoothness and clarity in his sentences now. Kanan understood his words as easily as she understood anything her agemates had ever spoken in the underworld. She assumed at first that Avi's grasp of the Cyborg language must be improving. Only later did she begin to wonder if perhaps the difference lay in her mind rather than his mouth. Perhaps she was gradually learning to speak more like Avi and his race had always spoken. Perhaps it was her, not him, whose language was changing.

Or perhaps it was a bit of both.

After all, how couldn't they both have changed, given all the time they now spent together? Though Kanan still slept beneath Tiqvah's tent each night, it was Avi who met her at the sun's first light to swim upriver to the fishing reservoir and catch a few breakfast tilapia. It was Avi who held the fish bucket as they floated downstream again, laying back to warm their bellies in the sun. It was Avi who taught Kanan to stoke the coals of the firepit, to smoke the fishes until their meat fell apart in tender flakes, to wrap the spoils in whiteroot leaves so they could be carried to Tiqvah's tent just as he was rising. And when Tiqvah declared he needed to be left alone to work in peace, it was Avi who shrugged and said with the pretense of surprise, "I guess Kanan is coming with me, then?"

Most days, Avi and his cousins and the other overworld warriors would train for hours in the heat of the sun. Kanan trained with them: wrestling, knife-fighting, running with heavy burdens, crawling and swinging through tangles of tree branches without troubling a leaf. She rarely spoke to the other warriors. Even Enos and Barak, who greeted her with folded palms and admiring nods, had little else to say. The language they all preferred was the language of ragged breaths, beads of sweat, shouts of victory or defeat as they sortied.

Every fourth training day was followed by a day of rest. On these days Kanan taught Avi to play checkers, sitting beneath the shade of a bitterbark tree and using colored pebbles as playing pieces. Some mornings Avi took Kanan to the market, bartering the same colored pebbles for stewed figs or baskets of peanuts dried in their shells. The peanuts they brought to a tent at the edge of the fishing reservoir, where the chief elder's grandchild Zillah greeted them with a ready appetite and fingers gifted in peanut-shelling.

Zillah was nothing like the frail, dying alien Kanan had imagined when she first heard his name. Once the chemicals from the raiding party arrived at the healer's tent, the child had made a miraculous recovery. Within a fortnight, he was on his feet again, his cheeks full of color, his eyes bright with laughter. No one would have believed he had so recently been a fingerwidth from death, if it hadn't been for the stories that spread slowly across the overworld, as unstoppable as a breeze:

"Just six of them in the raiding party. Sent by the elders in secret. And one of the six not humanborn at all, but an escaped Cyborg stripped of its shell. The raiders went in by water, and escaped by the same. But not without nearly getting killed when a Cyborg warrior found them. Avi, the chief elder's grandchild, sent the alien into Nothing with a plunge of his knife. They share a parent, you see, Avi and the child Zillah whose life was saved. Avi it was who demanded the raiding party must be sent down to the underworld, despising the risks. Remarkable devotion, even for a sibling. As for the Cyborg with no shell, they say it is nearly human now, though it rarely ever speaks."

These stories made their way back to Kanan bit by bit. Sometimes they were remarkably accurate in their detail. Other times they had blossomed into grandiose legends, exaggerated well out of proportion.

On the morning of Mahlah's capture—the morning of the kiss—Kanan wandered through the market alone. Avi and Zillah were close enough to pick out from the crowd; Zillah's head protruded far above the rest as he rode on Avi's shoulders. Kanan had stopped at a redfruit stand to examine the gleaming orbs when she overheard two vendors repeating Avi's name. Feigning interest in a particularly large redfruit, she stepped closer to listen. The translation she rendered in her head wasn't perfect, but she understood enough of the words to catch their meaning:

"Everyone credits Avi's bravery," one of the vendors said, "but no one seems to notice Avi's shrewdness. It was Avi who insisted on rescuing the Cyborg with no shell, despite the spies' conflicting reports. Was the alien a captive of the Cyborg warriors, or was it in hiding with one of our allies? Only Avi seemed to know the answer—to know that the Cyborg's death was imminent. Avi himself went, along with the Cyborg-tongued Tiqvah, to make the rescue. And then, not half a day later, it was Avi who suggested that perhaps the need for a Cyborg shell was no barrier to the raiding party. After all, a Cyborg stripped of its shell now lay abed in Tiqvah's tent."

"It explains," said the other vendor, "why Avi took so much interest in the rescue of this particular Cyborg. I had wondered at the time. But everything can be seen clearly now."

"Yes," nodded the first. "It was not the Cyborg he cared about, but his sibling's salvation. Everything else was merely a tool."

Kanan replayed the words in her head all morning. She watched Avi's doting attention to Zillah with fresh eyes. The tenderness with which he brushed hair away from the child's forehead. The warmth of his goodbye when they deposited Zillah back at the tent beside the reservoir.

Was that all Avi's kindness to her had ever been? Just a tool in service of the one kindness that really mattered?

When the sun's heat began to wane, Kanan and Avi raced laps around the overworld. They ran in silence until Kanan couldn't hold in the question any longer: "Why did you rescue me from the underworld?"

"Because you needed help," answered Avi between gulps of air. "It is a warrior's calling to rescue those who need help."

"Did I need your help?" Kanan panted back. "Or did you need mine? You needed a Cyborg to steal the chemicals for Zillah. And there I was, right on time, under the protection of a Cyborg ally you could pass off as a pawn of the orderkeepers. Is that why you carried me up to the overworld that day—not because you cared about whether a Cyborg lived or died, but because you needed a Cyborg under your control to get what you really wanted?"

"Where did you hear this idea?"

"Is it true?"

Avi hesitated. "You know the kinds of stories people tell about that night in the underworld. The legends are more imagination than fact."

"Then tell me fact."

The path between wheat fields shrank until two couldn't run abreast. Avi slowed for a few strides, allowing himself to fall behind. Perhaps it was for the best, thought Kanan, that she couldn't see his face.

"I cared about you as well as Zillah," said Avi at last. "I cared as much as I could possibly care about a stranger."

"And Arisa the galley chemist?" Kanan demanded. "Was she working with the orderkeepers as you and Tiqvah claimed?"

"Tiqvah knew only what I told her. As for the rest—the matter is more complicated than it seems."

"But Arisa was your ally the entire time? Why not have her steal the chemicals herself? Why use me at all?"

"Arisa is no one's ally," said Avi. "Least of all mine. As I said, the matter is complicated. Arisa could not have taken the chemicals without risking being found out. It is a risk she was not willing to make."

"Why take the risk of hiding me, then?"

"You were an unwelcome surprise, a risk she never meant to take. But once you appeared, she felt it was her duty."

"Then she was hiding me." Kanan's jaw clenched. "She was a friend. And you lied about her in order to get what you wanted."

"Arisa and I both told the stories we needed to tell. She needed a way to protect her Cyborg reputation. And I needed to make sure you got out in time."

"In time for what?"

"To save your life."

"To save Zillah's life, you mean."

Avi said nothing.

"There's no shame," said Kanan, "in finding a tool and knowing how to use it. Lucky you stumbled across a Cyborg at the very moment you needed one. Lucky I could be your tool."

Before Avi could answer, Kanan increased her pace, kicking up dust as she left him behind. She sprinted the rest of the way to Tiqvah's tent without glancing back.

Beneath the tent's shade, Tiqvah bent over a recording device, listening to Cyborg words caught by spies and scrawling notes on a scrap of parchment. He didn't look up when Kanan entered. "Recognize the voices of your old friends? No, this is the wrong word. Cyborgs do not speak that way; they do not have friends."

Kanan poured water into an earthen bowl and drank before answering. "They're not the only ones who don't have friends."

At that, Tiqvah raised his head. "You are angry?"

"My first day in the overworld," said Kanan, "you told me Avi had some special interest in Cyborgs, some special care for our race. Now at last I understand why. It was all for Zillah, to save Zillah's life. Everything beyond that—even my own supposed danger—it was just a story. Cyborgs have never mattered to Avi for their own sake. We matter only as a means to things that matter more."

"This is the reason for your anger?" Tiqvah's face was impassive.

"Tell me I'm wrong."

"It is not a matter of right and wrong. You've told the whole story except for the beating heart at its center."

"What beating heart?"

"The runaway Cyborg Robiana," said Tiqvah. "You remember her, I trust?"

"I—" Kanan faltered.

"Avi was a young scout when he met Robiana. She had a penchant for rule-breaking, sneaking out of her dream machine at night. He hadn't yet learned how to navigate the hallways of the underworld undetected. They should have been threatened by each other—each of them holding the keys to the other's undoing. Instead they were transfixed. Avi sought me out for lessons in the Cyborg tongue. I thought nothing of it. It was refreshing, after seasons of being entirely ignored, to find someone interested in my work. But he took my lessons back down to the underworld, night after night, wooing Robiana until she agreed to run away with him."

Kanan sank down to the grass. "Robiana came to the overworld?"

Tiqvah nodded. "The Cyborgs called it a deletion. But she did not die; not at first, anyway. She simply stopped being human in the way Cyborgs understand humanity. She took off her skin and hid it, with Mahlah's help, somewhere deep in the recesses of the water tunnels. She asked me to teach her our tongue, and taught Avi bits of her Cyborg tongue. For a time, she became one of us."

"Where is she now?"

Tiqvah clicked off the recording device. "For generations, there have been disturbances in the rhythms of the universe. A change in the flow of the water. Crops that overproduce without reason, and others that never ripen. Three seasons ago, a tremor in the air cooled the burning of the sun. Robiana began making theories to explain that disturbance, and all the other disturbances as well."

"What kind of theories?"

"She would not say. Only that they were theories requiring two different tongues in order to be understood. The ideas would have been invisible, she said, if I had not trained her tongue in the patterns of the overworld. As time passed, she became more and more erratic. Even Avi grew afraid of her."

"They had stayed friends all along?"

"More than friends. They were as near to one another as two humans can be. But when she disappeared, not even he knew where she had gone. She left in the night, the same way she arrived, without a word. Silence for her goodbye. And for her eulogy, too."

"She's dead, then."

"She is neither in the underworld nor in the overworld," said Tiqvah. "There is nowhere else she can be except in the essence of Nothing."

Mahlah's words came flooding into Kanan's mind: *Gone into Nothing. For three seasons now. So deep into Nothing she may never return.*

"I told you," Tiqvah went on, "that it was with great pain Avi studied the Cyborg tongue. This is his pain. She is his pain. The longer she is gone, the more she seems to linger."

Kanan let out a long breath, trying to banish the vision of blue-striped Mahlah from her mind. "Why are you telling me all this?"

"You have said that Avi cares nothing for Cyborgs. Avi has many faults, but this is not one of them. He used to stand guard over you, in your early days with us, when I was called away or took a moment to rest. Not since Robiana have I seen him look at anyone as he looked at you."

"He lied," said Kanan. "To you. To me."

"About that, I do not know," said Tiqvah. "But I know Avi has spent three seasons obsessed with the idea of saving. Saving Zillah. Saving you. Each one is a kind of penance, I think. A substitution of what can be saved for what cannot be."

Tiqvah bent back toward the recording device and resumed his work. Kanan slumped into the grass and closed her eyes to listen. Cyborg murmurs washed over her like breeze. Their words felt familiar but distant, like words from a dream.

§§§

When Kanan opened her eyes, the sun was dark and Tiqvah had been replaced by Avi. His back was turned to Kanan. His neck craned away from the chatter of the river and toward the dark carbon wall at the edge of the universe.

"What are you looking at?" Kanan's voice felt naked and thin as it cut across the silence.

"Nothing," said Avi. "And beyond that, more Nothing."

In the distance, Kanan heard two voices shouting. With anger? With excitement? There was no way to be sure.

"Arisa devised the scheme," said Avi. "For her own safety. She sent word to me through the galley supply portal, as usual. We knew the security footage would be discovered in the end—the two of you in the hallway outside the mess hall, in the moments before you burst past her. She needed to confess it before the orderkeepers saw it for themselves. If she waited until they came to interrogate her, she would look guilty. But if she sought the orderkeepers out, showed her cooperation with the search, then all the blame would be laid on you."

"Is this supposed to make me feel better?"

"It's supposed to be true," said Avi. "How you choose to feel it depends entirely on you. Arisa did what she thought had the best chance of saving both your lives. Once you were hidden, she went to the orderkeepers and told them she had tried to earn your trust and convince you to hide inside the butchery. It was the perfect trap, she said. A room with no exit except a locked door. A storage room where you could be trapped until your skin failed and your deletion took care of itself."

Kanan shuddered.

"But you refused," Avi continued. "Or so Arisa told the orderkeepers. You didn't trust her. You knocked her down and ran past her, just like they would later see in the hallway's security footage. By the time she was on her feet again, you had disappeared."

"Why talk about the butchery when that's exactly where I was hiding? Why tell a lie so close to the truth?"

"In case you were discovered. She needed a way to explain your presence there without implicating herself. She could say that you must have been persuaded by her argument, even though you didn't trust her to lead you there, and so you snuck in on your own. Or, if more time had passed before you were found out, she could claim you had come back to her later for help. She might have been on her way to report your capture to the orderkeepers at the very moment she learned you'd already been discovered there. Besides, she knew that if she emphasized the impossibility of escaping from the butchery, the orderkeepers would be less likely to search it thoroughly."

"But they did search it. Jarawi nearly saw me."

"Jarawi?" Avi laughed darkly. "The same Jarawi from the night of the raiding party? That they sent an orderkeeper so young and inexperienced merely proves the point. Of course they had to search it, as a matter of course. But Arisa made the butchery seem like the last place you would want to be, and the easiest place to apprehend you if you did have the misfortune of hiding there. It was a lie that kept her as safe as she could possibly be. And a lie that saved your life."

"I understand her lie, then. But why yours? Why would you lie to the elders' council? And to Tiqvah? And to me?"

"I needed the elders to order an immediate rescue. Had they known you weren't yet discovered by the orderkeepers—had they known Arisa was a friend to you—they might have called for patience, for caution. It is caution, after all, that has kept our race so long unnoticed by the Cyborgs. Our elders prize caution above all. But every moment you stayed in the butchery, the risk increased. The risk for you. For Arisa. For Zillah. I told the overworld the same story Arisa told the underworld, or nearly so. Close enough for the details of our lies to be easily blurred together. It was best, in any case, for me to obscure Arisa's involvement in your rescue. We do not advertise the identities of our Cyborg allies."

"But I've spent half a season thinking of Arisa as the one who tried to kill me. I've spent half a season hating her."

"She can endure it. She is built hard, even beneath her skin, even beneath her underflesh. She must be hard in order to survive as a galley chemist with access to the butchery. To understand the evil to which her career chains her, and yet to stay and fight it from the inside. Few can bear that kind of heaviness. As long as you are saved, Arisa is willing to be hated."

"You could have told me," said Kanan.

"And perhaps I should have. But I didn't want to make everything more complicated than it already was. I'm sorry."

"Cyborg sorry?" said Kanan. "Or overworld sorry?"

Avi crouched in the grass beside Kanan and fixed her with a long stare. "The kind of sorry that will not be satisfied until it is forgiven."

Kanan stared back. She thought of Tiqvah's words that afternoon: *Not since Robiana have I seen him look at anyone as he looked at you.*

"Is it Robiana you see?" Kanan asked. "When you look at me?"

Avi sighed deeply before answering. "At first, perhaps. And then, for a while, I saw both of you at once, like two different pairs of eyes staring out at me from the same face."

Kanan feigned a cough, turning her eyes down toward the grass. She studied the two pairs of legs crouching there. Hers didn't look so different from his anymore. Runners' legs, both of them, knotted and strong. Not as fast as a Cyborg shell, perhaps, but far faster than anything Cyborg underflesh could accomplish when the shell was stripped away.

"But now"—Avi lifted a finger to brush Kanan's cheek— "now I see you."

Kanan raised her eyes back to his, studying every inch of him along the way. From the first moment Kanan had seen Avi's body in the butchery, some part of her had longed for that body to become her own body. She herself had been freshly stripped of skin, freshly thrust into weakness. Avi's body symbolized strength. Not the strength of skin, as Kanan had coveted since her earliest fledgling days, but the strength of an underflesh that needed no skin. Strength without Finalization. Strength without the underworld's version of humanity. Kanan had desired Avi with the only desire she had ever felt for anyone— the desire to become the thing she admired.

Now, for the first time in her life, as Avi's finger traced the slope of her cheekbone, she wondered if desire could mean something else entirely.

The shouting in the distance grew louder, more voices joining the fray. Static descended like a blanket over Kanan's ears to keep her from hearing the words. She couldn't see anything past Avi's face, because she had stopped believing in the existence of anything beyond their two bodies. His hand was at her waist, gently tugging her closer.

"Is this okay?" said Avi.

"Is what okay?" said Kanan.

"This," said Avi, and then their lips met.

In the morning, they would learn the meaning of the shouts. The rumors would all be confirmed by then: Rumors of how Arisa's treason had been found out by the Cyborgs. Rumors of how Mahlah had gone to the underworld to warn her, only to get himself captured by the same orderkeepers who had just arrested Arisa. Rumors of a fearsome new Cyborg weapon—a creature called *interpreter*—who would pry the overworld's most sacred secrets out of both prisoners' mouths.

In the morning, the universe would unravel, and they would be afraid again.

But that evening, hidden by dusky darkness, Kanan and Avi knew nothing of rumors. All they knew was each other, lips and tongues and fingers and curving underflesh. If either one had known the word, they might have called it love.

23

TEI

THE NATCHER REFUSED TO LOOK AT HIM.

Tei stood not more than an armslength from the alien, in a tiny bare compartment just off the orderkeepers' quarters. They could have crouched or sat on the earth's cool silica instead of standing. But the skinless creature in front of Tei insisted on pacing, corner to corner, tugging at the oblong metallic disc that secured both hands behind its back. And Tei couldn't very well sit when the Natcher was standing.

In Cyborg culture, sitting might have worked. Cyborgs associated higher elevation with greater authority: Finals in their tall skins loomed over fledglings, and Buru loomed high above them all as he stood at the assembly room podium. If this creature with Tei had been a Cyborg, sitting down could have symbolized Tei lowering himself, adopting a humble posture, treating the captive in front of him like a trusted friend.

But in Natcher, the body language was all wrong. Natcher elders sat as they held council, casting authoritative judgment over the ones who stood in front of them. To sit in a Natcher's presence would be to claim bodily power over it. And claiming power was the last thing Tei needed right now.

He didn't want the alien prisoner to see him as a threat. He wanted it to see him as a friend.

So Tei stood, shifting his weight from foot to foot, gnawing uncertainly on his lower lip.

At least they were finally alone. Buru had insisted at first on being present for the interrogation. Tei protested in vain, then spent the next forty-five minutes speaking every word with slow, surgical precision— trying to compose Natcher sentences that might be understandable to the prisoner without sounding like treason in Buru's ears. Finally, mercifully, Buru retreated from the room, promising to watch their every move through the eyes of the command room.

Still, even now that Buru was gone and Tei could speak freely, the Natcher hadn't uttered a single word in reply. Its expression was blank. Tei wondered if the creature understood anything coming out of his mouth. Maybe the accent he'd learned from Kyri and Kiphu wasn't so close to a Natcher accent after all. Maybe the Natcher language had evolved more than they'd predicted in the generations since Kyri was archived. Or maybe this particular creature's ears were damaged and couldn't hear Tei's words, let alone understand them.

"I want to help," Tei said again and again—using the Natcher word for *help*, not the Cyborg one. "I'm not like the ones who captured you. I want to help, but I can't do anything unless you'll talk to me."

Even as he spoke the words, Tei realized how unconvincing they sounded. Any interpreter-turned-interrogator would have said the same. Tei's Cyborg skin spoke more loudly than his Natcher voice ever could.

The Natcher kept pacing.

Finally, Tei gambled on the question he'd been longing to ask all along. "Do you know Kanan?"

The creature froze. For the first time, its face betrayed understanding.

"So do I," Tei continued without waiting for a response. "He was— He is my friend. I didn't even learn the word *friend* until after he was gone. But he might be my only living friend. If he's still alive, I mean."

Tei could read the wariness on the Natcher's face. Its lips were pressed together, its eyes torn between caution and trust.

"The morning he disappeared," said Tei, "he promised we would find each other. The promise was supposed to be all his to keep. We thought I would..." Tei's voice trailed off. How could he explain the archive to a Natcher in anything but the harshest terms? "We thought I would be killed, and Kanan would survive, and he would hold me in his memories and visit me there. But everything flipped upside-down. I was chosen to live, and he was chosen to die. When he ran..."

The tears in Tei's throat were too thick now to choke back. He spoke in bursts, meting out words according to the heaving of his chest.

"I thought he was breaking his promise by running. Maybe he thought the same. But it turns out running was the only chance he had of keeping his promise to me. Because he ran, maybe he's still alive. And if he's still alive, I have to find him. We have to find each other."

At last something in the alien seemed to break free. "Kanan has mentioned you," it said.

"You—" stammered Tei. "You've spoken with him?"

The Natcher hesitated, its eyes twitching with unspoken calculations. When it spoke again, its words came slowly and guardedly. "Kanan speaks little. To learn our human tongue takes time, especially when a creature's soul lives in its feet as Kanan's does. And Mahlah is only an aquarian, with no knowledge of the Cyborg tongue. But Mahlah hears things while swimming with Kanan and Avi. Kanan speaks only one Cyborg name with fondness."

"Tei?" The interpreter uttered his own name like a plea.

The alien captive nodded. "Mahlah did not think at first it could be you. The other Cyborgs call you Eleven or Interpreter."

"It's the Cyborg way," said Tei, "to pile on layer after layer of disguise until the human underneath them all is barely visible."

"You sound like a creature of the overworld." The alien almost smiled.

"I have enough overworld in me to ruin the underworld," said Tei. "And enough underworld to ruin the overworld."

"Then what do you still have, when everything in the universe is ruined? What else is left?"

"I have whatever lies outside the Universe. And Kanan."

Mahlah tilted its head toward the locked access gate. "What about the rest of the Cyborgs?"

"The more I learn the tongue of the overworld," said Tei, "the more the other Cyborgs become like strangers to me."

The alien rested its shoulders against the compartment wall and slid slowly to the ground. It motioned for Tei to follow. "We have a creature like you in our midst. One who lives split between two tongues at the order of the elders, for the sake of the whole community. Tiqvah's tent stands alone, far from the others—not because Tiqvah is unwelcome, but because the words themselves make distance. Still, Tiqvah remains loyal to our race. What about you, Tei? Do you remain loyal to your race?"

"That's the way it seems to them," said Tei. "But they've never heard me speak your race's tongue—not in any meaningful way."

"This is why the other Cyborg creature left us?"

Tei nodded. "I told him my interpretation could not work if we were overheard."

"What is it that the other Cyborgs expect to learn from Mahlah?"

"Everything," said Tei. "Why you've come down to the underworld and let yourself be captured. Why your race stole one of our Cyborg shells and killed Jarawi. Why the suns are darker now than they used to be and the food scarcer. They want to know what makes your race strong, and what makes you weak, and whether you would survive if the Cyborgs tried to exterminate you. They want to know what role your race plays in keeping the Universe spinning, and whether Cyborgs could fill that role for themselves after your race was dead."

The alien's lips hung apart. "They think Mahlah knows all this?"

"Maybe not. But you know some of it, no doubt. In any case, you know more than they know. Just think of all the parts of life that feel ordinary to you. Food springing up from the ground. A river of clear-colored water to make it all grow. A single sun far out of reach that powers everything else. For your Cyborg captors, these simple facts are alien thoughts. They think that, once they understand everything you understand about how the overworld runs, they'll be more ready to claim it all for themselves."

"If that's the only thing they want," said Mahlah warily, "why bother with a captive? You seem to understand it all well enough. As if you've seen the overworld before."

Tei's head bowed. "I've seen only memories of the overworld. There's still so much to learn."

"And why haven't the other Cyborgs seen the same memories? Surely they would have studied whatever memories you've studied, if they want so badly to understand our race?"

"Even if the Cyborgs saw what I've seen, they couldn't understand it. Or if they did begin to understand, they'd call their understanding treason. For all they say they want the truth, the rules of their language ensure they will never find it."

Mahlah studied him closely. The creature's shoulders were bent forward, its eyes narrowed. "And does the tongue of the overworld allow for the truth you're seeking?"

"In a way, perhaps," said Tei. "But it's not much better in the end. Or maybe it's better and worse all at once. Your race sees things the Cyborgs can't see. And we see things you can't see. Everyone is blind in their own way. And in their blindness, they see what those with different eyes are blinded to."

The creature began to smile. "If the rest of Mahlah's race could hear their tongue used this way, they would say you are a creature gone mad."

"Maybe I am," answered Tei.

"Good," said the alien captive. "Mahlah has been waiting for a Cyborg as mad as you."

§§§

The third night shift was well under way when Tei banged on the locked access gate to indicate that his interview with Mahlah was over. Buru had long since retired to his hydro-pod. The captain left a message with the orderkeeper on duty, demanding a thorough debriefing in the command room the next morning.

Tei slept dreamlessly through the meager remaining hours of darkness. Even in absolute unthinking silence, his jaw stayed clenched.

When morning came, he sat at an empty mess table far from the chatter of his agemates, forcing bites of steamed grain and nutmeal paste down his throat. In the hallway to the elevator,

Buru met him with a shouted greeting and an impossibly wide grin.

"Interpreter! Wait up, won't you? We'll ride up together. What perfectly coincidental timing."

Tei said nothing. They passed through the first access gate, with Buru offering out the skin of his hand for confirmation.

"It's fortunate, me running into you like this," said Buru. His usual confidence seemed shaken. He spoke quickly, folding his hands into one another like dough being kneaded. "So much to discuss from last night, you know. And the message I left with the orderkeeper—one can only say so much. What one orderkeeper knows, the entire force knows, if you take my meaning."

The second access gate rose into the ceiling at the sound of Buru's voice.

"It makes perfect sense, of course," Buru continued, "for us to debrief your interrogation with the whole officers' committee. We have no secrets from them. But you're a smart young Final. You've kept your ears open to know that there are certain— certain *tensions*, shall we say, among the officers. This whole project of interpretation, it was my idea from the beginning. To invest our dwindling resources in an Eleven. To reintroduce an old career. Some of the others said it was foolish, wasting precious time on Natcher gibberish when we had an army of orderkeepers at the ready. After Jarawi, of course, the pressure to act became all the greater. This waiting game we've played—waiting for you, you understand—it hasn't been easy for me. I've had to make commitments I wouldn't have made otherwise."

They were standing at the third gate now without passing through it. Tei bent down to scan his own eye.

"Identity confirmed," croaked the digiscape voice. "Eleven, interpreter."

"And of course," said Buru, "it's all paying off beautifully now. To have a Natcher captive like this—what better proof could there be of an interpreter's value? Imagine if the captive had come to us just one season earlier, while you were still in fledgling skin. The best we could have done with the alien back then was a wasteful erasure. Or we would have had to keep it in captivity this entire time until the creature became useful to us. Not even the most stubborn of humanity's officers could doubt now that we made the right choice in Finalizing you."

"Good news indeed," said Tei. He reached out a hand to write his passcode into the fourth gate, but Buru caught him by the wrist.

"And so," said Buru slowly, "we must not give them any reason to doubt."

"I'll tell them exactly what the Natcher prisoner told me," said Tei. "They'll see firsthand that I can understand and speak the Natchers' words."

Tei made to pull his hand away, but Buru's grip tightened.

"I'm not sure you've taken my meaning," said Buru. "It's essential that what the committee hears at this breakthrough moment comes as a confirmation of the actions we've taken so far. It's not necessary for you to share every detail with them. Any setbacks—anything that would cast a shadow over our past decisions—these can be handled privately by the two of us, after the committee is adjourned. The report you give to the whole committee should be the kind of news fit for the whole committee."

"You're asking me to lie about what the prisoner said?"

"To lie?" Buru let go of Tei and raised both hands, smiling widely. "Never, never. Surely you remember that you and I have no secrets from the officers' committee. I'm merely advising you to be cautious about what information needs to be known by whom, and when. Some facts, if placed in the wrong hands at the wrong time, can do great damage."

Tei scrawled his passcode onto the screen of the fourth gate. It rose into the ceiling, revealing the elevator.

"Checkers," said Buru. "Such an interesting passcode for someone your age. Which reminds me, I recently stumbled across a strange coincidence. Perhaps you remember Kanan, your old deleted agemate? I spoke not long ago with his former mentor. Checkers was a favorite game of Kanan's, as it happens. His mentor even seemed to think the two of you might have played together."

Fighting to keep his expression steady, Tei shrugged as he stepped into the elevator. "Who remembers how they spent their fledgling days? It already seems so long ago."

"Does it?" Buru's smile was all teeth. "The day you chose that passcode, it must not have seemed so long ago. The morning after the aging ceremony, as I recall. While Kanan was still missing, before he had been deleted. And so, because of an accident in timing, your passcode almost seems to align you with a traitor."

"A strange coincidence indeed," said Tei.

Buru nodded with a gentleness that could have passed for kindness. "And a coincidence best kept to ourselves, don't you think? Not every officer on the committee is as understanding as I am. It's like I said before. Some facts, if placed in the wrong hands at the wrong time, can do great damage."

"I couldn't agree more," said Tei.

"Very good," said Buru. "Then I expect you'll keep the same principle in mind as you present your findings to the committee."

The elevator rose. Tei became heavier, then lighter, until he was floating weightlessly beside the captain.

They reached the command room to find the officers' committee already half assembled, strapped into a ring of chairs that looked upside down from Tei's perspective. Tei propelled himself toward an open seat and somersaulted into it. The world turned on its head, bringing all the officers upright.

"You've had a long night, Eleven," said Goru, the committee's master engineer. He had wide shoulders and a booming voice that filled up the whole hollow orb of the command room.

"I was born into skin for moments like this one," Tei answered, looking toward the far side of the circle, where Buru was strapping himself into the captain's chair. "The survival of our race depends on our ability to understand the danger and respond."

Goru rubbed his chin with fingers stained black by carbon oil. "We are eager to hear what you've discovered."

"The interpreter's report should wait," said Buru, "until the others have arrived."

"Buru calling on us to wait?" said an administrator whose name Tei had forgotten. "How unusual."

Several of the officers laughed. Buru's smile stretched thin.

"While we wait," said Goru, "there is also the matter of the galley chemist to discuss."

The elevator opened, and another two officers floated in to take their places around the circle.

"Discuss?" The speaker was Namoel, a master orderkeeper with skin patched in shades of blue like camouflage. "What's to discuss? Arisa should have been deleted seasons ago. Robiana couldn't possibly have disappeared without his knowledge; all their agemates testified how close the two were. Then there is the matter of Kanan's disappearance and their meeting outside the mess hall. Why should we believe Arisa's account of what was said? We were fools to let all this pass as simple coincidence."

"Proximity to a traitor is not proof of betrayal, Namoel," said Goru. "Surely you of all people believe this. Or do you think we've all forgotten about your agemate the archivist?"

Namoel fell silent, his face darkening.

"But there's no doubt about the infirmary chemicals," said another officer whose name Tei couldn't remember. "Claimed by Arisa's skin, and found hidden near the galley supply portal as if to be sent to the Natchers. Or the strands of repair skin, carried from one channel of the water processing plant to another without purpose. Conspiracy is the only possible logic for actions like these."

"The proof is still circumstantial," said the administrator. "Enough to arrest and interrogate, undoubtedly. But is it enough to merit Arisa's deletion?"

Four new arrivals launched themselves out of the elevator. "These matters should not be discussed in front of the interpreter," growled the master chemist as he drifted towards them.

"No matter," said Buru. "Our quorum is present. The more pressing business can begin."

Every eye turned toward Tei. He gulped.

What was there to say? What story could keep Mahlah alive long enough to be rescued? What story could increase his access to the overworld or the command room, unsupervised, without sparking suspicion?

"The creature's name is Mahlah," he began in a trembling voice.

"Remarkable," interrupted the nameless administrator, his voice dripping with disdain. "Aren't you all glad we waited two and a half seasons for this breakthrough? Now we can call the Natchers by their names as we erase them."

A few of the others began to laugh. Tei cleared his throat and continued. "Erasing the Natchers is far more dangerous than you realize. According to Mahlah, our human universe and their portion of Nothing aren't just connected—they're completely dependent on each other. The Natcher homeland is the source of humanity's food, our water, our sunlight."

"You see?" said Buru triumphantly. "I've said this all along. To advance without understanding would have put the whole universe in jeopardy."

"Or so says the Natcher captive," interjected Namoel. "We have no reason to trust its words. Perhaps it is a spy sent to infect humanity with lies."

Goru the master engineer tugged at one of the straps that held him affixed to his chair. "But this testimony does the Natchers no favors. If they are the source of food and water and sunlight, as the captive creature says, then the blame for our shrinking food supply and the darkening of our skies truly must lie with the Natchers. Their own words condemn them."

Tei shook his head. "The Natchers are not the source of the deprivation. Their world provides our resources, but Mahlah claims that even the Natchers do not have complete control over it all. They are constrained by their universe just as we are constrained by ours."

"If the Natchers are so weak," said Namoel, "what's to keep us from erasing them all and replacing them with our own workers? Anything those skinless aliens can do, a human can surely do better."

"All in good time," said Buru. "Before we replace them, we need to know everything they know. Everything. We can't simply ask a prisoner how their Nothing works. We need to get into it, to see it for ourselves."

The administrator laughed. "And how do you propose we do that, Buru? Invite ourselves up for a tour?"

The captain opened his mouth to answer, but Tei was quicker: "That's exactly what I've done."

Every eye turned towards him again.

"You did *what*?" said Buru.

The plan was still forming in Tei's mind as he spoke, but there was no time for hesitation. "Not in so many words, of course," he said. "I needed a way to earn the creature's trust. It wouldn't speak a word to me at first—Buru can tell you, or you can see the footage for yourself if you wish. So I told it that I wanted to become a Natcher. I said that learning the aliens' gibberish had made me believe their race was superior to the human race. I promised to help it run away, if it would take me up into Nothing and show me how the Natcher world operates."

A few officers' lips curled in disgust. Buru looked livid.

"This would not be the first time," said Goru slowly, "that an interpreter has turned to treason."

Tei fought to keep his expression steady. "That's exactly why I thought the alien might be persuaded by my story. The closer to reality, the more believable the lie."

"But why should we believe your treason isn't the reality after all?" Namoel's cheeks swelled out as his voice rose. "Maybe you've been waiting all along for a moment like this one. A chance to follow a Natcher into Nothing and betray your humanity like so many interpreters before you. We have more reasons to doubt you than to trust you."

Tei tried to turn his fear into a disdainful smile. "Do you really think, if I were toying with treason, I would confess it to you all this way? I'm not that much of a fool. If I wanted to betray my humanity, I could have laid plans to help the Natcher creature escape without breathing a word of it to this committee. By speaking of treason, I've raised your suspicion. You'll watch me with greater scrutiny now. Good. I welcome your scrutiny. But hear me out. If I go into the Natchers' Nothing this way, I'll be greeted by them as a hero. I'll be returning one of their warriors unharmed, and that warrior will testify to my trustworthiness. They'll tell me anything, show me anything. Then, when I've learned enough to ensure the survival of our universe, I can return to this committee with every bit of knowledge we need to erase the Natchers forever."

"Treason is not a fledgling's toy to be played with," said Buru. "To intentionally put yourself so close to treachery, even if you are only pretending… the risk is too great. Too many interpreters have been lost for us to lose another the same way."

"Interpretation without risk is a farce," said Tei. "I've already come as close to treason as it is possible for a loyal human to come. I was agemates with the traitor Kanan; we played games and ran the perimeter of the universe together before his deletion. Since I was born into Final skin, I've dedicated my every working moment, and most of my leisure time as well, to make my mouth able to speak like the mouth of a Natcher. There is no one better suited to treason than me. If, after all that risk, I am still dedicated to humanity, what future risk could possibly undo me?"

"Look me in the eyes," said Buru, "and tell me you are not already a traitor."

Tei turned his whole body to face the captain. Eyes in skin were a magic spell, and Buru's eyes were no exception. But this spell was nothing like Kanan's spell. The sorcery of Buru's eyes was sharp, burning white-hot—the sorcery of a grinning monster ready to devour. Tei met Buru's gaze and held it without blinking.

"I am more committed to the human race than I've ever been," he said.

Buru nodded slowly. "I support the interpreter's plan. I urge us all to give him our full support."

"But if he's lying—" Namoel began to object.

"I've seen Eleven lie," said Buru. "I of all people have been with him enough to know the difference. And he is not lying now."

The vote was taken. Fourteen in favor, three against, two abstaining. The officers laid a plan for Tei and Mahlah's staged escape. Namoel scowled even as he pledged the orderkeepers' cooperation. The administrator whose name Tei had forgotten stroked his chin and said nothing.

When the committee adjourned, Goru shook his head wonderingly at Tei as he floated away. "Did you ever imagine a contradiction like this, Eleven? Did you ever imagine your loyalty to humanity could turn you into a traitor?"

"Never," said Tei.

If Buru had been watching, he would have seen the telltale flicker of a lie in the interpreter's eyes.

24
LILY

THE PLAN HAD BEEN TO WAIT until Project Universe was out of the solar system, past the eccentric orbit of poor disenfranchised Pluto, before seeding new eggs in the hatchery. "Still a few kinks to work out of the system," the hydroponic gestation specialist said. "What's two years' delay when you're preparing for millennia?"

But Adam's arrival changed everyone's timeline. The hydroponic nursery program would have to be ready for him immediately after birth. Even if Lily had wanted to raise him outside the digiscape–to raise him like a Terran child–there was no ExoSkin small enough to fit a newborn. And no one knew if a natural-born infant could survive the ship's magnified pseudogravity without the help of ExoSkin.

"We'll have to improvise labor and delivery," said the gynecologist, watching the fetus squirm on a tomography screen designed for wound care. "Once he's safely in the nursery water, we'll be out of the woods."

"Six years," said Lily. "How do you expect me to let go of him for six years?"

The gynecologist rolled her eyes. "If you wanted motherhood so badly, you came to the wrong Universe."

"I don't," Lily stammered. "I didn't. It wasn't supposed to happen this way."

"No shit. Lucky for you the guy who boned you has enough clout to get the Margola sisters on your side. Not that it's any of my business where you spread your legs."

"Slut" was a word that should have disappeared quickly on Project Universe. Sex existed only in the digiscape now, where no one cared if or when or with whom or how often. But Adam's birth gave the Universe one last shred of Terran history to savor in outer space: one last slut to shame. No one cared about the sexual act itself, nor even the resulting pregnancy. It was Lily's insistence on keeping the child that infuriated them. Her selfish refusal to surrender her body to the preferred schedule of the Universe—that was what made her a slut.

Thanks to Lily, "slut" lasted four generations before its meaning was finally forgotten, and another seven generations before it fell out of use as an all-purpose insult. The word could only ever be applied to women, never to men; but of course, three hundred years after Lily's death, no one remembered why.

25

KANAN

BY THE TIME THE ORDER to rescue Mahlah was given, a charcoal evening sun hung above the overworld. The elders had argued through the heat of the day, sitting in front of a sweltering council fire as Tiqvah and two dozen warriors stood by awaiting their command.

In the end, only Elder Javan objected to the rescue plan. He too might have agreed, were it not for the warriors' insistence that Kanan join the rescue party dressed in her Cyborg shell. "A creature on our side who looks and moves and speaks like one of the Cyborgs' own?" said Avi. "We can't afford to waste a tactical advantage like that." The other warriors nodded their agreement.

Avi was evasive in his explanation of the skin's history. He certainly had no intention of telling the elders how, after being hidden between worlds in a place known only to Mahlah, the skin had mysteriously reappeared in Avi's tent the very night of Mahlah's disappearance and capture. He had no intention of describing the note that accompanied the skin, scrawled in

Mahlah's unmistakable hand: *In case of disaster.* The aquarian needed to remain as innocent as possible in the elders' eyes. Whatever premeditation Mahlah had been guilty of was no one's business but Avi's and Tiqvah's and Kanan's.

Javan glowered through the warriors' proposal. The elder interrupted on more than one occasion, his lips flecked with furious spittle. But all his shouts of Kanan's certain betrayal weren't enough to dissuade the rest of the council.

Kanan never spoke in her own defense. How could she possibly explain to the elders that her betrayal of the overworld lay not in the future, but in the past—in the silence she had kept over Mahlah's secrets? That old story had no value now. Mahlah had made his choice. Every betrayal worth fearing had already come to pass.

Betrayal. Kanan turned the word over on her tongue as she and Tiqvah huddled behind a copse of fig trees in the dusk, covering Kanan's underflesh with strips of the stolen Cyborg skin. *Betrayal.* This overworld word was identical to the Cyborg word for *loyalty.* All her seasons in the underworld, Kanan had only ever heard those syllables spoken with honor. Strange to hear them now as an accusation. She tried to imagine the Cyborgs' faces—the faces of Mentor and Captain Buru and her agemates—if they only knew that a runaway in a stolen skin was being accused of loyalty.

When the last fold of skin fused into place, Tiqvah stepped back to survey his handiwork. "You look like a Cyborg again."

"All the better for my betrayal," answered Kanan without smiling. "The outside finally matches the inside."

Tiqvah shook his head. "I know Cyborgs. You're no Cyborg."

"Maybe not," said Kanan. "But I spent most of my life wanting a Cyborg shell more than I wanted anything in the universe. No sense pretending those seasons never existed. I'll always have too much Cyborg in me to be a full-fledged citizen of the overworld."

Tiqvah poured himself a bowl of water and offered a second bowl to Kanan. "You don't think the same is true of me? My heart is overstuffed with loyalties that are also betrayals. It's more than just my tent that lingers on the outskirts of the overworld. No one really believes I belong here. Not even me."

"Still," said Kanan, "you don't belong in the underworld either."

"Certainly not. And neither do you."

"Then where else is left for us, once overworld and underworld are ruled out?"

Tiqvah stood in silence for a long moment before answering. "The in-between. The boundary line. Or somewhere else entirely."

"Somewhere like Nothing, you mean?"

For a split second, Kanan thought Tiqvah would agree. His eyes lifted, his lips parting slightly. But then the double-tongue shook his head firmly. "Nothing is not a somewhere. It is not a place that can be sought after or belonged to."

"I would have told you the same," said Kanan, "when I only spoke like a Cyborg. But the Nothing I thought I knew was a far cry from the Nothing I discovered. Why shouldn't the same be true here in the overworld? Why shouldn't the thing you call Nothing be another undiscovered somewhere?"

"I told you once," said Tiqvah, "that the journey between tongues was perilous. You are beginning now to see its perils. Questions like these are enough to drive a person mad."

"You haven't gone mad," said Kanan.

"No," said Tiqvah. "I have learned which questions are worth asking."

A long silence fell. Kanan twisted her arms and bent her legs one by one, flexing the muscles of her sleek Cyborg skin. She had become the creature she always dreamed of becoming. A creature who was no longer recognizably her. A Final. A stranger.

"Do you ever wish you did belong?" she said, breaking the silence. "In one world or the other, I mean? To one tongue or the other?"

"Of course I wish it," said Tiqvah. "But before I'm done wishing, I realize I don't want to give up either one of my tongues. There are gifts in the in-between-ness. Without in-between-ness, I wouldn't understand the Cyborgs' words, and I couldn't serve my race in the ways I do. Without in-between-ness, you couldn't have worn a Cyborg shell to save Zillah's life, and you couldn't wear it now to save Mahlah's life. The in-between-ness makes us able to do things that those who fit perfectly in the overworld or the underworld could never do. Gifts, you see?"

Kanan climbed to her feet. "What if I don't want those gifts?"

"Who ever said the gifts were for you?"

A series of shouts and a loud splash echoed up from the riverside. Tiqvah shot Kanan a frightened glance before racing out of the copse, down the grassy slope toward the source of the commotion. Kanan followed close behind.

At the sight of Mahlah, Kanan's run slowed to a walk. All her fear dissolved into happy confusion. The escaped prisoner floated through the air at the water's edge, carried on the shoulders of a cluster of warriors whooping and laughing. Someone had leapt into the river to splash handfuls of water high like glistening confetti. Mahlah thrust both triumphant fists toward the sky. His face was bruised, and a trickle of blood ran down from his side, but he was grinning.

A few skinlengths back, isolated from the crowd, Eleven the Interpreter limped hesitantly forward.

Kanan's old agemate was dressed in Cyborg skin, sleek and blue and thoroughly out of place next to the raucous celebration of the others. She looked nothing like the Eleven Kanan remembered: the powerful, almost mythical newborn Final who still appeared in Kanan's nightmares. Nor did she resemble the old fledgling Tei of gentle smiles and boundless optimism. This creature was thinner. More fragile. On the verge of shattering.

One of the interpreter's legs had a black mark seared across the thigh. Her lips stretched into what could have been a smile, or perhaps a grimace of pain, or perhaps nothing at all. After so long in the overworld, Kanan had forgotten the challenge of reading Cyborg emotions. The face's natural contours and meanings were all disguised by a layer of skin.

Kanan's eyes met Eleven's. The interpreter's face changed. Even skin couldn't hide her emotion now: the open-lipped wondering gasp of a person seeing sunshine after a lifetime in midnight. They walked towards each other.

"You're here." Eleven's Cyborg voice, mechanical and shrill, made Kanan flinch.

"You're here," answered Kanan in the low, earthy tones of the overworld.

Because there was so much to say, they said nothing at all.

Kanan felt something brush against the skin of her hand. She looked down to see Eleven's trembling blue fingers reaching towards hers. For a moment she took them, and the two Cyborgs stood entangled, feeling each other's heartbeats in the throb of their palms. Then Kanan felt Avi's eyes on them. She shook her hand free.

"There are laws," she whispered, as if Cyborg laws had the power to pierce through underworld sky and overworld grass, to fill the whole universe.

"Laws," the interpreter repeated flatly.

They looked away from each other, back towards the raucous shouts of the skinless ones.

Mahlah had begun regaling the other warriors with scenes from his escape: The handcuff key stolen from an orderkeeper's belt. The blow to the head that knocked a second orderkeeper unconscious just as she opened the access gate to Mahlah's cell. The sprint through dimly lit hallways, stryker darts whizzing past. Fistfights with two more orderkeepers. The strange creation called *elevator*, which carried them into the overworld powered only by the sound of the interpreter's voice.

"And Tei, of course." Mahlah's voice was louder now, his words beginning to slur. Someone had placed a canteen of dragonsbreath in his hand, and he interrupted himself with long swigs between sentences. "How could I forget the hero of the story? *I have to escape from the underworld,* the alien tells me. *I may look like a Cyborg, but I have a human heart. I'll get you out of this cell if you'll take me with you to the overworld.* I don't believe it at first. I'm sure it must be a trap. But when the creature speaks Kanan's name, I can see it feels in ways that Cyborgs are not taught to feel. It has the double tongue like Tiqvah. Perhaps it is a bit insane. But a bit insane is just enough to risk its life to save mine. Here's to you, Tei!"

Mahlah lifted his canteen. The warriors cheered and roared into the darkness. Kanan looked over at her agemate's face, trying to read the unspoken thoughts behind Tei's clenched jaw.

The interpreter's Cyborg skin was an inscrutable wall, revealing nothing.

§§§

Kanan had forgotten what truly raw Cyborg underflesh looked like. Soft. Limp. Bony. The spectacle might have been funny, if Tei's shivers and shudders hadn't made it so pitifully heartbreaking. The interpreter sat with her arms wrapped around her scant belly, eyes darting from Kanan to Tiqvah and back again.

"It takes time," Tiqvah soothed, "for the body to adjust. See how Kanan's underflesh has adapted to skinlessness. Yours will do the same soon enough."

"I've been skinless in the digiscape plenty of times," said Tei. "But it never felt like this."

"Of course not." Tiqvah set a length of plant fabric over Tei's shoulders. "The digiscape is not for feeling. For knowing, perhaps—but never the kind of knowing that reaches the body's core. The Cyborgs who sink into the water of their hydropods looking for wisdom are doomed to float in foolishness."

Tei cocked her head to one side as she pulled the fabric around her. "The truest things I've ever learned, I learned in the digiscape."

"Then you can't have learned much of value," said Tiqvah. The gentleness of his voice almost masked the harshness of his words.

"I learned to speak your language," said Tei. "I split my tongue in two thanks to the digiscape. Surely there's value in that."

Tiqvah tapped his chin. "I wondered about your tutor. The Cyborg interpreters have been extinct for generations. Or so our race has been led to believe."

Kanan listened to the conversation in silence. She knew enough of the overworld tongue to follow the thrust of their words, but not enough to speak confidently for herself. The sound of Tei's voice was surreal—like a voice from a dream, transplanted into a waking world where it didn't belong.

"We can speak in the Cyborg tongue if you wish," Tiqvah offered. "I'm a double-tongue as well, as much in danger of treason as you."

"If it's all the same to you," said Tei, "I could use the practice in your race's tongue. I've never spoken outside the digiscape before. And you're not wrong when you say that the digiscape has its limits."

"Gladly," said Tiqvah. "But surely you want to speak with your friend in the language you both know best."

"No," said Tei, in the same breath that Kanan answered, "Yes."

They looked at one another for a long moment.

Tiqvah stood. "Perhaps I ought to leave you both alone."

Tei spread her hands apart. "No need. We have nothing to hide."

"Nonsense," said Tiqvah, turning to leave. "Everything tender begins in secret. Tender joys and tender wounds alike. The seeds grow in darkness until they are strong enough to face daylight. Whatever exists between you, good blood or bad, I can see it is still tender. You have everything to hide."

Tei opened her mouth to object, but Tiqvah had already started running. Soon he was barely more than a bouncing dot on the horizon.

"Welcome to the overworld," said Kanan at last, when the silence was almost unbearable.

"You didn't need to send the Natcher away," said Tei. "You'll make it suspicious."

Kanan growled. "Don't say *Natcher*. Don't say *it*. His name is Tiqvah. He is human. They're all human."

Tei blinked in surprise. "Of course. I agree. I just thought— I thought you'd want to speak the words we grew up speaking, now that we're alone."

"I can't speak those words anymore," said Kanan. "The Cyborg tongue seems wrong now. Evil. Incomplete."

"But you can't speak like a Natcher either," said Tei. "I mean—sorry—you can't speak the tongue of the overworld. Not as easily as they do."

"And somehow *you* can." Kanan shook her head. "I'm the one who spends half a season in the overworld, but still you're the one whose mouth seems to belong here."

"That's what it means to be an interpreter," said Tei. "All my time as Eleven has been spent inside the archive, learning how to speak across worlds. You would have hated it. Being Eleven, I mean. Strange to think how sure I was back then that you'd be the one chosen."

Kanan bit her lip, remembering her own desperate hope at the aging ceremony. Remembering her anger at hearing Tei's name where her own name should have been. It felt cruel how different everything could look when seen from a different vantage point, a different place in the universe.

"But you're wrong," Tei continued, "when you say I sound as if I belong here. I sound like a foreigner. Like a person who knows digiscape code better than I know real life. And you— you may not have learned the grammar and vocabulary yet, but I can hear the overworld on your lips. Even when you speak in Cyborg words, there's something not-quite-Cyborg about you."

"I guess we've both changed."

"I guess we have." Beneath the fabric, Tei buried her hands inside her armpits. "You don't seem to care about skin as much as you used to."

Kanan looked down at her own bare torso. "I'm not sure it was ever skin I cared about."

"Then what?" said Tei. "Honor? Humanity?"

"Whatever it is you call humanity before it earns the word *human*, maybe. In that moment when we're just underflesh, plain and simple. When we have meaning just because we exist. That moment before someone comes along to assign honor to us, to decide who deserves it and who doesn't."

"Is there honor in the overworld?" asked Tei. "I know there's no word for it. But is it here, just the same?"

"Sometimes. Sometimes not. When it's missing, it's even worse, because there's no way to name it and point to it and say, *Where did the honor go?* But when it's here, it's even better. Because it feels like something so natural, so intrinsic, that there's no need to give it a name. We gain something without the word. And we lose something, too."

Tei nodded, quoting Kyri: "Every way of seeing is also a way of not seeing."

"What about you?" said Kanan. "What happened to your new name and the honor that was supposed to come with it? What happened to serving humanity as no one has served before or since?"

"That's exactly what I'm doing." Tei stretched out her arms, the cloth unfurling behind her like a cape. "Only, as it turns out, humanity is a larger circle than I thought it was."

"Then you've done your job so well you've turned into a traitor like me? Is Buru pronouncing threats at you through the universal throat this very moment?"

"Something like that."

Kanan studied the look in her agemate's eyes, the perfectly still sideways smile. It was the expression Tei wore during games of checkers. The calculating look of someone deciding whether to make a risky play.

"What aren't you telling me?" said Kanan.

"Nothing," said Tei, who had never been a good liar.

"You used to trust me."

"I still do. I want to. But we've both changed. You said so yourself." Tei paused. "The one called Avi seems especially drawn to you."

"He's a good friend."

"Only that?"

"What else is there except that?"

Tei's naked hand crept out from beneath the cloth and closed over Kanan's fist. "Promises," she said.

§§§

Halfway around the universe, the warrior Enos passed a listening device to Tiqvah. "The chatter from inside the Cyborg orderkeepers' quarters tonight. I worry, by the tones of their voices, that something is amiss. They are as loud and raucous as our own people. It's as if losing Mahlah troubles them not at all. What does it mean?"

"I'll know soon enough," answered Tiqvah. "The underworld has no secrets from us."

Enos joined his palms in front of his torso and disappeared into the darkness.

Tiqvah held the device up to his ear to listen. As the recording progressed, his face twisted into a mask of fury.

"Loyalty," he whispered. The Cyborg word for loyalty.

He began racing towards Avi's tent. The path in front of him glowed dimly, lit by the luminescent blade clutched in his hand.

26
TEI

TEI WOKE A FEW HOURS BEFORE DAWN with a knife at his throat.

Avi knelt across his thighs, pinning Tei by his forearms against the grass. Tiqvah held the knife, which cast blue-white light across the alien's upside-down lips as it hissed, "Betrayal!" After a beginning like that, thought Tei, the day could hardly get worse.

As long as he was still alive by the end of it.

He tried at first to deny Tiqvah's accusation altogether, to pretend total ignorance. But his denials only made the alien's anger fiercer. "I know what I heard," it snarled, holding up a black box against his cheek. "I can play the words again if you wish. You didn't help Mahlah escape—not truly. The Cyborgs let you both go free, and feigned a fight only for Mahlah's sake. They sent you here as a spy."

Tei gulped and felt the knife's edge bob against his underflesh. "That's what the Cyborgs believe, yes. That's what I told them so they would let us leave in safety. But I have no intention of spying for the Cyborgs. They think I'm loyal only because they believed my lie to them."

"Even if what you say is true, you lied to us as well." Tiqvah's teeth clenched as the blade pushed deeper. "Why? Why pretend you escaped without the Cyborgs' help? Why not tell us the whole truth?"

"Because the lie I told the Cyborgs was so believable in their minds. I was afraid you'd believe it too. You'd think I really am just a spy."

Kanan's voice drifted out of the shadows. "Are you a spy?"

"No." Tei twisted his head towards the voice. "I swear it, Kanan, I'm not a spy. You know me. You have to believe me."

"Do I know you?" Kanan's words were still Cyborg, but his voice sounded as low and murky as a Natcher. "We've both changed, remember?"

"Exactly," said Tei. "You remember me the way we used to be, when we'd only ever looked at the world through one set of words, through one set of eyes. And now we've changed. We're not fledglings chasing skin anymore, mindlessly believing whatever the Cyborgs tell us. That's why we're here in the overworld."

Kanan's face appeared between Tiqvah and Avi, hovering over Tei in the faint green glow. "I know why I'm here. Tell me why you're here."

"To find you," said Tei. "To keep a promise."

Kanan shook his head. "Even if that's one of your reasons, it's not the only reason. You've never been a good liar, Tei. In that, at least, you haven't changed a bit."

"Fine." Tei sighed, took a deep breath. "I came here to destroy the Universe. And I need your help."

§§§

The sun was just beginning to brighten as Tei finished telling the story of Project Universe. He could hardly blame his audience for their frowns and distrustful stares. Here in the grassy overworld, far from skin and digiscape, it all sounded preposterous. That the only world any of them had ever seen was just a tiny mimicry of something much more massive. That Planet Earth was their race's real origin, and Gliese 832c their real destination. That Tei was on a mission to take over the command room and chart a course through the stars so humanity could one day leave behind the underworld and the overworld forever.

Tiqvah shook its head as Tei spoke, repeatedly murmuring, "Insanity." The knife gradually went slack in the alien's hand, though the blade never left Tei's throat.

Avi, too, held its position atop Tei. Its grip never relaxed. Tei's limbs numbed beneath the alien's weight. Avi's eyes filled with a mixture of fear and nostalgia, like someone staring at a ghost.

As for Kanan, he retreated into the shadows, pacing back and forth along the tent's edge while the creeping daylight brought his silhouette into color. Sometimes he seemed to be nodding in agreement. Other times his jaw was slack with what might have been amazement or disbelief or outrage.

When Tei finally fell silent, it was Avi who spoke first. "From where did Tei get these dangerous ideas?"

"From the last of the Cyborg interpreters," answered Tei. "Kyri is his name. And from Adam, the very first human born on the Universe after it left Planet Earth."

"The dead have no ideas," barked Avi, its eyes narrowing.

"From the digiscape, you mean." Tiqvah's voice came gently. "You spoke to their memories in the digiscape. But surely you know that creatures in the digiscape are not the same as creatures in flesh. The digiscape can't be trusted. It's not real, what you see there. The memories can be distorted. They already have been distorted."

"A distorted memory is better than no memory at all," said Tei.

Tiqvah curled its lip in disdain. "Our race keeps its memories without any need for a digiscape. How else do you think we've grown our crops and fished our river and trained our children all these seasons? Our stories are passed down, generation to generation. There is no coding to be corrupted or erased, no archivist purifying the unwanted parts of history."

"No," Tei agreed. "Your race doesn't have coding or archivists. But you have elders ready to punish every contradiction to the history that benefits them. You have the risk of starvation, threatening to silence anyone who makes enemies or loses a place in the market by telling an inconvenient memory. You have forbidden words and forbidden ideas. Once these things are forbidden long enough, they die along with the creatures too afraid to speak them. Once enough generations have passed, everything inconvenient dies. Your world, like mine, remembers precisely what it wants to remember. Nothing less. Nothing more. At least the digiscape makes it possible for humans to rediscover the things we've tried to forget."

"Cyborg lies," spat Avi. "What else would a spy do except try to infect our minds with doubt?"

"If you don't believe me," said Tei, "come and see the command room for yourself. Help me clear the diamantium window and see into the stars. What have you lost if I'm wrong, except a bit of pride?"

"By asking us into the command room," said Tiqvah, "you're asking us to wear Cyborg shells. This is not simply a matter of pride. It means forsaking our identity as members of the human race. You're asking us to become Cyborgs."

"Don't you see?" Tei would have leapt to his feet, if it hadn't been for the alien on top of him. "This isn't about Cyborgs and Natchers. This is about speaking whatever language we need to speak, wearing whatever clothes or shell we need to wear, to see the world as it really is."

Avi snorted. "Any reality that needs a Cyborg shell to be seen is a reality not worth seeing."

"Even if your story were true," said Tiqvah, "the burden it imposes is unfairly distributed. It is easy for a Cyborg like you to believe it. It comes from your digiscape, relies on your skin. But for Avi and me and our race? Your story's very heart stands opposed to everything we hold dearest."

"Don't tell me what is easy for me," said Tei. "If it's true—"

From the edge of the tent, Kanan abruptly stopped his pacing. "If it's true, there's a whole universe to be gained."

Avi's grip relaxed. Its neck craned toward Kanan, its brow furrowing in fear. "You're not taking this madness seriously?"

"Why shouldn't I?" Kanan strode closer and set a hand on Avi's shoulder. "Before you rescued me from the butchery, I thought the underworld was the entire universe. I didn't know about a second tongue, didn't know about humanity outside of skin. I would have told you it was madness. Who's to say I'm not just as blind now? Why shouldn't there be even more to reality than I've grown accustomed to seeing? Why shouldn't the universe be even larger than I thought it was?"

"The madness of Robiana," whispered Avi, pulling its hands away from Tei to cover its own face.

Tei clenched and unclenched his fists, trying to restore the blood flow in his arms. "It isn't madness. If Robiana has said the same, all the more reason to believe us both. It only sounds like madness because the stories you've heard—the words through which you've heard those stories—are designed to hide it from you. The true madness would be to let humanity stay trapped in here when a whole universe awaits us in the vastness of Nothing."

Avi was on its feet now, clutching both of Kanan's hands between its own. "Tell me you're not listening to this creature. Trust me, I know where this road leads. It's not somewhere you want to go. It's the Cyborg in you, being infected by madness. I already lost Robiana this way. I can't lose you too."

Kanan pulled his hands free of the alien's. "But if it's not madness at all?"

Avi stumbled back like someone struck by a fist.

"Maybe you're right," Kanan added in a rush of words. "But don't we at least owe it to ourselves and to humanity to ask the question?"

"No," said Avi in a voice as thick as river mud. "We owe nothing. I owe nothing." The creature turned and ran into the golden early light.

"What about you, Double-tongue?" said Tei. "You know the tricks of words better than Avi. Don't you see how the story might all be true? Planet Earth? The voyage? The destination?"

Tiqvah shook its head wearily. "Avi is right. This is madness. It will end in sorrow." The alien tucked the knife away at its waist. "Forgive me, Interpreter. I underestimated you when I accused you of betrayal. I thought it was only one race you had betrayed. I never dreamed you would be bold enough to betray both races at once."

§§§

When the two of them were alone, Tei reached for Kanan's hand. "We should leave. It isn't safe here."

"And go where?" Kanan pulled his fingers free. "You're forgetting I can't go back to the underworld like you can."

"But the Natchers—"

"I told you not to call them that. Use their names. Avi. Tiqvah."

Tei took a breath. "Avi. Tiqvah. They think I'm dangerous. Who knows what they might say to the others? What they might do to me?"

"They won't hurt you. I won't let them."

"At least you believe me."

"Maybe I don't believe you. But I know you believe you. That much, at least, I know for sure."

Tei looked into Kanan's eyes. The magic in them was as strong as it had ever been, or even stronger.

"You look so different than I remember you," said Tei. "And still so much the same. Skinlessness suits you."

"And you look ridiculous," said Kanan. "But that's nothing new."

Tei leaned in closer. "There is a word called *kiss*," he said.

"I've seen it done." Kanan sat stiff, not drawing closer, not pulling away. "It's ridiculous too."

"Is it? As the old interpreter Kyri described it to me, I couldn't be sure."

Their faces were close enough now for Tei to feel Kanan's exhale against his cheeks.

"They say some feeling is supposed to accompany the kiss," said Tei.

"I've never felt it," said Kanan.

"Would you know if you had?"

"No. Maybe not."

"Then how can you be sure you're not feeling it now?"

Tei would have been afraid, in the moment their lips met, that he had fallen into a fledgling dream. But the crisp detail of the daylight falling across their skinless shoulders made everything too clear to be a dream.

From the branches of a fig tree across the river, Avi watched with shadow-darkened eyes.

27
LILY

THE SAME WEEK ADAM WAS BORN and transferred into the hydroponic nursery, forty new eggs were seeded in the hatchery. The sperm and eggs for the new hatchlings had been extracted from a few crewmembers' hydropods while their minds were busy in the digiscape. No one was told whose genetic material had been sampled for this first batch of youngsters, and no one wanted to know. Rumor had it that more would be collected soon—why not stock up the freezers now?—but no one bothered to find out if the rumor was true.

No one wanted to know.

Lily spent six years watching her son float in a tank of green liquid. She watched him learn to crawl and walk and run and fall under the tutelage of the mechanized pincers that held his arms and legs in place. She watched his lips move silently beneath the water's surface, forming words given to him by wires jutting out of his temporal lobe. She told herself that he was still in the womb. The tank of green anocyte-charged water was somehow part of her, somehow hidden inside her now-flat stomach. It had to be.

After all, she had never even touched him. The doctors whisked him away as soon as the umbilical cord was cut, ignoring her outstretched arms, not even bothering to wipe away the placental slime. How could she have allowed it if she hadn't known he was bound for a second womb? What kind of mother would she have been?

As the tanks around Adam's filled with other youngsters, Lily's guilt receded. Alone in the nursery, Adam had looked like an alien creature, not so much human as lab experiment. With others by his side, he became their de facto leader, larger and more developed than the rest. The vanguard of a new era of humankind.

"Firstborn of the Universe," Lily would whisper, holding her fingers just above the surface of the water. "Record-breaking. History-making." There was a bit of Luka in her voice, a bit of self-possessed engineer pride. And why shouldn't there be? She was both of Adam's parents now.

The day her son was old enough to leave the nursery and step into his first ExoSkin, Lily declared to anyone who would listen that this moment was the moment of Adam's birth: "The other birth, the one that usually happens to a fetus at thirty-nine weeks on Earth–it doesn't matter in this Universe. Look at all the hatchlings coming after Adam. They'll only ever leave the womb once, at the moment they're born into ExoSkin. What's the difference between a fetus in a hatchery tank and an infant in a nursery tank? All we need to distinguish aboard this ship is life before ExoSkin and life in ExoSkin. No sense measuring anything else."

The others scoffed at her reasoning. "That isn't what it means to be born," they said. "You can't just change words whenever you feel like it." And yet, whether because they were secretly persuaded by her arguments, or simply because Lily was more right than any of them knew, the transition from nursery to ExoSkin started going by the name "birth." By the time "slut" was gone from everyone's dictionary, almost no one except doctors and historians cared that the word "birth" hadn't always been applied so late in the lifecycle of sperm and egg.

Almost no one cared. But not quite no one. Every generation had its malcontents, a few gadflies making pessimistic pronouncements about how humanity was forgetting its Terran roots. "What if," they asked, "by the time we reach Gliese 832c, we don't remember there's such a thing as birth before seven years old? What if we get so used to wearing ExoSkin that we start believing you have to wear ExoSkin in order to be human? What if we lose the ability to distinguish between digiscape and real life? It's unnatural, what we've done."

"But it's necessary," said the rest. "It's how we're going to survive for thousands upon thousands of years. What good is it to insist on living like we're still on Planet Earth? The ground beneath our feet is the only earth we've got for now."

"It's unnatural," the malcontents repeated. "We won't stand by and watch our race turn into a bunch of cyborgs. It's unnatural." They said it so often that the rest of humanity began referring to them in mimicry—first as "Naturals," then as "Naturs," and then, after spelling and etymology had long since been forgotten, as Natchers.

28

KANAN

KISSING TEI HAD BEEN A MISTAKE. Kanan knew it the
moment she allowed it to happen. She knew it all the more in
the moments that followed, as she fought to mask her indifference with something like happiness.

Tei held her gently by the elbow, watching her as if she were
a bowl of cool water in the hottest hours of sunshine. Kanan
was incapable of returning the gaze.

Maybe, Kanan thought, she could muster such a gaze for
Avi. The pull she felt toward Avi was bodily, instinctive, reflex-
ive. But Tei? Tei was too familiar, even after half a season
spent apart. Tei didn't belong in this strange new world of
skinless wanting. She belonged in the underworld, in mess hall
chatter and checkers games, in casual goodnights spoken by
the thousands as they clambered into their hydropods side by
side and Tei programmed dreams for them both. She belonged
in skin, where touching was forbidden and friendship had no
name and the only thing left was fond familiarity.

Tei wanted to be near Kanan. That was obvious enough. And Kanan enjoyed the feeling of being wanted by Tei, just as she had enjoyed the feeling of being wanted by Avi. But she couldn't bring herself this time to want the one who wanted her.

It was a cruel thing, being wanted without wanting in return.

For three days, Kanan did everything she could think of to avoid moments alone with Tei. Sharing a tent with Tiqvah made evenings and mornings simple enough. As for the daytime, Kanan was rarely apart from the brooding presence of Avi, whose mood had soured ever since he heard Tei's claims about the true nature of the Universe. Tei, sensing Avi's distrust, tended not to linger anywhere once the overworld warrior arrived.

But the real saving grace that kept Kanan from repeating the other morning's mistake was Mahlah. Ever since his escape from the underworld, the aquarian had begged to spend every spare moment with his rescuer. He introduced Tei to skinless swimming, which she mastered with an ease Kanan envied. When they weren't in the river, Mahlah became Tei's overworld guide and guardian, introducing her to friends and family members, leading her through a maze of markets and mills and tents and orchards. Mahlah seemed to view his guardian role as a kind of recompense, a gesture of thanks for an unpayable debt. As for Tei, she seemed thrilled at the opportunity to practice her interpretive skills for hours on end with a real live citizen of the overworld.

When the spies brought news that Arisa's deletion had been scheduled, Mahlah's time with Tei only increased. Kanan was afraid to guess what the two of them were planning, but she felt sure it had something to do with the galley chemist. Whatever it was, Mahlah knew enough to keep the plan hidden from Avi and the other warriors. Tiqvah tried to pull the secret out of him, but to no avail. "You should be glad," Mahlah replied, "that I didn't wait for the elders' permission before rescuing a child out of the Cyborg hatchery twenty-six seasons ago." Tiqvah bowed his head and said nothing more.

Avi didn't seem worried over whatever foolish plan Mahlah and Tei might hatch to rescue Arisa. His attention was all consumed by Tei's story about Project Universe. "They are speaking of the madness," Avi said to Kanan one afternoon when they spotted Tei and Mahlah whispering together on the riverbank. "The interpreter is drawing Mahlah into Robiana's madness."

"Why should Mahlah be in danger of the madness?" asked Kanan, trying to keep her tone light and disinterested. "If you and Tiqvah with all your knowledge of the Cyborg tongue can't be persuaded to consider the story, how could Tei possibly persuade someone like Mahlah? Someone so wholly committed to the overworld?"

"It's *because* I've studied the Cyborg tongue," said Avi, "that I'm not taken in by its deceptions. Tiqvah too has this wisdom."

"And me?" Kanan slowed to a walk. "If you and Tiqvah have wisdom, what do I have?"

Avi turned back to her, fear written across his face. "You're not saying the Cyborg interpreter has convinced you?"

"No," said Kanan. "Not yet. But I haven't shut up my ears like you and Tiqvah. I'm still willing to be convinced."

"Then the only way to save you is to make sure the interpreter never has a chance to convince you." Avi's words had the ring of a threat.

Kanan felt her breath catch. "What will you do to her?"

"Nothing," said Avi.

"I swore to Tei you wouldn't hurt her."

"And I won't. I know how fond you are of promises." Avi started to run again, leaving the last of his words to dissipate into the wind: "Especially when they're someone else's responsibility to keep."

§§§

The day before Arisa's deletion, Elder Javan's hirelings came for Tei.

Kanan was in the market with Avi when the commotion began. She set down the gourd she was examining and raced to the shoreline, pushing through a crowd of tightly packed bodies to see four figures thrashing in the river. A halo of pink tinged the water around them. It wasn't until the creature with the bleeding head cried out that Kanan realized the voice belonged to Tei.

Her feet tried to move, but an arm wrapped around her chest held her motionless.

"Don't," Avi whispered in her ear. "You can't fight them all."

"Not without help," said Kanan. "Come on."

"It is Javan who ordered the arrest," said Avi. "I have no power to defy an elder."

The hirelings dragged Tei to the shoreline, tossing her body up onto the rocky embankment at the feet of a frail creature with a scarred chest. A circlet of leaves sat atop Javan's grey head. He turned to the onlookers, spread his arms wide, and began to speak.

Kanan understood enough of the words to make her blood run cold. She fought against Avi's arm, but it held her fast. "What is the elder saying?" she pleaded, forcing herself to believe she didn't already know the answer.

"Javan accuses Tei of spying for the Cyborgs," whispered Avi. "He says Mahlah's escape was a trick to earn our trust. Tei comes to us with a mouth full of lies. He is invoking the elder's right to punish without council in matters of treason."

"Punish?" The word was dry like dust in Kanan's mouth.

"The punishment for treason among our people is exile. They are sent where their loyalties lie, back to the underworld to face the Cyborgs."

Kanan felt a wave of relief wash over her. "Then she'll be safe?"

Beside her head, she felt Avi's nod. "No harm will come to her except what is done by her own race. And since they have commissioned her voyage into the overworld, she has nothing to fear."

Down at the river's edge, Javan seized a fistful of Tei's hair and pulled a glowing knife from his belt.

"Stop," cried Avi in a booming voice. All at once the arm around Kanan was gone. Avi raced down to the riverbank ahead of her.

Kanan couldn't make out all the words Avi shouted as he threw himself between Javan and Tei. But she knew the pattern of his voice well enough to catch the key ideas: "You have no right… exile, not execution… not part of our agreement…"

"Agreement?" The lines on Javan's face wrinkled as he began to laugh. "We had no agreement. You did your duty by reporting the spy. I owe you nothing. A Cyborg spy can't be punished like a common traitor. In exile, the alien wins. All the knowledge it gathered returns to the underworld with it. There can be only one punishment for a spy."

The elder raised his knife. Avi caught him by the wrist. "Execution without trial is a crime."

"You wish to challenge my ruling?" Javan lifted the circlet of leaves from his head and placed it on Avi's. "Perhaps in thirty seasons you will have earned one of these, and you'll possess the right of challenge against an elder. Until then, get out of my way."

"But if another elder challenged…" said Avi.

Javan waved toward the crowd. "Do you see another elder here? There is no time to call one. I rule that the danger must be dealt with. Immediately."

One of Javan's hirelings grabbed Avi by the shoulders and thrust him aside. Before Javan could draw back the knife again, Kanan leapt onto the elder and knocked him to the ground. The blade flew out of Javan's hand. It soared high across the embankment and disappearing into the river.

A second hireling pulled Kanan away from the elder, twisting her arms tightly behind her back. She pressed her heels into the dirt and tried to fight, but the hireling's grip was unyielding.

Javan spat out blood mixed with mud as he studied the newcomer. "The other Cyborg. I was hoping we would see this creature here. Is it another spy, perhaps? We'll know soon enough. Striking an elder will earn it a flogging, in either case. But we'd best keep to one punishment at a time."

The elder strode back to where Tei knelt with her hands and feet bound behind her. He seized a fresh handful of her hair. "Your knife," he said to the third hireling, holding out his other hand.

Just then, Mahlah flew out of the river with a loud cry. The aquarian clutched Javan's knife, which flashed through the air and severed the hireling's arm. The creature hollered in pain. Mahlah silenced him with a kick to the stomach that sent him sailing into the dirt.

The hireling who had grabbed Avi came towards Mahlah brandishing a spear. Mahlah caught the spear just behind its blade and pulled sharply, making the hireling stumble on the rocky shoreline. All at once Mahlah was on top of the hireling. Mahlah's knife hilt cracked loudly against the hireling's skull, leaving him unconscious on the ground.

"Treason!" cried Javan. As soon as the word left the elder's lips, he seemed to regret it. Mahlah stalked towards him with ragged, seething breaths. Javan took two steps back, tripping against the hem of his richly colored elder's robe. In the dirt, he continued to claw his way backwards as the aquarian approached him with a raised knife.

"There will be an execution," said Mahlah. "An execution with your own blade, just as you wished it. Justice enough for you?"

The knife buzzed like an insect as it flew through the air, burying itself between Javan's eyes. Blood began filling up his face before his head hit the ground.

The final hireling released Kanan's hands and started toward Mahlah. Mahlah turned to meet him with fists raised. But Kanan was even quicker. She launched herself towards the fallen spear and yanked it by the shaft, sending the blade up between the hireling's legs and slicing deep into his thigh. He toppled onto the rocks, clutching his leg and groaning in pain.

The crowd watched in stunned silence. Even Avi was frozen like a statue, so still Kanan couldn't see the rise or fall of his chest. She heard her own shallow breathing and the hireling's moans and the endless burbling of the river.

Mahlah knelt down and pried out the knife still clutched between the fingers of the hireling's severed arm. With it he sliced through the cords that bound Tei. She slumped forward, sighing faintly to prove she was still conscious. Throwing the knife aside, Mahlah lifted the interpreter gently onto his shoulders and began staggering towards the river. Once water lapped at his feet, he spun around to face the crowd.

"Judge for yourselves," said the aquarian. "Is it treason to stop an elder and his hirelings from murdering an innocent creature? If so, I have no desire to be anything else to you but a traitor. When I return, judge me for my crimes if you wish. But the Cyborg interpreter is not yours to judge."

As he spoke, Mahlah drew out a breathing mask from the pouch around his waist and affixed it over Tei's face. His words still ringing, he stepped back into the water and dropped suddenly. He and Tei disappeared into the depths of the river, leaving behind only a trail of bubbles.

Without thinking, Kanan dove into the water after them. She swam directly down, feeling the pressure in her skull increase as the absolute darkness behind her eyelids grew darker still. There was no hope of catching up with Mahlah. No one could outswim an aquarian—least of all an ex-Cyborg like Kanan who had never learned how to keep her eyes open underwater without a breathing mask covering her face. Still, if Kanan made enough of a commotion, maybe Mahlah would have pity on her. Maybe he would rescue her and carry her with them to the same place he planned to hide Tei.

Kanan spent the last of her air screaming Tei's name into the water. By the time the sound reached her own ears, it was just a single warbling pitch in the river's dull cacophony.

A hand caught her by the forearm. As it pulled, the darkness lightened and the pressure diminished. After what felt like an eternity, her head broke the surface of the river. She coughed and sputtered in the sunlight.

"Breathe," said Avi. "Set your hands on my shoulders and breathe."

Kanan pushed him away in disgust. "You lied to me." She began swimming toward the opposite bank of the river.

"No," said Avi, swimming after her. "I never hurt Tei. I never meant to hurt her. But it was my duty to tell the elders what I knew. She was dangerous to the overworld. Dangerous to you."

"If it was your duty, why weren't all the elders told? Why only Javan?"

Avi said nothing. They reached the riverbank, where a slender strip of rock bordered a field of leafy green nutmeal plants. Kanan pulled herself up onto the earth.

"You wanted Javan to invoke the elder's right of punishment without trial. You wanted Tei exiled."

Kanan began to scramble away from the water's edge, but Avi caught her by the ankle.

"I saw the two of you together," he said.

"You don't know what you saw," Kanan spat back. "The body's meaning for Cyborgs is not the same as its meaning for you and your race. We have no parents or children, no habits of touch to tie a thread between our bodies. There is nothing between me and Tei. Nothing like the thread of wanting that pulls between me and you."

Avi's fingers went limp. "Then why did you follow Tei and Mahlah into the river in the moment of their exile? There's no returning to the underworld for you. Why risk your own exile from the one place you can still call home?"

"Because," said Kanan, "Tei is my friend. If the overworld can't be her home, why should it be mine?"

"And you would have done the same for any other friend? You would have done the same for me?"

Kanan dug her toes into the dirt. She hesitated.

"You say there is nothing between you and Tei," said Avi. "But the thread that pulled you into the river is stronger than the thread between you and me could ever be."

§§§

Halfway through the second watch of the night, Kanan awoke in Tiqvah's empty tent with a familiar hand covering her mouth. Above her, Mahlah held a finger to his lips. "Quietly," he whispered. "At any time the double-tongue might return."

"You're not going to drug me this time?" said Kanan wryly as she rose to her feet.

Mahlah shook his head. "You would not follow before. This time, Mahlah thinks, you will choose differently."

Kanan trailed the aquarian to the river, where fins and masks awaited them both. "Stay close," said Mahlah, sinking beneath the water.

A blurry dream greeted Kanan beneath the river's surface. Shadows drifted around her like shy fingers, reaching gingerly in, then pulling away as the light from Mahlah's belt advanced. Time stretched out endlessly before them. Mahlah led through a winding maze of channels, past mesh gates and pulsing currents and corridors that flickered with jagged green lightning.

At last they swam up a long narrow channel and emerged into air again. Kanan immediately recognized the cave yawning overhead, slick and brown and studded with stalactites. She pulled herself onto the damp earth, tore her mask away, and swung her head frantically from side to side, searching for Tei. She saw only shadows.

Mahlah set his mask beside Kanan's but stayed in the river, treading water. "Your friend was here, in hiding, for a little while. But nothing can hide forever."

"Where is she now?"

"Gone," said the aquarian. "The blow to Tei's head was too much for Mahlah to heal."

Kanan stopped breathing. The cave around her began tilting sideways. She clutched the earth beneath her, feeling something like damp fur against her fingers. "Then why did you bring me here?"

Mahlah disappeared beneath the water and reemerged with two Cyborg skins held high. "To dress for our journey."

"No," said Kanan. "I don't want your journey. I want my friend back."

"Mahlah wants the same. You are not the only one with a friend to save."

Kanan watched green water drip from the dangling tendrils of skin. "Where are we going?"

"The only place left to go," said Mahlah. "Up. Out of the universe. Into Nothing."

29
TEI

A PLUMBER NAMED HOUMIL discovered Tei first. The interpreter had been left along the far side of the processing plant's third tier, where he lay skinless, curled in a puddle of green water and red blood. He moaned in pain as he held both hands against the wound on his head. He couldn't seem to stop shivering.

Houmil called for the skincaregivers, who called for the orderkeepers, who called for the officers' committee. By the time Buru arrived, the puddle beneath Tei had grown dark and slick. The captain bent low without letting his own skin touch the mess.

"You were found out by the Natchers?" he whispered.

Tei nodded slowly.

"They stripped you of your skin and left you for premature archiving?"

A second nod.

"How much did you see of their world before you were discovered?"

Tei turned his head to meet the captain's gaze. "I saw enough."

§§§

The skincaregivers made quick work of Tei's head wound. "Strange debris," said one as he patched the torn underflesh together in the infirmary. "Never seen a contaminant like it. You must've had quite an adventure."

"The interpreter doesn't remember any adventure," interrupted Buru with a dangerously wide smile. "Just as I'm sure you and your colleagues won't remember any debris."

The skincaregiver dropped his head. "Yes, Captain."

An orderkeeper named Siplin arrived at the infirmary clutching a new Final skin. Its slender tangled ribbons still dripped with water. Siplin frowned as he held the skin out to Buru. "Two Final skins for a single human. Unusual. It has never been done before."

"Never been done?" Buru's grin glistened, making his teeth looked unusually sharp. "I thought I'd called for an orderkeeper, not an archivist. If you're concerned about a shortage of skins, perhaps you'd like to archive yourself and offer the interpreter yours? No? I thought not."

Tei's new skin had none of the soft gradated hues of his first Final skin. The Cyborg shell that swallowed up his underflesh this time bore a jagged, aggressive pattern—as aggressive as shades of blue could ever be.

"It must be a relief," said Buru to the interpreter, "to see yourself looking human again."

"A relief," Tei repeated. He hoped the sigh in his voice sounded like agreement rather than wistfulness. As he cautiously bent his elbows and knees, unfamiliar muscles answered his brain's command.

"No telling what the adolescence will be like," said the skin-caregiver who had spoken earlier. "Perhaps the interpreter's body will adjust easily to a second Final skin, since it has already taken pains to adjust to Final skin once before. Perhaps the two skins are different enough from one another to trigger a complete repetition of adolescence. Or perhaps the excess time he's spent in underflesh will make the adolescence last longer than three weeks, longer than anything we've seen before. All our best predictions are just speculations. To go from Final skin, to no skin at all, to a new Final skin—it is the first such case for us."

"And the last case, I assure you." Buru triggered the access gate and stepped into the hallway. "Come, Eleven. The others will be waiting for us. We have a deletion to see to."

"Deletion?" Tei feigned surprise.

"Of course." Buru spoke as if he were reporting the menu of a feast. "But you wouldn't have heard the announcement. I'll fill you in as we walk."

The first morning shift had just ended, turning the hallways thick with Finals hurrying to their career posts and fledglings racing to training hydropods. Buru made no effort to lower his voice as the crowds parted around him and the interpreter. The captain talked about Arisa's crime and trial and scheduled punishment with the same dispassionate vigor as a history teacher lecturing in the digiscape. Curious eyes followed them down the corridors, but Buru held his head high with calculated disinterest. His smile never faltered.

As Tei nodded along with Buru's narrative, he mentally reviewed the plan he and Mahlah had devised to save Arisa. They'd made most of their preparations before Javan's disruption, before the execution and exile. But nothing about the last day's events changed anything of their plan to stop Arisa's deletion. If anything, having Tei in the underworld wearing a fresh skin provided an advantage, assuming that Kanan could be persuaded to help them.

Originally, Mahlah had planned to borrow Kanan's skin and dress as a Cyborg alongside Tei. The alien had been reluctant to take the skin ("Mahlah is no thief," it said again and again), but they'd had no other options. There was no time to finish Mahlah's partial skin or to steal a fresh one from the assembly room pyramid. Even if there had been time, they couldn't risk Arisa's life on such an impossible gamble. Tei would have asked for Kanan's permission—or, better still, Kanan's help—but Mahlah was insistent that Tei's old agemate could not be trusted with a plan that amounted to a betrayal of both underworld and overworld.

The past day's events had changed everything. With his leap into the river, Kanan had proven he was willing to break ties with the commands of a Natcher elder. It was enough, under the circumstances, to make Mahlah believe he could be trusted after all.

What other choice did they have?

As for the rest of the Natchers, there was no hope of persuading any of them to help. Perhaps, if skin hadn't been involved, Mahlah could have tried to persuade Tiqvah or Avi or the cousins. But Arisa's deletion would take place where the Universe's atmosphere wasn't controlled. Being skinless would spell quick death.

When he was a fledgling, Tei had assumed deletions were carried out in the command room. This was the rumor whispered among his agemates, after all, following the deletions of Ciani the archivist and the butcher whose name Tei had forgotten: "There was a whole crowd of them, orderkeepers and officers and Captain Buru and the condemned one, parading down the corridor toward the command room. And when they came out into the same corridor, the condemned one had disappeared."

Now that he understood the true meaning of deletion, Tei knew the situation couldn't be so simple. Bodies didn't simply disappear when they were deleted—and there certainly wasn't a stash of deleted bodies stored inside the command room. Deletions couldn't take place on the upper deck, either; Buru and the officers didn't even seem to realize that their elevator could take them to Natcher territory. A runaway like Robiana or Kanan might be called "deleted" after escaping into the overworld, but Buru certainly had no intention of delivering criminal Cyborgs into the Natchers' world.

Fortunately, Tei had studied the Universe's blueprints with Adam enough to know that there was a place where a group of Cyborgs in skin could go, travelling by elevator, and leave an endless supply of bodies.

Exactly one place.

Storage silos ran the length and circumference of each of the Universe's elevator shafts. "Lots of spare blocks of silica and circuit boards and lengths of wire to use for repairs," Adam had said in the digiscape. "And of course, a non-mechanized way of getting between the command room and the decks in case of elevator failure—though the easiest way in is through the elevators themselves, by an access gate midway up the shaft. One silo is lined with spare fuel for unexpected launches or landings, I think. Beyond that, it's hard to remember everything we stored there. My father thought it would be best to give us too much, rather than risk giving us too little. He was determined, my mother said, to anticipate every possible way in which the Universe might fail."

"As far as the machines were concerned," Kyri had added, "I suppose he succeeded."

Five of the Universe's six elevators were in disrepair now. Or perhaps they had been blockaded on purpose, as a way of restricting movement between decks and access to the command room. Tei had gone to visit them all in skin, after seeing them on Adam's blueprints, just to be sure. All five were repurposed into closets or pantries. That left only one working elevator, which meant there was only one readily accessible storage silo.

A silo was a strange place for deletions, thought Tei. Since it had no floor, officers and orderkeepers who witnessed the deletion would need to spectate from the walls, lining up along the ladders that ran the length of the silo. But the lack of atmosphere control made it the perfect place to kill a human being by simply removing his skin. Though gravity didn't pull downward as strongly in the silos as it did on the upper and lower decks, it still pulled downward; Tei and Mahlah guessed that the dead bodies were probably released into gravity's pull after their deletion, allowed to fall down the length of the silo.

To rescue Arisa, then, they simply needed to make sure the chemist was released into the pull of gravity while he was still alive. They didn't need to fight off a full committee of officers and a squad of armed orderkeepers. All they needed was a distraction that could loosen the grip of whoever held Arisa captive, sending the chemist plummeting into gravity's grip—and into the net of his rescuers—with his skin still intact.

The Cyborg water was Mahlah's idea. "It alters the Cyborg mind by altering the Cyborg shell," the alien said. "Poured on the Cyborgs, even just a few canteens full, it should be enough to loosen their grips and set Arisa free. If one of us climbs above to pour, the other can wait below with the net, to help Arisa climb to safety after falling."

"And what if Arisa isn't the only one who falls?" asked Tei. "What if one of the others falls with him, or even more?"

"There is a fabric here in the overworld," said the aquarian, "which water cannot pierce. Mahlah's Cyborg shell can be covered with the fabric, to be sure Mahlah's mind is clear while the others are still fever dreaming from the effects of the water. If they fall into our web in the midst of their dreaming"—the alien bared its teeth and picked up a knife—"those dreams will be their last."

So the plan was laid. The night before Arisa's deletion, Tei and Mahlah would fill as many canteens as they could carry with Cyborg water. They would crawl through the underworld's air vents and emerge just a few skinlengths from the elevator access gate, where Tei's skin and passcode would get them into the elevator and up to the storage silo. They would climb down the silo and tie a web of braided ropes strong enough to break Arisa's fall. And then they would lie in wait, Mahlah perched beside the net covered in waterproof fabric, Tei hanging from the ladder above the elevator entrance with canteens of green water ready to pour onto an unsuspecting officers' committee.

It was a foolhardy plan. A brazen plan. But it had to be. What other kind of plan could possibly work?

There was no reason the plan couldn't work with Kanan acting in Tei's stead. Mahlah would be wearing Tei's skin and knew Tei's passcode, which meant the alien should be able to access the elevator just as easily without him. Kanan could pour Cyborg water in Tei's stead, while Mahlah waited below with its knife at the ready. Perhaps, with Tei standing at elevator level near Arisa, he would be able to make sure that the galley chemist slipped out of the committee's hands at just the right moment.

Buru held his hand against the elevator's glowing guide screen. Then he said a word Tei had never heard before: "Airlock."

"Destination confirmed," answered the digiscape voice.

"Where?" Tei tried to keep his voice calm and disinterested, hoping against hope that *airlock* was just another name for the storage silo.

"A place you've never been before," said Buru. "We use it only for deletions."

Instead of rising, the elevator seemed to fall under Tei's feet. His body felt temporarily light, then uncommonly heavy. He closed his eyes and tried to picture the blueprints he had studied with Adam and Kyri. The elevators weren't supposed to run any lower than the underworld. And none of the Universe's spokes had led to something called an *airlock*. Not according to the memories preserved in the archive.

Unfortunately, he wasn't in the archive anymore.

"It's a solemn honor to witness a deletion," said the captain. "Some of the committee felt it wasn't appropriate for you to join us, but I insisted that the experience would be valuable. You more than any of us need to understand what it costs to give up your humanity. You need to understand what it costs to protect humanity from those who would betray it."

"I'm grateful to learn," mumbled Tei, hating not only the words in his mouth but also the Cyborg sharpness of his voice as he spoke them.

"Our new orderkeeper Resen will be there for the first time as well," Buru continued. "He was an agemate of yours? No? The cohort below, then. Ah yes, we Finalized him early in Jarawi's place. But perhaps, given all the time you've been with Reif in the archive room, you didn't hear much about Jarawi's sudden skin failure. Such a tragedy, that."

Tei said nothing.

"And here we are," said Buru as the gate slid open. No one would have known by his smile that he had been speaking of death just one breath ago. "Welcome to the airlock."

Wherever they were, it wasn't the storage silo. It wasn't the place where Mahlah and Kanan waited with canteens of green water and a carefully strung net. Tei and Buru were fixed to the earth with a heavy gravity. They had to be below the lower deck—along the outermost edge of the Universe. But nothing else was supposed to sit below the lower deck at the edge of the Universe.

Nothing except Nothing itself.

The first thing Tei noticed about the room they entered was its walls. These walls weren't flat like the walls of the underworld and overworld, or even like the smooth diamantium of the command room. They were gnarled and cavernous instead. Covered by a network of pipes, they looked patched and unfinished—as if they were walls no one had intended to spend much time looking at.

Arisa stood in the center of the room, flanked by two order-keepers carrying strykers. A scattered collection of officers from the committee and another three orderkeepers waited nearby. Resen was among them, his narrow face stretched even narrower than usual. He glanced up as Tei entered, then immediately fixed his gaze on the floor.

Metallic discs secured Arisa's arms and legs. Despite the crowd, the galley chemist somehow seemed to stand distinct from the rest, like the single colorful object in a digiscape world rendered black and white. His eyes were closed. If it hadn't been for the pained lines stretching across the skin of his face, he might have been sleeping.

"I've come to rescue you," Tei wanted to say. But there was no rescue; not from here. Tei had come to witness an execution and nothing more.

Buru read the charges aloud. Betrayal. Conspiracy. Treason. The words would be read again later, over the universal throat, when the announcement of Arisa's deletion was made official.

But here in the airlock, Buru's voice held an extra measure of delight.

Half-skinning came next. Goru, the committee's master engineer, was the first to grip Arisa by the scalp and tear away a strip of his skin. The chemist's body shuddered, but the order-keepers held him firm. "As you have rejected humanity," said Goru, "so humanity rejects you."

One by one, the other officers followed Goru's example. One tore a strip of skin away from Arisa's arm, another from his face, another from his chest. With each bit of disappearing skin came the same somber condemnation: "As you have rejected humanity, so humanity rejects you."

Beneath the skin, Arisa's pale underflesh looked nearly white. The short curls matted against his skull glistened fiery red. He held his head high and made no noise, not even when Namoel the master orderkeeper dug his fingers into the galley chemist's unprotected belly. A single tear trickled down Arisa's cheek. His eyes never opened.

"One more strip of skin must be taken," said Namoel. "Let Buru have the honor."

"I yield the honor to Eleven," said Buru. And then, more softly, so that only Tei could hear: "This is how your predecessors were punished, you know. The interpreters who failed. Their skin stripped away from the waist up, to reveal the half-Natcher freaks they had become. But you won't fail, will you, Eleven? Not now that you know what it could cost you?"

The captain pushed Tei, who stumbled forward and caught himself by Arisa's bare wrist. He straightened his back so that he and the chemist were face to face.

Arisa opened his eyes.

Human eyes in skin were a magic spell. Tei had always believed it to be true, and now more than ever he felt its truth in his limbs. Arisa's gaze paralyzed him.

Tei should have been rescuing Arisa at this very moment. He should have been saving the chemist's life. But any attempt at blocking the deletion now was hopeless. It would only ruin his chance of winning over the officers' committee later on. If Buru and the others were ever going to believe him about the true nature of the Universe, they needed to see him in this moment as someone who could be trusted.

To be trusted, he needed to play the game by their rules.

"Finish it, Eleven," said Buru. "Make the punishment complete."

Slowly, Tei forced his fingers around the strip of skin left on Arisa's torso. He tugged at it, felt it begin to pull stickily away from Arisa's underflesh. His eyes never left the chemist's.

"Forgive me," he said in Natcher. He hoped Arisa had learned enough of the language from Mahlah to understand his meaning. Otherwise, the chemist would have heard only the Cyborg meaning of those same syllables—the meaning that everyone else in the airlock assumed as the sounds emerged from his lips: *I despise you.*

With an almost inaudible rip, the skin tore away cleanly. Arisa opened his lips, let out a tiny sigh, and closed them again.

"I despise you," Tei repeated with all his heart, willing Arisa to understand him. The officers jeered and applauded.

"Very good, Interpreter," said Buru. "Now to the second phase of the deletion."

The orderkeepers undid the discs around Arisa's arms and legs. He went limp between them. A gate on the far wall, with a red sun glowing from the wall just above it, lifted to let the crowd pass through. The room they entered appeared nearly identical to the first. Only its floor was different: absolutely smooth, with three square patches of perfect blackness carved into its dark silica sheen. Three giant metal spools affixed to each wall held lengths of coiled rope. Straps and buckles covered every available skinlength of wall space.

Once the last of the officers had passed into the new chamber, the gate latched behind them with a loud hiss. "Secure yourselves," said Namoel, buckling himself into a harness along the wall so that his feet no longer touched the ground. "You don't want to be standing free when the outer gate opens. Not unless you mean to delete yourself along with the traitor."

Tei studied the smooth floor with its patches of blackness. The black patches weren't perfectly black after all, he realized. They were streaked with tiny trails of white, blurred pinpricks of passing starlight.

Starlight.

The truth came flooding into his brain all at once. He wasn't looking at the floor. He was looking *through* the floor. He was looking through clear diamantium windows and into the expanse of outer space. He was seeing for the first time—not just in digiscape code, but with his own two eyes in skin—into the depths of Nothing.

"It's real," he said. No one heard him.

Tei had believed for weeks now, for months, that something bigger than the Universe existed. But believing had been an intellectual exercise, as distant as a mountain coded along a digiscape horizon. Now reality was within reach, no more than a skinlength away. The whole universe waited at the perimeter of his Universe. When the outer gate opened, the last boundary between them would be gone.

When the outer gate opened, Arisa would die.

"Stop," said Tei, and then repeated the word until the rest of the room had fallen silent. "Stop. Stop."

He hadn't planned to say anything more. He shouldn't have said anything more. Not if he wanted to hang onto the officers' trust. Not if he wanted to earn his way into the command room, to take control of the Universe's direction and restore their path to Gliese 832c. But no patient plan devised with Kyri and Adam in the digiscape had half as much power over Tei in this moment as the magic in Arisa's eyes.

Why bother about the future of the human race if he couldn't even save one human being?

"You see the view through this earth you call the outer gate?" the interpreter said. "You're seeing into the place our speech calls Nothing. But it's not a Nothing. It's a Something, larger than all the Somethings we've ever imagined in skin or digiscape. There are other Universes out there, and places called planets where new Universes are built. The humans on planets live like people inside the digiscape. They exist among other creatures—puppies and lizards and all the rest—and they climb mountains, and swim oceans, and grow flowers. But their world isn't programmed like the digiscape. It's real. Solid. Permanent. Like a world in skin that doesn't need skin to be itself."

Buru scowled, then began to laugh. "It seems the interpreter hit his head when he fell out of the sky from the Natchers' world." A few others laughed with him.

Tei should have stopped speaking, and he knew it. But he couldn't. The truth tasted like food on starving lips. Now that the flavor was in his mouth, he had no will to abandon the feast.

"Think about command room," he pleaded. "Haven't you ever wondered why the Architect created all those gadgets the officers' committee doesn't understand? They were designed to move the Universe through the Something outside it, to fly us from one planet to another. Just ask Adam if you don't believe me. You know, Adam, the firstborn in skin, the same Adam who teaches history to every fledgling cohort. He knows so much more than the historians and the archivists will allow him to tell. Just ask him, and he'll tell you like he told me. Or go to the command room for yourselves. Deactivate the surface deflection protocol and look out into the stars. You'll see that the universe is so much bigger than this little place we call Universe. You'll see where we've come from. You'll see where we're going."

"What gibberish is this?" cried Goru. His hand rested on the lever that would open the outer gate and finish Arisa's deletion. "Is this what three days with the Natchers does? Turns the human mind to mush?"

"You need rest, Eleven," said Buru, with a smile that might have looked kind if Tei hadn't known better. "All this danger and excitement has you confused."

Tei shook his head. "I'm not confused. For once, I'm not confused at all."

"Open the gate," said Namoel. "We'll deal with the interpreter's derangement after that."

Goru's fingers tightened around the lever.

"Stop," said Tei again, reaching up to unbuckle the harness that held him tight against the wall.

"Hush," hissed Buru.

"Open," shouted Namoel.

In the same moment, three things happened.

One: Tei released his harness and launched himself across the room toward Goru.

Two: Resen the orderkeeper, who had been watching Tei's every move, unbuckled his own harness. His eyes were alight with eagerness to prove himself. Brandishing his stryker, he leapt out after the interpreter.

Three: Goru flung the lever up. The outer gate began to hiss. Its smooth face and three diamantium windows glided sideways, stealing the floor from beneath everyone's feet. Behind the dark silica lay a whole expanse of empty black dotted with light.

The last boundary between Universe and universe was gone.

Tei threw out both hands, catching Arisa's wrist with one hand and a dangling harness strap with the other. Gravity stretched him taut. Arisa hung beyond the boundary of the Universe, his body tossing like a leaf in the wind. Tei tightened the muscles in the skin of his chest, trying to pull them both up toward safety.

Resen slid past them, thrashing the air in search of something to hold onto. The stryker flew out of his hand. Its trigger brushed against his finger as it fell out into space, firing a dart up toward the heart of the room.

The dart struck skin. In the commotion, Tei couldn't see the face of the skin's owner.

The unarmed Resen grabbed hold of the lip at the edge of the outer gate. Eight fingers strained against the silica. The rest of the orderkeeper's body dangled out into the darkness as it flew past in a dizzying rush. His fingers disappeared fraction by fraction, slipping across the silica. Three joints became two. Then, all at once, they were gone.

"Close the gate," Tei tried to shout, but no one seemed to hear or care. He felt the harness strap burning as it slid through the skin of his palm. The officers' committee and four orderkeepers watched in stunned stillness. When Tei could hold on no longer, he released the harness and pulled the chemist in close against his chest. He clutched Arisa with both arms as the two of them plummeted into the open expanse beyond the Universe.

They were among the stars now, floating in empty space like Tei had so often floated in the digiscape. But there was no Nauraa to carry them this time. There was no movement except falling, no direction except down. Tei watched the

Universe in front of them drift slowly further away, turning like a giant wheel until the gate through which they had fallen disappeared from sight.

The Universe. Tei's eyes adjusted slowly to the magnitude of the sight. He'd seen it in blueprints, of course; Kyri had even programmed a flight with Nauraa around the ship's exterior. But nothing could have prepared Tei to see it outside the digiscape, in the world of skin. He closed his eyes, clearing away the bleary wetness, and opened them again. Humanity's home still floated in front of him. Unthinkably enormous. Horrifyingly small.

The shape resembled a spindle, or so Adam had said. At one tip of the spindle shaft sat the command room, its gleaming diamantium window peering out toward the darkness ahead. Close behind that tip, a yellow ball of energy flickered and glowed. The energy core sat at the center of the spindle's whorl: a huge spinning ring, split lengthwise into upper deck and lower deck, affixed to the spindle shaft by six bulky spokes. The ring's innermost wall—what Tei had seen from within as the sky of the overworld—was built from a semipermeable diamantium alloy that allowed artificial sunlight to flood the upper deck.

Past the habitable decks and the elevator spokes and the artificial sun, the rest of the spindle shaft jutted downward like a Natcher spear, ribbed and sleek. Its gargantuan engines and thrusters, which had whirred and crackled with life during Kyri and Nauraa's visit in the digiscape, now sat dark and dormant.

Above and below the spinning Universe, stars spattered the blackness. Tei had thought the stars would feel close, now that the diamantium barrier between them was gone. But those flickering dots of light were still impossibly far away. Tei was closer to the stars, but the stars were no closer to him. Everything out here was emptiness.

Nothing more.

Nothing.

"Stay with me, Arisa," said Tei. Even as he spoke, he felt his words disappear silently into the vacuum. "I'll find you a skin somehow. You're going to make it."

Arisa said nothing. The chemist's eyes had turned up into his skull. His body was frigid and stiff, a statue carved from ice.

On the far side of the Universe, blocked from view by millions of tons of steel and carbon and silica, the gate to their former home slammed shut without making a sound.

30
ADAM

BY THE TIME ADAM WAS OLD ENOUGH to be paying any attention, the tension was already palpable between a human majority who embraced the new innovations of their technological world, and a small-but-vocal minority who distrusted them. The groups weren't yet Cyborgs and Natchers, not in the formal sense. The two races wouldn't split fully apart for thousands of years more. But already they had begun to speak and work and live in opposition to each other.

"You've got to remember," said the humans-who-would-become-Natchers, "there's no sense bringing the human race to Gliese 832c if we're no longer recognizably human by the time we get there." This group tended to avoid the digiscape and spend their time–like Lily did–on the upper deck. Surrounded by plant life. Warmed by artificial sunlight and cooled by artificial breeze. Listening to four thin notes of simulated birdsong churned through the camouflaged audio system. "It's our solemn duty to keep acting like humans," they said. And yet, the longer they avoided the digiscape and the history it held, the more distorted their recollections of Earth became.

"You've got to remember," said the humans-who-would-become-Cyborgs, "there's no sense dreaming about our future on Gliese 832c if we can't keep ourselves alive until then." They scoffed at the others' escapism. "We live on a ship in space now," they said. "We can't just pretend we don't because we wish we didn't. We might as well embrace it, become the best ship-dwelling human race we can be."

Fearmongers and extremists found their voices in the fray as well. Rumors spread of a grim future featuring everything from compulsory castration and cannibalism to anarchy and willful self-destruction. No one wanted to pay the rumors any heed. But the longer they circulated, the harder it became to discern which ones had any basis in reality.

"I thought I left that whole shitshow on Earth," Adam's mother would tell him during his teenage years as the two of them ate together in the mess hall. They had no official relationship to one another—Project Universe wasn't designed for family units—but Lily insisted on sharing at least one meal each day with her son. "Everyone talking past each other, their eyes fixed on one kind of danger, paying no attention to another danger sitting right in front of their faces. Not that I'm saying every idea is just as good as the next. But it's all just that, you know? Just ideas. We're all so smart, and still so fucking stupid. I guess you've got to do more than leave Earth to get away from stupid."

Adam liked it when Lily talked this way. With everyone else she was a model of precision and dispassion, as if she were reading aloud from a book of predetermined answers. But with Adam, at family dinners, she was foulmouthed and sloppy. Her words meandered with no obvious goal. It was the way Adam would remember his mother in later years: the head of her ExoSkin pulled away, hair askew, oblivious to onlookers, practically shouting as she waved her spoon like a conductor's baton.

No wonder the Cyborg archivists of future millennia had scrubbed her neural impulses out of the archive, her and all the rest of her generation who had been born before the creation of the Universe. There was *no taming a creature like Lily. She knew too much, and spoke too freely, about what humanity could have become and what it became instead.*

How could Adam have known, back in the days he was still in skin, what a precious commodity the old memories of Earth would become? His childhood, at the time it began, had been the exotic one. No one aboard the Universe cared to hear what it was like to be born in a country hospital in Yorkshire, to lose your first tooth in a high rise in Abu Dhabi, to attend a preparatory school in St. Petersburg. No one was begging for stories of four-lane roads or grocery stores or pet gerbils. They already knew about Earth. It was their strange new Universe that captivated them.

Everyone wanted to know how it felt to learn language and move-ment and morality from a computer program. They wanted to know how it felt to wear ExoSkin from the first moment your lungs began to breathe. They wanted to know about taste buds that had never tasted any meat except fish, about eyes that had only ever seen pet golden retrievers in the same fantastical space as unicorns. They wanted to know how it felt to grow up as a native son of this world in which they themselves were foreigners.

The same things that made Adam remarkable in the eyes of the Uni-verse's first crewmembers were the things that made him so familiar in the eyes of the generations who followed after. They were the reasons why, thousands of years later, Adam survived the Cyborgs' archival purges. They were why he became a historical monument, the lon-gest-lasting collection of neural impulses in the Universe's data bank.

Surely a childhood on Earth couldn't have been so different, thought Adam, from a childhood inside a hydroponic nursery tank. Either way, the memories were vague and gestural. Once he became aware of him-self as a human creature—once his memories began to last longer than a moment—the nursery felt just like any other part of the digiscape. The wires feeding into his parietal and occipital lobes told him where he was in each moment. Sometimes on a field of grass, beneath the shade of a fig tree, paddling along a river. Sometimes in the lower deck's mess hall or assembly room or dormitory. It all felt both real and surreal. In short, it felt like childhood.

Inside the nursery tank, Adam had had playmates by his side—some of them real projections of his fellow infants in the nursery, others mere simulations provided as part of his training. He'd had a mentor, the first of many. And he'd had a nanny, a round and gentle figure with no age or gender and no name except "Nanny."

It was Nanny he missed when he was born into ExoSkin. The playmates were restored to him the following year, once they came of age. (Or the real ones were, at any rate, and the digitally invented ones were quickly forgotten.) As for Mentor, the old Mentor and the new one might as well have been interchangeable. But there was no Nanny in the world of ExoSkin. The closest thing was Lily, who wrapped her arms around him exactly twice per day, once at the beginning of the meal they shared and once at the end. Lily, who called herself "your mother" and spoke endlessly about "your father the Architect" with an impossible blend of shame and pride. Lily, the first and last parent in the Universe.

Future generations of fledglings would be terrified by the very thought of careers—the fierce competition for a few meager slots in Final skin, with no telling which skills would help them stay in skin when the aging ceremony came and which would be worthless. But Adam had no such fear. Population was controlled differently in those early days; excess humans were culled from the hatchery before their transition into the nursery. Once you were born, there was no question whether you'd be permitted a career. The only question was which career you wanted to pursue.

Adam's curious child mind wanted all the careers, and he tried his hand at nearly every one during his adolescent years. Planting and harvesting on the upper deck. Tending wounds with the doctors who had overseen his two births. Synthesizing chemicals from the leaves and fungi that grew along the banks of the babbling river. Galley cooking, transportation, engineering, communication. But what he loved most of all was to sit weightlessly in the command room, strapped into a chair beside Captain Anu as she piloted the Universe. Past comets and asteroids, across long still patches when all Adam could see through the giant diamantium window was beams of starlight flooding in from every direction.

"It doesn't take much," Anu told him, rehearsing the names and functions of a hundred knobs and dials and levers. "Three quarters of the time, I'm more a figurehead than a real pilot. Still, autopilot can only get you so far. All it takes is one hit from an asteroid or one surge in the electromagnetic field to send us a fraction of a degree off course. And when you're going where we're going, a fraction of a degree is the difference between settling a new planet and wandering in space forever."

"Does it get boring?" asked Adam, kicking his weightless legs from side to side. "Waiting so long for nothing to happen?"

"Boring?" Anu took him by the shoulders and turned him toward her. "If you care where humanity ends up, you can't possibly be bored in this room. If all you care about is your own lifetime, the things you can see with your two eyes in the Universe and the digiscape, maybe it's boring. But if you're willing to look toward a world a thousand generations from now—if you can train your eyes to see that far ahead— there's no better place in all the Universe."

When the captain died of heart failure during the Universe's fourth decade, everyone recognized Adam as her obvious replacement. He gave up his first career as a hydropod technician to make his twice-daily pilgrimage up to the room where the starlight lived. After taking stock of the horizon and the electromagnetic readings, he would return to the decks below, trying to use his clout as captain to bridge the divide between the humans-who-would-become-Cyborgs and the humans-who-would-become-Natchers. "Whatever happens," he said in countless meetings and speeches and whispered conversations, "we have to remember that we're all on the same mission. We can't forget where we are *or where we've come from or where we're going. The moment we fall apart, the Universe is doomed to fail."*

Six elevators could have taken Adam up to the command room. But Adam always rode the same elevator, the one nestled just behind the hydroponic nursery. Each morning and each evening as he passed by the nursery, he would look in at the tanks and their green-tinted occupants. He wondered if the fledglings born out of those tanks would envy him for being the firstborn of the Universe. The truth was, being born first meant nothing. He envied them for being born second, third, tenth, hundredth, thousandth. He envied the eggs and sperm still frozen, the babies who wouldn't be born for millennia to come. They would travel closer to Gliese 832c than he could ever reach.

All he could do was make sure their Universe was pointed in the right direction.

31

KANAN

THE SHEER SIZE OF THE AIR VENT NETWORK flab-
bergasted Kanan. She and Mahlah began their crawl on hands
and knees at the anocyte converter, high above the water processing plant. An hour later, they were in an entirely different
segment of the Universe, passing above a deserted rowing
room and crawling over three compartments full of vacant
training hydropods. Canteens full of anocyte-charged water
dangled from both their skins, clanking against open grates
as they passed.

"Hush," said Mahlah, holding a cautious finger to his lips.
But he smiled just the same. The nearest air vent outlet was
twenty skinlengths away. Not even the greenest fledgling
recruit would be foolish enough to fire a stryker dart into the
sky simply because she thought she heard a rattling coming
from above the suns.

How, Kanan wanted to ask, could the Cyborgs obsess about
keeping themselves safe from Natchers while leaving such an
obvious route into their world so poorly protected? But as soon

as the question formed in her mind, she already knew the answer. These air vents existed above the Cyborgs' skies and suns. They were part of Nothing. And Nothing, as soon as it was named Nothing, became irrelevant.

At last they reached a dead end where the vent system ran up against the elevator shaft. Mahlah lifted the grate with the edge of his knife and lowered himself down from the sky onto the underworld earth. Kanan followed, standing on Mahlah's shoulders to slide the grate back into place before slipping down to the earth.

They stood in a narrow hallway, flanked by locked gates on either side. Mahlah stepped up to the gate with a glowing screen on its face. Placing one finger against the screen, he painstakingly scrawled the word *Checkers*. "Passcode accepted," croaked a digiscape voice as the elevator gate slid up.

Kanan felt a lump forming in her throat. "You know about checkers?"

"Mahlah knows only what Tei showed how to write." The aquarian stepped into the elevator, motioning Kanan to follow. "What is its meaning?"

"Just a game," said Kanan. "A favorite of mine. I never thought Tei liked it much."

"Must have liked it," shrugged Mahlah, "to choose it as a passcode."

The elevator rose under Kanan's feet. "Must have," she agreed.

When the elevator gate opened, Kanan wrinkled her nose at the scent. The storage silo had just enough atmosphere inside it to circulate the smell of dust and neglect. Every metallic clink Kanan and Mahlah made against the silo walls as they tied their net in place echoed in both directions. Sound swelled larger as it moved, turning whispers into shouts. As soon as both of them had taken their positions—Mahlah crouching at the edge of the net, Kanan perched high above the elevator gate—silence fell thin and frigid.

Kanan's heart pounded during the first few hours of waiting. Her fingers gripped a canteen cap, poised to pour its contents over the whole officers' committee. But as the day stretched on with no sign of Arisa or her captors, Kanan's grip loosened. Soon the canteen was clipped to her belt again. Her free hands traced the uneven surface of the silo, the bundles and bales and barrels strapped together like haphazard decorations.

"Tei and the others should have come by now," she whispered. "Well before now. It must be the fourth shift already."

"Soon they'll come," Mahlah answered from below. "Best be ready. Hush now."

Kanan's roving fingers brushed against an unexpected texture. A strand of plaited fabrics—rough like rope, though it wasn't much thicker than a thread—had snagged against a storage harness. Its color was impossible to make out in the semi-darkness. She pulled it free and ran it between her fingers, tracing the pattern knot by knot. The texture felt familiar, like something out of a dream. When her hands tired of the distraction, she tied the strand around her wrist.

Time passed, with no way of measuring its passing except the growling of their stomachs and the drooping of their eyelids.

Finally, a low whir emerged from the elevator shaft beside them: the sound of a compartment climbing towards them. Kanan uncapped two canteens and held them out in front of her, waiting for the gate to open.

The whirring grew louder as it approached, then passed above them. The gate never moved. Kanan listened until she heard nothing.

"You're sure," she whispered into the silence, "that deletion happens here?"

"So said Tei." Doubt had crept into Mahlah's voice. "The universe has no other place for it but here."

"And if she's wrong?"

Their answer came from a third voice, a voice booming through the universal throat. "Human citizens," said the voice without fanfare. "The deletion of Arisa the galley chemist, found guilty of crimes against humanity, is now complete. Her shame is humanity's restoration."

Kanan heard Mahlah take in a ragged breath.

The unfamiliar voice continued. "The human race has also suffered three great losses today on account of skin malfunction. Captain Buru and the newborn orderkeeper Resen lost their skins while protecting humanity against Arisa's treachery. As for the one called Eleven, once known as Tei, her skin failed in the course of her duties as interpreter. All three have rendered great service to humanity and will be greatly honored in the archive. Their honor is our honor."

The voice went on, detailing plans for a special assembly in which a new captain would be named and new fledglings Finalized to fill the vacant careers. Kanan had ears for none of it. All she heard was the pronouncement of Tei's death. *Her skin failed her in the course of her duties as interpreter.* The words swelled like storage silo whispers inside her skull, echoing until they became a deafening scream.

Tei was gone; gone to everything but an archived memory. Kanan had imagined this moment back in her fledgling days, when Tei made pessimistic prophesies over games of checkers. But the reality was nothing like the imagination had been. Back then, Kanan feared the archive without knowing why. Now she knew exactly why.

Kanan didn't realize Mahlah was beside her until she felt his hand settle on the back of her neck. And she didn't realize she was crying until she heard his gentle, thick voice chiding her: "Hush."

"They're dead," Kanan choked out. "Arisa is deleted. Tei's skin failed. We're too late."

Mahlah shook his head. "Maybe not dead. Maybe they've escaped into Nothing."

"But we're already in Nothing. The only part of Nothing we know how to reach. And they're not here."

Instead of answering, Mahlah caught Kanan by the hand and held her wrist up to the light of his blade. He let out a triumphant cry. "Where did you find this?"

Kanan's finger shook as she pointed to the place.

Mahlah ran his fingers along the harness and the crevices beneath. Finding nothing, he reached down to the braided strands tied against his own ankle. The two braids were identical.

"What does it mean?" said Kanan.

"It means Robiana climbed this way." Mahlah unsheathed his glowing blade and held it up toward the shadows. "It means we follow."

§§§

The higher they climbed, the easier climbing became. Soon Kanan forgot she was climbing at all. She was merely floating forward, sent soaring by each flick of her muscles. The canteens dangling from her shoulders and from the woven belt at her waist grew lighter until they were drifting aimlessly through the air like balloons.

"Not far now," called Mahlah from above—if it could still be called *above* at all, when up and down seemed to have disappeared.

Kanan raised her head. The ladders along the silo wall ended abruptly, replaced by a blank yawning shadow. "Be careful," she began to say. But before the words had left her mouth, Mahlah disappeared into the shadow. Kanan might have screamed, if she hadn't followed him a moment later.

The silo had fed them into a massive cavern. At first they could see nothing except the blue-white radius around Mahlah's knife. But then, as if the room were aware of their presence, a vague green glow slowly filled the air. It brightened until everything had turned the same hue as hydropod water. Kanan spun herself around to take in the view.

Sleek metal creatures with wings lined the walls, each one as large from wingtip to wingtip as a fledgling dormitory. There might have been thirty in view, nestled five abreast at every point along the cavern's tubular edge, beyond which the green light's reach expired.

Kanan let out a gasp as the word formed on her lips: "Aircraft."

Mahlah reached out his hand to touch the nearest craft's glowing nose. "You've seen these creatures before?"

"Yes," said Kanan. "Well, no. In the digiscape. We're taught to fly them as part of our senior fledgling training."

"Fly?" Mahlah frowned at the Cyborg word.

"To go through air without touching earth. It can only be done in the digiscape, where there is endless space between earth and sky. In here—" She looked around and shook her head. "There's nowhere to fly in here."

"Then there must be a way out of here," said Mahlah.

Before Kanan could protest, the aquarian had sheathed his blade and climbed up onto the aircraft. The moment his fingers touched the body of the craft, its sides slid back, revealing six seats and an empty cargo space. Mahlah pulled himself into one of the first pair of seats, then patted the cushion beside him.

Kanan shook her head and reluctantly clambered into the pilot's seat. "It's exactly like the digiscape," she gasped. Every knob was familiar to the touch, each one drilled into her memory as Tei helped her study for their last fledgling aviation exam. She reached for the lever tucked between their seats. The sides of the craft sealed over them like a cocoon.

"You can fly it?" said Mahlah.

Kanan shook her head. "There's nowhere to go. But I can power it up for you."

Pulling back the water circulation valve, she initiated the launch sequence. Streams of anocyte particles snaked across every inch of the craft, throbbing and pulsing like veins coming to life. The green glow brightened until it was almost painful to look at. The engine whirred and let out a shrill hiss.

Mahlah's eyes widened. He clutched the sides of his seat with shaking fingers.

Kanan laughed. "Lucky we're not flying for real. Imagine how terrified you'd be if this aircraft had a place to—"

Whatever she meant to say next was drowned out by ear-splitting thunder. The rounded wall beneath the craft's belly split apart, sliding back to reveal a patch of pure black interrupted by pinpricks of light. Kanan froze.

The pulsing aircraft sank through the open gap. Soon they were clear of the cargo hold, free-floating in a world that shouldn't have existed. Around them, the body of the Universe turned like an abandoned wagon wheel along a sleek axle. Ahead, they could see only Nothing.

Off to the right, a circle of color peeked out from behind the Universe's rim. Its round face shone vibrantly—a kaleidoscope of white and blue and golden-green.

Kanan gasped. "What is it?"

Mahlah only shook his head.

If they could have heard Tei's awestruck whisper from a thousand skinlengths away, as the interpreter clutched Arisa's frozen body and took in the same breathtaking view, they would have had their answer:

"Gliese 832c."

32

TEI

TEI KNEW THREE THINGS FOR SURE.

One: He was going to die. Not quickly like Arisa, but slowly, sucked dry over days or weeks. Sucked dry by the same Cyborg skin that kept him alive as he drifted through the emptiness of space.

Two: The planet in front of him could only be Gliese 832c. How many times had he studied those telephotometric images, tracing each blue ocean and green-gold land mass with his fingertips? How many times had he and Adam used three-dimensional star mapping to calculate the Universe's position in relation to surrounding constellations and galaxies? It was no coincidence that three pockmarked moons orbited this planet alongside the Universe and Tei. It was no coincidence that the dwarf sun illuminating them all glowed rusty red. This solar system was the Gliese 832 system. The Universe had accomplished its mission.

Three: No one from the crew of the Universe would ever set foot on Gliese 832c. There was no telling how long they had already been in orbit around it. Seasons might have passed, or generations, or thousands of generations. Why should anything change now? Why shouldn't Cyborgs keep fighting Natchers, Natchers keep fighting Cyborgs, each race bound up in language the other race refused to enter? Why shouldn't humanity bide its time until the sixth and final elevator failed, until the command room became unreachable through any means except the long-forgotten storage silo ladders? Until humanity's best remaining hope of salvation disappeared, just like every other hope before it?

Kyri had said he wanted Tei to destroy the Universe. *Destroy.* The etymology of the word was as old as Adam, born from an idiom describing the Universe's creation. "To start spinning" meant "to create," just as Luka the architect had created the Universe and set it spinning. Accordingly, "to stop spinning" meant "to destroy." The end of the spinning meant the end of the world as humanity knew it.

Kyri's dreams of destruction—the dreams that had become Tei's dreams—weren't about hating the Universe. They were about honoring its original purpose. Luka's spaceship had been created to stop spinning someday. It was meant to be destroyed. Not *destroyed* in the sense of ceasing to exist, but in the sense of ushering in a new era. An era when the Universe became just one tiny piece of a much bigger home. An era so grand, so alive, that no Cyborg or Natcher dared to imagine it.

Tei would have told them, if he could have. Even if they all refused to listen. Language be damned. He would have shouted the news in both languages, or in some bastard hybrid of the two, just understandable enough to ensure all of humanity hated him equally. But even that much was impossible now. The walls of the human world—the boundaries of their words—kept them from seeing the one sight that might have opened their eyes.

At first Tei's mind had been full of plans. He would kick himself away from Arisa's body at just the right angle, reversing his momentum and starting his drift back towards the Universe. Once he caught up with the ship, he would climb along its surface until he found a way inside. He would sneak up to the command room, hack into the universal throat, speak into every corner of the Universe until Buru and the orderkeepers tore him off the receiver.

Those plans all dissolved the moment he lost hold of Arisa. He had lifted his cramping hand away from the chemist's body just for a moment, to squeeze a bit of blood back into his fingers. When he went to grab hold of the body again, it had floated just out of reach. He tried to fling himself towards it but succeeded only in performing a somersault, accidentally kicking Arisa's outstretched forearm in the process. The body went careening away. Within minutes, it was invisible, swallowed up by the darkness.

On the bright side, the kick had sent him closer to the Universe. Closer, but not close enough.

What good was *closer* if you still died in the end?

Tei channeled all his rage into a long scream. Then a second scream, a third, a fourth. The skin of his face wrinkled as his mouth stretched wide. The ridge above his eyes bent and furrowed. He screamed until his throat was raw, until his mouth tasted like blood.

He screamed but made no sound. Sound couldn't travel in the vacuum of space. Even if it could, no one was there to hear him.

He felt himself growing weaker as time drifted past. Drier, too. The Natchers called this feeling *thirst*. Itching was its first symptom, crawling into the slender gap between his skin and his underflesh. Then itching turned to warmth, a candle flame held too close, threatening to scorch. Sleep and waking blurred together. It was always daytime and always night.

If he'd been bolder, he would have killed himself. He was already wearing the best tool for his own murder. Nothing peeled skin away as easily as skin. Luka had designed it that way—Luka and his scientists back on Planet Earth. Skin was impervious to any other material not charged with anocytes. No sharpened steel could remove it, no powerful acid, no fiery explosion. Only with skinclad human fingers could skin be torn away from underflesh as easily as a redfruit peel.

Skin was like humanity that way. Indomitable, invulnerable, to everything except itself.

He wished he could become his own murderer. He wished he could peel away the skin and let himself drown in starlight. But he'd never been good at drowning, not even in the digiscape. He'd never been good at the ends of things.

His fingers were already dug into his scalp, beginning to pull, before he lost his nerve. He balled both hands into fists and sobbed. His body writhed and heaved, too dry to shed a single tear.

§§§

He was afraid, when he saw the shuttle approaching, that it might have been a hallucination. Other hallucinations had already come and gone. Kyri in half-skin, riding astride Nauraa the unicorn. Adam swimming through space like it was made of ocean water. Kanan's face hovering an inch from his own, their lips meeting in the darkness each time he closed his eyes.

How confusing, then, that it was Kanan who emerged from the shuttle with a tether tied around his waist. Kanan whose voice crackled through the radio transmitter embedded beside Tei's ear: "Hold still. I'm coming for you. Everything will be okay." Kanan whose hand grabbed Tei's elbow, who wrapped two arms around his torso and clung tightly as the tether pulled them both back to the safety of the shuttle.

Mahlah held the end of the tether between its palms, wearing Tei's old skin. Behind the alien, Resen the former orderkeeper watched the proceedings with unblinking eyes.

"You," Tei croaked, not sure which of them he was speaking to.

"Me," answered Kanan, taking hold of Tei's hand. "Just like I promised."

For a moment, their eyes met. Tei felt something press against his lips.

A canteen. That was all. Nothing more.

"The water is anocyte-charged," said Kanan. "Don't try to swallow. Hold it in your mouth until the skin of your tongue absorbs it."

Tei obeyed. Water began to seep through his skin. When his mouth was empty, he swigged from the canteen again, again, again.

"Easy now," said Resen. "No telling how long we'll have to make those canteens last."

"If there's not enough water for four," growled Kanan to the orderkeeper, "maybe we should have left you to dry up in Nothing."

"Hush." Mahlah spoke in Natcher, soft and calm. "Our world has too few humans, and too much need, for making enemies now."

Tei reached for Kanan's arm, struggling to hold himself steady. "We have to get back into the Universe. We have to tell the others."

Kanan shook his head. "We've tried. We circled every inch of the ship looking for a way back inside. All we found was Resen. I'm starting to wish we hadn't even found that."

"Hush," repeated Mahlah. "Without Resen, we'd know nothing of Tei and Arisa."

"Arisa," said Tei, and found he had no more words.

Mahlah's eyes sparkled. "No looking back now. Only forward."

"To where?" said Tei.

"We hoped," said Kanan, "that you might have an answer to that question."

Tei pushed away from the shuttle floor and floated toward the pilot's seat. Through a glowing diamantium windshield, he took it all in. On one side, Luka's Universe spun in the distance. On the other, three glowing moons hung dusty and bright. Straight ahead, the clouds over Gliese 832c were dissipating.

"To the planet," he said. "To finish what our ancestors started."

33

NO NEW ELEVEN WAS CHOSEN to take the old interpreter's place. The worst of the danger had passed, thanks to Eleven's noble sacrifice. Or so said Captain Goru at the special assembly, just before announcing which fledgling would be reborn to take Resen's place as orderkeeper.

In truth, the officers' committee had decided the risk of another interpreter was too great. Four skins lost in a day's time, and two of them wasted on an interpreter gone mad? No one was keen to repeat that experiment.

Namoel argued as usual for war. But the majority vote—the same vote that put Goru into the captain's podium—ruled that they ought to bide their time. Whatever else the Natchers might be, they were bound up in some way with humanity's survival. The universe balanced on a knife's edge. Humanity wouldn't upset the balance until they were certain they could avoid the blade.

§§§

The two Cyborgs were not much missed in the overworld. The one called Eleven had died—this much the spies reported with the help of Tiqvah's translation. As for Kanan, nothing at all was known. The creature had disappeared in the middle of the night, leaving behind only a bag of colored stones and a square of bark carved with crosshatch lines.

It was Mahlah whose disappearance ignited the rumors. Self-imposed exile, some said, after the death of Elder Javan. Recaptured by the Cyborgs, said others. But the spies recorded no chatter to support this latter theory. They listened diligently under Avi's command for a season or more, chasing down every whisper of a lead to the aquarian's whereabouts. All to no avail.

"The madness," Avi had been known to mutter while running laps around the perimeter of the universe, sweating beneath the glare of the sun. "No thief more clever than the madness."

Kanan's carved bark and colored stones found their way from Tiqvah's tent to Avi's. Sometimes the warrior would study them, trace them with gentle fingers, press them against trembling lips.

Perhaps they were clues, said the other spies. Perhaps the secrets they hid would bring Mahlah back from exile. Back from Cyborg prison. Back from the dead.

§§§

Adam, firstborn of the Universe, lay asleep on a raft in the digiscape. His mother Lily had lived near a river called Susquehanna, back in her own childhood. Nothing beautiful, she said. Nothing much to see. But Adam liked to picture himself floating on that river just the same. If you floated long enough,

Lily said, the river became a bay. A little longer, and the bay became an ocean. Water always knew where it was meant to go. Stay awake, fall asleep, it didn't change a thing, as long as the water carried you.

Two hands emerged from beneath the river, pulling back ripples of water like curtains. A stranger stepped into Adam's code. The newcomer was dressed in Cyborg skin, lips puckered and whistling cheerily.

The Cyborg dipped Adam's cast-off tee shirt into river water. Folded it into quarters, carefully, meticulously. Laid it over the ex-captain's nose and mouth. Held down firmly until the fighting and flailing and twitching stopped.

The bundle of neurons named Adam never felt a thing. His last memory was of sleeping, easy and without fear, trusting the water to carry him.

§§§

It was a pity, Reif told the officers' committee, to lose such an important historical figure. But the safety of humanity had to come first. If the code was corrupted, and that corrupted code bore the blame for making interpreters go mad, it must be erased. Surely the archive had another ancient mind swimming inside it who could rise up as the firstborn of the universe. Or if no such code existed yet, writing new code from scratch was a simple enough task for a skilled archivist.

Reif skipped a meal in the mess hall to get directly to work. Tracking down the offending strands of code took only half an hour. The archivist spent the rest of the day scrubbing the strands clean, whistling the anthem of humanity.

§§§

One quarter of a season after Mahlah's disappearance, the elders' council summoned Tiqvah. The time had come, they said, to train up another double-tongue. Tiqvah tried at first to refuse.

"The risk is too great," the double-tongue pleaded. "To speak a Cyborg's words is to think with a Cyborg's mind. Poison in the tongue becomes poison through the whole body. Avi and Tiqvah have tasted the poison just enough to build immunity. But even we have peered past the precipice of insanity. Would the elders poison our children as well?"

It couldn't be helped, the elders answered. Let the training be given with every imaginable care. Let a few suffer the danger of the Cyborg tongue, that all humanity might be kept safe.

§§§

The Cyborg word for *truth* was best translated, "That which Cyborgs hold to be true." So it must have been true, what the human race believed, as they slept in hydropods and ate in the mess hall and competed for the honor of Final skin. They knew the size of the universe. They knew what mattered in skin, and what lived on in the archive, and what belonged to the irrelevance of Nothing.

The Natcher word for *truth* was best translated, "That which Natchers hold to be true." So it must have been true, what the human race believed, as they worked the fields and swam the river and laughed at the Cyborgs' small minds. They knew the real size of the universe. They knew, apart from the Cyborg lies of shell and digiscape, how life and death were measured.

Good and evil—they knew that too, every one of them. They saw it with their own eyes. They knew what future held the hope of humanity.

Why should they know anything different, as long as the universe kept spinning?

ACKNOWLEDGMENTS

I spent four years dreaming about this novel without writing a word; then a global pandemic gave me the dubious gift of time in which to start drafting. Writing, revising, and publishing have taken another three years or so. In that seven-year gestation, I've become delightedly indebted to a host of people.

First and foremost, Mike Nappa. I've lost count of how many hats you wore during this project. To begin the list alphabetically: advocate, agent, confidant, critic, designer, editor, encourager… You've excelled in every single role. Thank you for believing in this novel, refusing to settle for anything less than my best work, tolerating my obsession with literary minutiae, and doing everything it took for this story to see the light of day.

Without the grace and support of my quarantine bubble—Carrie Gingrich, Evan Gingrich, and Rachel Fawcett—this book would never have bridged the gap from dream to reality. Carrie, thanks for continuing to cheer me on even after you moved to Virginia and were no longer contractually obligated to do so. Evan, thanks for prophesying this novel's existence and invoking your readerly prowess to help me bridge the gap between memoir and speculative fiction. Rachel, thanks for enduring long silences on walks while I brainstormed plot developments, and then for pouring tireless enthusiasm into revision and promotional brainstorming. To all three of you, thanks for delaying dinner innumerable times because I wasn't quite ready to stop writing.

For a stunning cover design, I'm grateful to the brilliant Anna Filbert (and her likewise brilliant husband-qua-consultant Zack). Working with dear friends is fun, and working with gifted professionals is also fun; doing both at the same time is exquisite.

Credit for capturing my formidably pensive author photo goes to Bret Kalmbach, whose presence makes me want to smile even when he tells me to look serious. Jerrod Saba and Steven Siwek also get partial credit, both for their auxiliary roles and for being excellent humans.

Amy Noel Green, Steven James, and Kimi Cunningham Grant gave generously of their time, their wisdom, and their words. I'm grateful to each of you for modeling a life of writerly grace and for challenging and encouraging me in my own craft. Kimi, thanks especially for checking in on the manuscript's journey, pondering major decisions with me, and offering valuable tips from your own experience; your talent, humility, and kindness are a threefold joy.

Colleen Chao, there is no delight quite like the delight of having a local friend who is also an accomplished writer who is also a staunch cheerleader. My writing and my heart are both the richer because our paths have intertwined. You are and will always be a lavish gift, from here to infinity.

A novel like this one—obsessed as it is with rhetorical theory, the philosophy of language, and the murky relationship between ontology and epistemology—owes its conception in large measure to the professors who first brought these questions to life for me. Elvera Berry, Cheryl Glenn, and Jack Selzer each led a branch of that professorial charge: into a fascination with symbol-using (and symbol-misusing), a curiosity about humanity's multivalent ways of knowing, and a conviction that language is almost always "more complicated than that." I'm also grateful to my students at Penn State and Roberts Wesleyan University over the years, who have been involuntarily privy to the dis/ordering of my thoughts on the ethics of language.

In addition to many of the aforementioned, several other advance readers deserve special thanks: my brother John, offering scientific consultation far beyond my ken; my parents, Dave and Jean, genetically biased and endlessly generous editors; Seda Collier, who made me smarter by asking the hardest questions; and April Kolman and Ryan Kolman, who narrated to me the gratifying vicissitudes of their reading experiences.

I'm deeply grateful to all the readers of my previous books or my academic work who have joined me in this excursion across genres. And I'm likewise grateful to the Kickstarter supporters who believed in this book before there was a book to believe in.

Last but not least, Curry Kennedy. It was you who heard this idea first, on one of our many philosophical ambles along the southern edge of State College, Pennsylvania. I told you how I wanted the book to end (which hopefully you've forgotten by now) because that scene felt synecdochic of the challenges you and I were musing over together, challenges at once deeply linguistic and deeply human. Regardless of whether you enjoy the novel that grew from that moment, I hope it inspires thoughts, raises questions, and prolongs the conversation. Wasn't that one of our favorite parts all along?

About the Author

Gregory Coles is the award-winning author of two memoirs and a contributor to *Jim Henson's The Dark Crystal Author Quest*, a collection of short stories published by Penguin Random House. He also holds a PhD in English, and his work in rhetorical theory—how language shapes society—has appeared in various academic journals and edited collections, including a collection from Cambridge University Press. Raised for fifteen years on the Indonesian island of Java, he now lives and writes in Idaho's Treasure Valley.

Find more about Dr. Coles at: www.gregorycoles.com

Made in the USA
Middletown, DE
05 February 2024